Visit us at www.boldstrokesbooks.com

By the Author

Sometimes Quickly

Veritas

Runaway

The Acquittal

A Date to Die

A DATE TO DIE

by

Anne Laughlin

2017

A DATE TO DIE

ISBN 13: 978-1-63555-023-8

THIS TRADE PAPERBACK ORIGINAL IS PUBLISHED BY
BOLD STROKES BOOKS, INC.
P.O. BOX 249
VALLEY FALLS, NY 12185

FIRST EDITION: OCTOBER 2017

CREDITS
EDITOR: CINDY CRESAP
PRODUCTION DESIGN: SUSAN RAMUNDO
COVER DESIGN BY SHERI (GRAPHICARTIST2020@HOTMAIL.COM)

Acknowledgments

Every book written is a labor of love and I'm lucky to have plenty of love around me to make it to the end. Thanks to all the people who support me and my writing, including Linda Braasch, Beth Brandt, Patricia Barber, Carol Anshaw, Joan Larkin, Carol Kennedy, Ann Farlee, Ann Stanford, Rita Balzotti, and my sister Liz. That's not a complete list.

I also want to thank retired Chicago homicide detective James Hennigan, who was epic in his patience with all my questions and contributed whatever authenticity there is in the novel about police procedure. I loved working with Jim and can't adequately express my gratitude. I also got medical advice from Dr. Len Barot and Dr. Josh Baru.

I also must thank the team at BSB, including my editor Cindy Cresap, my publisher Len Barot, and all the designers, line editors, and proofreaders who made the book a better one.

All thanks go to my wife, Linda Braasch. She's an unfailing cheerleader for my writing and also a perceptive first reader. Most of all she's Linda, which for those who know her says everything.

Dedication

To Linda, always

CHAPTER ONE

A pril didn't feel like spring in Chicago. The sun shone, the buds were popping, the days were longer, and still it was hat and gloves weather.

"Goddammit," Kay said as she stepped outside the Area Four headquarters. "I'm sick of this coat." She shivered as her partner Adam led the way to their unmarked car.

"I'm sick of this fucking city," he said.

They were both complaining in that way cops did. The words came out of their mouth without any real heat to them. It was midafternoon, close to the end of their shift, the worst time to catch a new case, especially when she had plans for the evening. They got in the car, Adam behind the wheel. Kay strapped in as he gunned the car west on Addison.

She wasn't in the best of moods, nervous about her brother's dinner party that night and the date he was setting her up with. She'd agreed to it reluctantly, hoping the woman would be less disappointing than the online dates she'd been going on. Those had been truly horrible. It was like a bait and switch scheme. A profile of a nice looking woman working in education would turn out to be a cafeteria worker living with three roommates. And so on.

"What's the address?" Adam asked. It was noon on opening day at Wrigley Field, a couple of blocks from Area Four. He was forced to slow as Cubs fans holding red plastic cups swarmed the streets as if Addison were a pedestrian mall. He turned on the lights and siren.

"Great job traffic's doing here," he said.

"They don't have enough officers. It's hopeless." Kay looked at the scrap of paper in her hand. "Clifton and Roscoe. Go left on Sheffield."

"I know where I'm going, Kay."

Adam was new to the Chicago police from Albany. He'd moved for a girlfriend and the relationship busted up almost as soon as he'd unpacked his boxes. He was thirty or so, tall with a stocky build, his hair a smidgen longer than a buzz cut, his suit slightly ill fitting. He'd shown he knew what he was doing and didn't pull any macho crap, her minimum requirements for a tolerable partner. Everything beyond that was gravy. After three months together they'd started to find a groove.

"You can cool it with the lights and siren," she said. "The call said the victim's been dead for at least a day. The evidence isn't what you'd call fresh."

Adam killed the siren and turned right onto Roscoe. They pulled up at Clifton, where a cluster of patrol cars crowded the street corner. Crime scene tape cordoned off the sidewalk in front of an old apartment building. It was turreted at the corner with a carved cornice and decorative stone at the entrance, but black soot wept down the façade, and only a few chips of Dublin blue paint clung to the weather-beaten front door. She popped out of the car and strode toward the uniformed officers gathered in front. Adam trailed behind her.

"What've we got?" she said to the group. Officer Ed Carey stepped forward, notebook in hand. He was standard issue Chicago cop—an expanding midsection covered by a Kevlar vest, no hat, burly shoulders, meaty hands. She'd worked with him many times. "Tell me this is an easy one, Ed."

"It's pretty bad. Deceased female is in unit 312, top floor. Looks to be in early stages of decomposition. Someone cut her throat."

"Sounds delightful." Kay smiled at the group as if she were standing with them at a barbecue, which she had often enough.

Officer Carey continued. "The body was found by the landlord after he got a call from the vic's mother. Said she hadn't been able to contact her daughter for over a day." He pointed to a man in shirtsleeves, standing inside the tape. "That's him."

"Thank you, Ed," Kay said. "Will you tell the witness we'll be with him shortly?"

"Will do."

"Do we have a name for the victim?"

Carey looked at his notebook. "It's Nora Sanderson."

She felt her gut drop. "Oh, shit. I think I know her."

"How?" Adam said.

She looked up at the apartment building, debating what to say.

Officer Carey shifted his weight. "Do we start guessing who she is or what?"

She turned toward him. "She's the sister of my ex-husband, if it's the same Nora Sanderson." All was quiet. This was the first anyone had heard of Kay Adler having an ex-husband. The fact that she'd ever been with a man probably shocked everyone there. A few feet started to shuffle.

"Ex-husband? You've never said anything about being married." Adam sounded almost hurt.

She shrugged. "It's not anyone's business. At least not until now. I haven't seen Nora in a long time." She prayed it was a different woman, not the girl she'd known only slightly when she was married to her brother Griffin.

Everyone was silent for a moment, waiting for her orders.

"Did anyone find her phone?" she said.

"It was in her bag with her wallet and about a hundred in cash," Carey said.

She turned to Adam. "Get the cell records ASAP. Ed, you're in charge of the canvass."

"Already in process," Carey said.

"Excellent. Please sign Detective Oleska and myself in. Let's go see if it's the same woman. Is anyone up there with the body?" Kay said.

Officer Carey gave her a withering look. "Of course. Donovan's there."

"Well, Jesus," she said. "If the corpse wakes up he'll scare her to death." Everyone laughed, the joke about Donovan's homeliness being well known. She walked into the building with Adam and put on paper booties from a box by the door. "How squeamish are you?"

"I don't think we ever got a decomposing body while I was in Albany. But I have a pretty strong stomach."

"We'll see." Kay had seen too many dead bodies to be squeamish, but she wasn't above dreading a slashed throat on a decomposing body.

There were two apartment doors at the top of the stairs, one of them open with an officer standing by. They stepped over the bloodstains on the carpeted landing. She could see several footprints pointed toward the stairs. It was going to be messy. They entered straight onto a living room. It was square except for the semicircular area where the turret was. Furniture crowded the room—a small seating area with large couch and coffee table near a startlingly huge TV. Next to it was a spindly dining table piled with books, papers, and a laptop. A couple of pairs of high heels lay under the coffee table, which was littered with Thai takeout. Clothes were thrown over the back of the sofa. She couldn't understand living in such a mess.

The body lay several feet from the entrance, the wall next to it spattered deep red brown with blood. Thick streaks of it ran along the floor from the entrance to where the body lay on its back, the gash across her throat a gaping maw. Blood had pooled into viscous puddles on both sides of her body. She recognized Nora's distinctive face, despite her contorted expression. She had tight red curls that spread in blood soaked clumps around her head. Her nose was broad and flat and her chin short and wide. She wasn't a pretty girl, but it looked like she put work into making the best of things. She wore full makeup and elaborate clothing. She had on thick leggings under a plaid pencil skirt, a gauzy white shirt and bolero jacket, and more accessories than she could count—wide belt with ornate buckle, a brace of silver colored cuff bracelets, several long beaded necklaces, earrings pierced all the way up her ear.

Kay usually felt a momentary sense of rage when she first looked at a dead body. A sense of loss and fury followed instantly by an analysis of the sight before her. Now she thought back to the ten-year-old girl in pigtails who'd seemed afraid of her much older brother. She remembered how eager Nora had been to see Griffin when they first visited the family home as a married couple. She stood tentatively in front of him and handed him a record album of her favorite band. He glanced at it after giving her a terse hello and tossed it on the coffee table. She could see the disappointment in Nora's eyes. It was the first time Kay had frowned at her husband's behavior.

"He pulled the body farther in the room so he could close the door, as if he was standing behind her and struck the instant she opened the door to the apartment," Kay said.

"Why would he risk being seen or heard by anyone in the building?" Adam said.

"The element of surprise, I think. Once he got inside it would be weird if he stood behind her. Or maybe he couldn't wait."

"And we don't know whether he came in with her or she answered the door to let him in," Adam said.

"But if they were face-to-face, I don't think he would have struck her in the doorway. The cut tells us he attacked from behind."

Kay squatted and touched her gloved hand to Nora's. The corpse's fingers were pliable. Rigor had come and gone.

"My guess is she's been dead at least a day, probably longer. It's late afternoon now. This most likely happened the night before last. She's starting to ripen." There was the early smell of decay coming from the body, which was starting to break down into the various gases and chemicals designed to eat the corpse from the inside out. Adam's jaw was clenched tight and his eyes darted away from what remained of Nora Sanderson. He was acting like a rookie. "Hold a latex glove to your nose. It'll help mask the smell."

"I'm fine," he said. He didn't look fine.

She opened both of Nora's hands to check for defensive wounds. There were no cuts or other markings on her hands or arms. Unless forensics found something she couldn't see, it didn't appear she'd had any chance to defend herself.

Standing farther in the living room was a huge man dressed in a uniform slightly too small for him. His head was long like a horse's, with a jaw jutting toward his knees. He wore big glasses over small eyes and his blond hair stuck up in a wiry fringe.

"What's the story, Donovan?" Kay said. She continued to stare at the body.

"You know what I know, boss. I'm making sure she doesn't get up and walk away."

"Well done, then. Hang tight here."

She studied the deep gash across Nora's throat. "Looks to be a left to right cut, so the killer's right-handed. There's no knife around the body, so it probably isn't suicide."

"Suicide?" Adam said. He was standing slightly behind Kay, the latex held to his nose. "Who would slash their own throat?"

"I don't think it's many people's first choice of ways to kill themselves, but it can be done. The key is to have a very sharp knife." Donovan snorted.

"You think she brought a stranger home?" Adam said.

"I don't think anything yet. Nora falls forward after he makes the cut and now he has a body blocking the door. He drags her into the apartment, turns her over, and leaves her here. That's the limit of my speculation at this point. She was wearing a lot of complicated clothing. It doesn't appear she was raped."

They stood there a moment longer, staring at the body. Part of her felt despair that this brutal murder had happened to Nora. The other part was anxious to get to work. She clapped her hands, as if breaking from a huddle. "Okay, let's get this operation going. Adam, go downstairs and make sure Carey's called in forensics and the ME, then interview the landlord so we can cut him loose. I'll start poking around here."

She moved into the bedroom to look around before the forensic team arrived. A woman's bedroom revealed a lot. Nora's was not the room of a woman with even a smidgen of decorating sense. The dresser had a thrift store look about it, the sea foam green walls were bare and needed paint, and there was no rug on the scuffed hardwood floors. The queen-size bed was unmade, and the sheets a dirty white. Kay liked a well made bed herself. It made climbing in at the end of a long day that much sweeter. Next to the bed was a rickety nightstand with two drawers. Sitting on top was a photo of her family, Nora and Griffin, along with their parents, all staring straight ahead without smiling. It was like a group passport photo. In the top drawer of the nightstand was lotion, manicure equipment, condoms, and a diary. The bottom drawer held a rather elegant vibrator. Kay contemplated it for a moment, wondering how much it cost and wasn't she ready for a new model? Tucked underneath was a paperback porn novel with a stern looking man standing over a naked, collared woman. Interesting what you don't know about people.

Kay opened the diary to the last entry, on Monday.

Another shitty day at work. That bastard Connelly was all in my face the entire day. I hate him. I wanted to go out tonight to get him out of my head, but I got home too late. Can't wait for tomorrow night. It's round one of the trivia tournament at Pinky's. We're going to kick ass.

She'd need to talk to this Connelly person. It didn't sound like there was any love lost between him and the victim. And they'd swing by Pinky's right after they informed the mother of her daughter's death. There'd be heat from her lieutenant about working a case where she was related to the victim by marriage, but she'd do so as long as she could. She had no desire to be thrust into Griffin's world again. It had been over fifteen years since she'd made her escape from it. But she also clung to every case she started. They were hers.

She moved around the room. There was a cardboard jewelry box that looked untouched. Bracelets and necklaces were slotted next to each other, no spaces in between. A strand of pearls looked like they had some value. She was ruling out robbery as a motive. The laptop and phone weren't taken, the TV, the cash in Nora's wallet. She checked all the dresser drawers and the small closet. Nothing unusual or noteworthy. The whole room would need to be dusted for prints, and she'd need to read the diary.

Adam came back into the room.

"Let's turn this over to forensics for now and go talk to some people," Kay said. "You can tell me about the landlord on the way."

Outside, a crowd had gathered, including the news trucks from the local network affiliates. She saw her lieutenant talking to the patrol officers and made her way over to fill him in. She didn't mention that she'd known the victim. Then she and Adam walked through the crowd to their car. She looked at the time on her phone. Four o'clock. If they hustled, she'd still get to her brother's dinner party on time. She'd broken many dinner dates with her family because work always came first. But she was ready to meet an interesting woman and this was the best way to do it, despite Tom's poor track record. Her date was a new painting instructor at the Art Institute and Tom's wife Louise had given her a thumbs-up. She was curious.

"I remember where the parents lived, but they could have moved. Griffin and I lived in Normal back then," she said as they walked to their car on Roscoe.

"Griffin?"

"The ex-husband. And don't ask me any questions."

"You'll have to answer questions, Kay." She didn't look at him. "I got the mother's number and address from the landlord. She's out in Jefferson Park," Adam said. "I don't know whether there's a dad or not."

"There was. An incredibly antagonistic brute. I've no idea whether he's alive or not."

She got behind the wheel and pulled into traffic. "What did the landlord say?"

"He doesn't live on the property so he doesn't know much about Nora. Said she'd lived there a year and always paid her rent on time. Never got any complaints about her."

"What did he say about finding her?" She got back on Addison and headed west for the Jefferson Park neighborhood on the northwest side.

"He got a call an hour ago from the vic's mom. She was freaking out."

"She convinced the landlord to open the door up," Kay said.

"Yeah. He said he about puked when he saw the body. He slammed it shut and called nine one one."

She frowned as they started to bog down in traffic. "There was a diary in the bedroom. She had a beef with her boss we'll have to look into. We need to read the whole thing, so be sure to get that from forensics after they've dusted it. Also, contact the ME and see when they plan to do the autopsy. And then check on the uniforms to see if they found anything during the door-to-doors."

"Are you going to start acting bossy?" Adam said. His look said he thought her capable of any monstrosity.

"You think that's bossy? Were you raised in a commune or something?"

Adam looked offended. "Not a commune. More like a dictatorship. I'm sensitive to bossy."

She laughed. "You're in the wrong business then. What did you do when you were in uniform. Cry?"

Adam stared straight ahead. Kay didn't know why he was bringing this up. She'd been ordering him around for three months. "You can't be a cop and be sensitive at the same time." She snuck a look at him. His lips were pinched together. "Why haven't you brought this up before?"

"Too new. But now I feel you should treat me more like a partner."

"You surprise me, Adam. I thought things were running smoothly between us."

He shrugged. "They are. I don't want to be treated like a subordinate, that's all. I think I've earned that."

"Well, guess what? You are my subordinate."

Adam slumped back in his seat. "I don't want to make a big deal out of this."

Kay couldn't understand where all this was coming from, but she didn't have time for sensitive partners. "You're my partner, okay? I'm sorry you doubted that. But I need you to follow my lead, and if you can't do that, I'll ask for a new partner, it's as simple as that. I'll try not to bark at you, if that'll make you feel better. Do we understand each other?"

"Yeah, yeah. That's not a problem. Sorry I even brought it up." He stared straight ahead.

She let it drop and drove up Milwaukee Avenue to the side street Mrs. Sanderson lived on. It was the same street they'd lived on when she was married to Griffin, lined with identical brick houses and mature trees—the heart of Chicago's bungalow belt. She glanced at the time again. They could talk to the mother and then the bartender at Pinky's by six o'clock, easily. She should be able to make her dinner and come back to work after.

Theresa Sanderson was holding her screen door open as they pulled into her driveway. She'd aged since Kay last saw her nearly sixteen years earlier. The lean frame that once wore clothes so well was now tiny and bent. The salt had outrun the pepper in her short layered hair. She'd been an ally of sorts during Kay's marriage. She seemed to disapprove of Griffin, her eyes narrowing when he said something self-serving, which was often. She would sit close to Kay during their visits and go out of her way to be kind, as if she was afraid Kay would think she was anything like her son. Kay hadn't yet twigged on to the fact Griffin was a bully.

"Thank you for coming," she said. "And so fast. I just called the police about my daughter." Her face twisted in confusion as they approached the house. "Kay?"

"It's me, Theresa. I hope I haven't startled you. I'm with the police now." She felt a sudden sadness. The time she was married to her son was one Kay wanted to forget, but she'd had a connection with Theresa. She took her hand and squeezed it gently.

"I just called the police minutes ago about my daughter. You remember Nora, don't you?" Kay looked beyond Mrs. Sanderson's shoulder into the living room. The TV was on with the sound off, tuned to a cooking show.

Kay was confused. "You called the police?"

"She's missing. They wouldn't listen to me before, not until she'd been gone twenty-four hours. They said they were sending someone."

Kay took hold of her elbow. "Can we go in and sit down, Theresa?"

They followed her into the room. She'd only been in Griffin's house a couple of times, but not a thing had changed. A sectional sofa took up most of the space, a huge curio cabinet dominated one corner of the room, crammed with Hummel figurines. Griffin had seemed embarrassed about his parents, his home, and she'd felt anxious when they'd visited. Adam sat on one end of the couch. Kay took a seat by Theresa on the other.

"We understand you called Nora's landlord because you were concerned about her whereabouts," she said.

"I'm expecting to hear back from him and I'm scared what he's going to say. I asked him to look because I haven't been able to get hold of her."

Kay drew in a breath. "I'm afraid I have some terrible news. Your daughter was found dead when her landlord entered her apartment. I'm so sorry for your loss."

Kay had delivered similar lines countless times, and it always felt awkward and inadequate. It felt especially cruel now. She couldn't anticipate how the news would be taken. Some looked at her as if she'd murdered their loved one herself. Others broke down immediately. Some wailed. There's no predicting how someone will respond when a few words change their life forever. Theresa simply stared at her, frozen in place.

Her eyes slowly shifted to Adam and back to Kay. Her hand reached for her throat. "She was murdered?"

"Yes, I'm so sorry. Is your husband out somewhere, Theresa? Can I call him and get him home for you?"

Theresa had the look of an automaton. It was as if she had no reaction at all. "My husband died a year ago. Heart attack."

Kay wasn't surprised in the least. The man always looked like he was about to blow a gasket. Theresa gave Adam her sister's number and he stepped away to make the call. Theresa stared blindly at the wall.

"I know this is a shock, but I'm wondering if you're able to answer a few questions. We'll have an officer take you downtown to identify the body a little later, after your sister gets here."

Adam nodded as he walked back to the sofa. "She's on her way."

"We need your help finding who did this to Nora. Will you tell us what you know?" Kay said.

Theresa shut her eyes for a moment, as if coming out of hypnosis. "I talk to my daughter at least once every day. Sometimes it's only voice mail, but one of us always calls. I last talked to her on Tuesday while she was at work. Everything seemed normal. She complained about her boss, but she was excited about some trivia tournament she was going to be in that night. She plays every week with her friends. After that, nothing. I called her best friend last night and she was worried, too. I tried her at work this morning and they said she hadn't been in since Tuesday. I was worried. But she's an adult. There could have been something else going on, maybe a new boyfriend. I didn't want to interfere."

Adam got the names and numbers for the employer and best friend.

"Has that ever happened before? When she went silent because of a boyfriend?" Kay said.

"Once or twice." She was quiet for a beat or two before her whole face dissolved and she started crying. And then sobbing. Kay wasn't going to get anything more out of her. She wouldn't try.

"Adam, how long before the sister shows up?"

"She said it'd be a few minutes. She lives a couple of miles away."

Once the sister arrived, Adam and Kay got back in their car and called for a squad to take Theresa to the morgue to make the ID. They drove to Pinky's, not far from Nora's apartment. It wasn't one of the pseudo-Irish bars that now sprinkled the city, serving gastropub food and craft beer. It was an old-school Chicago tavern, one block off a main street, surrounded by residential properties. It was home to two sets of regulars—tradesmen who knocked off work around three and drank until six. Then the younger crowd who came in later. Kay had been there a number of times with other police.

The inside was dark and smelled like the bottom of a keg of Old Style. She waited at the door for her eyes to adjust. She saw a few men hunched over the bar and a group of four huddled around one of the tables. Credence Clearwater played on the jukebox. The bar ran the length of the left-hand wall. A bartender stood at the far end, playing with his phone. They approached him and identified themselves.

"What do you want?" the bartender said. "If this is about the liquor license, you'll have to talk to the owner."

Pinky was long gone, and Kay didn't know the new owner. She leaned across the bar toward him. He was in his thirties, portly, wearing the scruffy beard that was the fashion of the day along with a flannel shirt and skinny jeans that made him look fat. He was trying for hipster but fell about four feet short of the mark.

"We're not here about your liquor license," Kay said. She saw the three men at the bar watching her, but she was far enough away not to be heard. "What's your name?"

He looked nervous, which almost everyone did when they talked to a detective. "Chris. Chris Steiber."

"Okay, Chris. We're here to ask you a few questions about one of your customers." Adam showed Chris the photo of Nora he'd taken from her apartment. She was bundled up in ski gear, her arm flung around another girl's shoulder. It wasn't the best photo for identifying someone. "Do you recognize the woman on the left?"

He scrutinized the photo for a moment and handed it back. "Sure. That's Nora. She's here a lot."

"When did you last see her?" Adam asked.

Chris chewed his lip, which was nearly hidden in his mountain man beard. Kay was pretty sure she saw some Dorito crumbs in there.

"It was Tuesday, because that's when we have trivia night. She never misses that."

"Were you tending bar?" Adam asked.

"Yeah. She hung out after the tournament ended. She was here until pretty late. I remember asking her if she had the next day off work," Chris said.

"Did she?"

"No. But she was talking with some guy. I think she was waiting to see how that would go. Usually she leaves with her friends."

Kay glanced at Adam. "Let's hold up there, Chris. Tell me more about this guy. Did you know him?"

"Never seen him before. He was drinking at the bar, had his stool turned around so he could watch the trivia game. I remember Nora coming straight over to the bar after it was done and climbing onto the stool next to him."

"By herself?"

"Yep. They started talking right away. I don't know if they'd been sending smoke signals to each other during trivia or what."

"Did it seem like she knew him?" Adam said.

"I don't think they knew each other. That was the sense I had, anyway." He wiped the bar with a gray rag. "I guess they hit it off. They talked for a long time and then they left together."

She liked the direction this was going. "Did you get his name?"

"No. He didn't introduce himself and I didn't ask."

"Could you describe him for me?" she said.

"He was probably six foot, blond hair in a ponytail, tinted horn-rimmed glasses, goatee. His eyebrows were huge."

"Fat, skinny? Dark skin or light?" Adam said.

"He was a skinny white dude."

"How old would you say he was?" she said.

Chris squinted. "It was dark. Maybe mid thirties?"

"What was he wearing?"

He paused and reached for his phone as if the answer was in his Notes app. She guessed it was an autonomic gesture, the iPhone as a security blanket. "I think he was wearing a black sweatshirt. I didn't see anything below bar level."

Kay turned to Adam and motioned him aside. "I want you to get him in to see the sketch artist ASAP. Tell him someone has to come relieve him at the bar. Then take a statement from him. Pump him for more." She grinned at him. "Please."

"Okay. What are you going to do? We still have to interview her teammates, right? Her best friend?"

"True, but first hook him up with the sketch artist so they can come up with a portrait. We may have a surprisingly dumb murderer. In the meantime, I need you to hold down the fort. I've got something at my brother's I can't get out of." Adam opened his mouth as if to protest. "Don't say it," she said. "I'll do the same for you. We're partners, remember? I'll be back in a few hours."

"Is this the brother who teaches at the Art Institute?"

"I only have the one." She brushed by him on her way out the door. She could see Adam had more questions. What was she doing at her brother's? How come he didn't know she'd been married before? Why didn't she ever tell him anything? She knew it was the way of most partners to be like a second skin to each other. They not only knew all about the people in each other's lives, but got the blow-by-blow on every moment in each other's days. She wasn't built that way. She liked to chat, but generally operated on a need to know basis. She was content listening to Adam prattle on—he was single, worked hard, and was a lifelong Mets fan and couldn't abide the Cubs. He liked to tell her all about his disastrous dates from Match.com. She heard all about his breakup. She didn't feel compelled to reciprocate.

She hailed a cab on Belmont, feeling mildly guilty about leaving the investigation for even a short time. The dinner party was at seven, which gave her plenty of time to get ready. She started to feel nervous. She knew Tom and Louise would be scrutinizing her, looking for her reaction to the woman they'd invited. Why had she been looking forward to this earlier in the day? She could use work as a way to get out of it, but that's exactly what they expected. At least it gave her a good reason to leave if she wanted to bail out early.

Tom and Louise lived in a gigantic apartment in the Loyola University area, where Louise was a professor of art history. Tom taught painting downtown at the School of the Art Institute. When they buzzed Kay into the building, it was precisely six fifty-eight, two minutes by the clock, but three minutes late by Kay's internal timekeeper.

"Get in here," Louise said, pulling Kay into the living room. "We have lots to talk about."

The room was filled with pillows and throws, rugs and wall hangings, floor lamps and easy chairs. It wasn't as much warm and cozy as it was like an overly dressed stage set. She admired it, but worried something would crash down from the walls or topple over whenever she moved around. Paintings covered the walls, everything from large abstract works to small, photo realistic portraits. It made her think of Gertrude Stein's apartment, crammed with art from floor to ceiling.

Louise led the way into the enormous back room, where the couple spent most of their time. At one end was a couch and a frumpy old chair pointed toward a TV set. Books and papers littered the coffee table, with tea mugs perched on top. The other side of the room held the kitchen, where Tom was stirring a pasta sauce.

Kay looked with dismay at his polo shirt and Dockers, wondering when such a well dressed man started looking like a suburban dad. His middle was thickening as he approached his fortieth birthday. Maybe he was giving up.

"My God, you're here," he said, glancing at her before adding something to the sauce. "I had a bet with Louise you wouldn't show up."

"I win," Louise said. She looked smugly at Tom. She was tall and bony and looked completely urban. Her black tunic covered half her thigh, her boots half her calf. In between were her knobby knees. Kay had carefully dressed in her date uniform—slim black pants, a sensible heel, a long open knit sweater over a boat necked shirt—and shown up with a smidgen of hope Tom had got it right for once.

Louise handed her a beer. They sat on the kitchen stools and watched Tom put a pot of water on to boil for the pasta. He poured a glass of wine and joined them at the island.

"Kay has come because she wants to check out Diane," he said. "She's wisely handed her love life over to those more qualified to manage it." This had to have been a joke. Every woman he'd introduced her to had been inadequate in some way—no sense of humor (twice), limited conversational abilities, no ambition, or quirky in ways that didn't amuse her, like the one who licked her lips repeatedly. How could Tom not have caught that? She was like a reptile.

"Her name's Diane?" Kay said. "Tell me."

"You'll love her," Tom said. "She's a new instructor at the school and a fine painter. You're here to help celebrate her appointment and, of course, to fall in love."

"I've met her a few times," Louise said. "Tom's right—you'll love her. She's friendly, smart, and very funny." She turned to Tom. "Would you call her cheerful?"

"I would, but that would scare Kay away."

"I don't scare that easy. I can handle cheerful." Kay took a drink of her beer. "Does she know you're setting her up with me?"

Tom went back to his sauce. "I thought you two could figure it out together."

Kay turned to Louise. "I almost wasn't able to come tonight. We caught a case this afternoon." She didn't mention who the victim was. The last thing she wanted was to bring up anything to do with Griffin in front of Tom and Louise. They'd disliked Griffin from the moment Kay first brought him home to meet her family. Their opinion only worsened with time.

"I'm surprised you're here, then."

"My partner's covering for me. I'll have to get back after dinner."

Tom drank his wine. "Clever. An exit strategy lined up in case Diane's not to your liking. That's a page right out of Dad's playbook."

"Don't compare me to him," Kay said. "I don't think Dad even likes people."

"He doesn't," Tom said. "And that includes me and you."

"Let's concentrate on the business at hand," Louise said. "It's nothing but trouble when you two talk about your parents."

"Do you really think that?" Kay said, surprised.

"It's always the same. Always complaints. It's not a good look on either of you."

"Christ." She felt deeply embarrassed.

"I've heard this before," Tom said. "I keep telling Louise she wasn't raised by our parents. She couldn't possibly understand."

They were silent for a moment. Maybe she needed to get into therapy. She didn't realize how she and Tom might sound to others and didn't want to come across as a complainer. She didn't believe in that victim crap. "Okay. Let's get back on track. Anything else you can tell me about Diane?"

"I don't think we should influence you," Louise said.

"Here's one thing I know. A painter and a cop make an odd pairing," Kay said.

"Yeah, but you're not like a cop," Louise said.

"What's that supposed to mean? I'm totally like a cop."

"I think she means you're not a cultural Neanderthal, which is a terrible stereotype, I know." Tom set the sauce to simmer and poured more wine. "Let's move into the living room."

The buzzer sounded as Kay settled into a deep, tomato red couch. She sprang up to stand behind Tom and Louise, waiting patiently while they greeted Diane. Finally, she walked into the room and Tom closed the door.

Kay was trying to find a posture that made her look politely welcoming and not as nervous as she felt. Or as surprised at what she saw. She was a gorgeous woman with thick wavy hair, startling blue eyes, and a crippling smile. Tom made the introduction and Diane closed the space between them to shake hands. Her grip was firm and lingered two seconds too long for a casual shake. She felt the extraness of it. Louise was right about her warmth. She put Kay immediately at ease.

"I'm so glad to meet you," Diane said. "Tom's said wonderful things about you."

"Really? That genuinely surprises me. They've said wonderful things about you. Do you think they were setting us up?" Where the hell had that come from? It seemed all her misgivings were gone.

She laughed. "I wasn't sure if that's the direction they were headed, but for fun's sake let's say they were."

"Excellent," Kay said. She led her to the kitchen, leaving Tom and Louise staring after them. "I hear we're celebrating your appointment to the Art Institute's faculty." She poured her a glass of wine. There was a slight tremor in her hand and the bottle knocked against the glass. "Congratulations."

"It's exciting. Are you interested in art?"

She certainly was now. "Yes. I love painting in particular."

Diane stood at the corner of the kitchen island and Kay sat on a stool. They weren't very far apart. She tried to slow her galloping thoughts, which were reckless and a little juvenile. She'd only heard two sentences from her, but if she had a diary she'd be drawing hearts around her name. She'd not had a visceral reaction like this in a very long while.

"You're a homicide detective? I thought Tom was kidding," she said.

"No, it's true. I'm police. Have been for a long time."

Her eyes glinted as she looked at Kay. "People probably tell you it's kind of sexy, don't they?"

She hoped that meant she thought so. "TV shows make people think that. You wouldn't believe how mundane my job is in comparison."

"What a relief. A modest cop. I don't think I could have handled a boastful one. How could painting compete?"

"Quite well, I think."

"I'd be happy to show you my work, though I don't suppose you can show me yours. I'm not very good with dead bodies."

Kay felt a little tug, that feeling of something falling inside her. This was trouble. She tried to determine how old Diane was. Maybe early forties? Not so large a gap from her own thirty-eight.

"I'd love to see your paintings sometime," she said.

Diane was quite a bit taller than her and looked down with her killer smile. "Let's find a day then."

Tom and Louise came into the kitchen as Kay realized they'd just made a date. She knew she wanted to see more of her. The buzz she felt was growing by the moment. They all helped Tom get dinner on the table and sat to eat. They got through some art department gossip and looked at photos of Tom's new paintings, figurative work clearly inspired by Hopper. All the while she could feel Diane's eyes on her. They'd avert when Kay looked at her. Once, they exchanged a long glance that made her chest tight.

Conversation stopped as they finished their dinner. Kay knew Tom wouldn't allow silence to last for any length of time. He held up his wine glass.

"To Diane, who's a good sport to let herself be ensnared by my little sister."

"I have not ensnared her," Kay said, incredulous. She turned to Diane. "Have I?"

"Ensnared is not the word I'd use at all. Charmed, perhaps." Diane tipped her glass toward her and drank.

"Shut up, Tom," Louise said, her tone light with the hint of an edge to it. Tom ignored it. He drank more and looked at Diane.

"You don't know much about Kay, so I thought I'd tell you a story," he said.

"No, you won't," Kay said, trying to catch his eye to warn him off.

"Don't worry. It's not a bad story. Did you know Kay is a hero?" he asked Diane.

She started to protest again, but Diane spoke over her. "It doesn't surprise me at all. I'd love to hear about it." She looked at Kay with a mischievous grin.

"Oh, I love this story," Louise said. She topped off her wine.

Kay looked down at the hands in her lap and bit her lip.

"There you go, Kay. You're outnumbered," Tom said. She shrugged in defeat.

He settled back in his chair, clearly happy to have center stage. "When Kay was a rookie cop, and I mean right out of the academy, she walked into a 7-Eleven while off duty. She was probably there for smokes since she was a regular chimney back then. It was at Belmont and Racine in Lakeview. A guy walks in while she's in line, raises a gun, and shoots the ceiling. He screams for everyone to get facedown on the floor. He has the clerk lock the door. There were six people in the store—the clerk, two middle-aged women there for the lottery, an old man with a cane and a pint of Jim Beam, the Hostess deliveryman, and Kay. She's lying there on the floor wondering what the hell she's supposed to do. She's a cop. It was her duty to take care of the people in the store."

Kay snuck a look at Diane, who sat with her chin in her hand, staring at Tom with a faint smile on her lips. Tom carried on.

"The man works his way down the row of people, patting them down for weapons and cell phones. Kay always has a small gun at her ankle, both on duty and off." Diane looked under the table at her ankles, and she lifted her pant leg to show her the revolver. Her eyebrows climbed up her forehead. "As the bad guy got closer, she sees that he's not patting down their legs. She's hopeful he won't find the weapon, and he doesn't.

"Now they're all lined up in a sitting position, leaning against the Big Gulp station. He tells them to keep their hands on their knees. She worries about the old man, who could barely get down on the floor while clutching his pint. Once he was down, he cracked open the bottle. The gunman calls nine one one to get the attention of the police. He was there for the hostages, not robbery. Already there are a few people peering in the window, wondering why the door's locked. He waggles his gun at them and they scatter.

"While he's waiting for the first cop cars to arrive, the man addresses his hostages. He introduces himself as Luke Bandemere and tells them that they'll be safe as long as they don't try to do anything stupid. The usual. Then, as squad cars are pouring into the store parking lot, he starts lecturing them about some crackpot religion. It might have been Scientology. Who knows. Maybe Kay remembers what he was saying. Gobbledygook. But he goes on and on. The store's phone is ringing, the building's surrounded by an army of police, and he seems as unconcerned as if he were swinging in a hammock.

"Meanwhile, Kay's sitting with her knees pulled to her chest. She's inching her hand toward her ankle while keeping an eye on Luke. He's marching back and forth in front of them in full rant. Finally, he notices the ringing telephone and when he goes behind the counter to answer, he turns to look out the window, trying to see if it's someone in the parking lot making the call. Kay pulls her gun and shoots him in the shoulder. His gun leaps from his hand and skitters away. She's up and has her own little gun trained on him as she kicks his out of reach. The clerk unlocks the door and the cavalry roars in. And there you have a hero, decorated before she's even out of her training period."

Kay buried her head in her hands as Diane and Louise applauded. Tom had embellished the story. There was no Hostess deliveryman there. But it was largely accurate, a story that had followed her throughout her career. She hated it. She was no hero.

Diane turned toward her and made a fanning motion in front of her face. "I don't care what you say. That's smoking hot."

Tom looked satisfied with himself. "I can only imagine how many women Kay's seduced with that story."

"I have never..." Kay sputtered.

"Relax, I'm kidding. Kay's modest to a fault. She's a good egg, but there's lots going on under the hood." He looked affectionately at Kay.

Diane placed a hand on Kay's arm and brought her glass to her lips. When Tom and Louise carried dishes to the kitchen, she leaned in. "Can we leave soon?"

"Yes. Absolutely."

"Like right now?"

"As soon as coffee's done. We'll drink fast."

The talk over dessert and coffee seemed endless, but fifteen minutes later, they were out the door and pounding down the stairs to the street. She felt the first surge of real promise since she'd started dating again. She was so excited to see what the night would bring. They burst through the door of Tom's apartment building and onto Albion Street. To the right was the dark of Lake Michigan. To the left the lights and bustle of Sheridan Road. They turned toward the lights, walked past the Loyola campus, and crossed the street. She looped her arm through Diane's and pulled her close. When they got farther along Albion, Diane stopped and drew her close for a kiss. Kay was percolating.

"I'm parked a block away," Diane said. "I couldn't find anything closer."

She looked up at her, ready to suggest they go to her place. Two streetlights were out. Only the full moon lit the street. Big apartment buildings lined both sides, interrupted by the el tracks overhead. A train pulled into the Loyola stop, drowning out any other sounds. As they kissed she felt hazy, as if they'd already made love. Diane pulled away suddenly with a curious look on her face. Kay felt something jam into her back.

"Wallets," a hissing voice said. "Drop them to the ground." He had the eerie sound of someone disguising their voice with a voice box. She froze, more shocked than fearful, though she didn't doubt it was a real gun pressing on her spine.

"What the hell?" Diane said. She pulled on Kay's arm, unaware the man had a gun and was holding her fast by the back of her collar.

"Step back or I shoot her in the spine. Your choice."

"Diane, listen to me," she said. She tried to maintain a level tone, but she knew anything could cause the man to shoot. "He has a gun at my back. Do what he says. Exactly what he says." Diane looked torn, as if unwilling to let her go, but when the gunman yanked hard on Kay's collar, she released her arm and slowly pulled her wallet from her jacket pocket and dropped it. Kay tried to turn around to face the man, but he pulled her even closer, his gun poking hard against her.

"My wallet's in my front pocket," Kay said, the pressure of her collar against her throat made her voice sound strangled.

The man's mouth was against her ear. "Take it out. Slowly." Kay slowly reached into her pocket. He was peering over her shoulder, watching every move. She could smell his cologne— not Old Spice, but something else on the drugstore shelves. Paco Rabanne? She used to buy it for her brother at Christmas. She pinched her wallet between her thumb and finger and slowly drew it out, hoping Diane would be quiet and still. She had no intention of trying any heroics, not with a civilian present. Reaching for her ankle gun would be suicide. Trying to flip him over from behind was a low percentage move. It worked much better on TV than in real life. The safest thing they could do was hand over the money. She let go of her wallet and stayed as still as possible.

He moved the gun from her back and shoved her toward Diane, who quickly stepped up and stood in front of her, apparently forgetting Kay was a police detective. She took a good look at the gunman. There was a silencer on his gun, which made it seem all the more likely he intended to use it. He wore a huge black sweatshirt with the hood up and baggy blue jeans. He had on red Converse Chucks that looked new. She couldn't see his hair, but he had a full, dark beard, well cared for. He wore mirrored sunglasses in the dark. She saw from his ungloved hand he was white.

"Move back five steps," he said. She tried to commit his tinny voice to memory. It sounded gravelly, almost intentionally so. She stepped backward and Diane followed suit, still standing in front of her.

"Quit with the chivalry." He pointed at Diane. "Move to her side." He waved the gun between them. As Diane stepped next to her, he scooped up the wallets. He was not a street person or a gangbanger, for whom the word chivalry rarely came up in a sentence.

As he stood straight and brought his gun arm up, Kay felt a frisson that told her everything was about to go to hell. She pushed Diane aside at the same instant the silenced shot was fired. She reached for her ankle gun as Diane crumpled to the ground without a sound, blood instantly blooming on the front of her white shirt. As the man took off running, Kay fired twice at his receding back, both shots missing as he zigzagged down the street as if he were on military maneuvers. He disappeared down an alley.

She dropped to her knees beside Diane and put her fingers to her neck. She felt a thready, weak pulse, but she looked more dead than alive. Her body was limp, her face pale in the dim light. Her eyes were barely moving. She grabbed her phone from her pocket and called it in. She tried to keep from screaming.

"This is a 10-1. Police involved shooting. I'm Detective Adler off duty from Area Four. My friend was just shot during a robbery. We're on Albion just west of Sheridan. Victim has a serious wound to the chest and has lost consciousness. Please get fire rolling immediately. Offender is a white male, medium build, wearing a black hoodie, baggy blue jeans, and red sneakers. I fired several rounds as he ran from the scene, headed west on Albion and into the alley past Lakewood. Victim is in bad shape. All speed on this."

She dropped the phone and crouched next to Diane. Blood was still pouring from her wound, which at least meant she was alive. She was almost unable to believe what had happened. She looked desperately around and saw several people staring down the street from Sheridan. A squad car screeched to a halt in front of them. She stood, holding up her star as they approached. She held her gun loosely in her right hand.

"Detective Kay Adler, Area Four. We need an ambulance. She's been shot in the chest."

"We heard the call. Other cars are in pursuit," one of the officers said.

One officer studied her identification while the other kept his gun trained on her. "Lower your gun to the pavement, Detective." Kay did as asked. The first officer came to her and picked up the gun. They were following protocol, but she knew they didn't suspect her. Not another cop. Nor did she much care. She was rigid with shock, surprised at the hollowness she felt about a woman she didn't even know. She heard sirens in the distance.

The other officer knelt beside Diane and felt for a pulse. He looked up at them and shook his head. She was gone.

CHAPTER TWO

K ay sat in an interrogation room facing two detectives. She was on the side of the table where people wore handcuffs. She was still dressed for the dinner party—her long sweater and pale blue shirt were rumpled, as if she'd wadded them up and thrown them in a corner. Three empty coffee cups sat before her, the only objects in the room not bolted to the floor.

The detectives said they only needed information from her, and it was true they didn't seem to suspect she had anything to do with Diane's death. Her backup gun was a revolver, and a shell casing from an automatic was found at the scene. Still, she wasn't exactly free to go. She'd have to talk to the internal affairs detectives next. She kept her expression neutral to hide her disbelief that Diane was dead. She'd known her three hours, but the grief seemed so real. She stared at her hands pressing down on the table, the nail beds white from the pressure.

Detective Simpson was leaning toward her, his massive body covering half the table. His face looked doughy, his hands pudgy, and he wore a toupee that sat on top of his head like a yarmulke. "Let's do this one more time before we cut you loose."

Kay groaned. "This is stupid. I can't believe I do this to people myself."

Detective Arroyo leaned back in his chair, trying to avoid Simpson's bulk. He was thin and anxious. He kept jumping up and moving around the room. "I still don't get why this guy would shoot and kill your friend. It doesn't make sense, especially the way you've described him. He doesn't sound like a banger, or even an addict."

"You expect me to know the answer to that? I'm not a mind reader. Why did he shoot Diane and not me? I wish I knew. I've told you this already."

Simpson shrugged. "You know the drill. The lieutenant will make us come after you for another run-through if we don't get it now. You're doing great."

"I'm not doing great." She looked directly at him and turned to include Arroyo in her gaze. "Why are you sitting here instead of looking for the motherfucker who did this?"

"I'm going to get you more coffee, Kay," Arroyo said. He left the room.

"The uniforms are still looking, but I doubt they'll find him," Simpson said. "The guy's in the wind."

"Are they doing a canvass?" She had to make sure of even this fundamental step.

"Of course," he said. He sounded like his patience had run out. "We know what we're doing."

She said nothing.

"You're not the only detective in the Chicago Police Department. I've been around the block a few more times than you." He pushed away from the table and walked out the door. Arroyo walked in with a steaming cup of coffee that smelled like a newly tarred roof. He gingerly put the cup in front of her, as if afraid she'd reach out and grab him by the throat.

"Where'd Simpson go?" he asked.

"Probably for a smoke. It's how he stays so thin." Kay moved the cup back across the table to Arroyo. "Let's get on with this. The sooner I'm out of here, the sooner I can find this piece of shit."

Arroyo looked alarmed. "I don't know about that, Kay. I'm sure your lieutenant won't allow you to work this case."

"I don't care what he says, I'm working it." Kay leaned back in the uncomfortable chair and glanced at her watch. It was just past midnight. She felt like she'd never slept before and never would again. "Did forensics find anything at the scene?"

"They're still down there, but I don't think so. No footprints anywhere, no cigarette butts, no dropped matchbooks. They'll check for prints on the shell casing."

She gave him a long look. "Get Simpson back in here so we can get on with it."

Arroyo left the room. Kay rubbed her face in her hands, itching to get out on the street. Itching to do something. But what? What would she do that the assigned detectives weren't doing? A disguised man pops up out of nowhere, robs and kills, and disappears without a trace. He wasn't hopped up on anything, he stayed calm and in control, he kept his identity well hidden. He was not an amateur. His face was almost entirely obscured by his beard and sunglasses. The sketch artist used her description to draw a face that could be almost anyone's. Why kill Diane? That was more the act of an out of control thug or a kid in a panic. There was no reason to shoot her, not after he'd gotten the wallets.

The detectives made her wait twenty minutes. She knew they were pissed at her. She didn't care. But when they finally came back, Simpson looked apologetic. "IPRA is here to give you the once-over, the bastards."

"Fuck me," she said. No one liked the internal affairs cops, but they appeared like rats after every police involved shooting. She was more annoyed than worried.

"One thing I'm curious about," Arroyo said. "You seem genuinely upset about this gal's death. Didn't you meet her a few hours ago?"

She didn't answer. She couldn't explain her feelings. She didn't want to admit how out of touch with her surroundings she'd been while Diane was kissing her. A circus parade could have marched past and she wouldn't have noticed. The killer had either been lying in wait for a random victim to walk by, or he'd been following her and Diane and waited until they got to a dark street to jump them. The latter seemed more likely to Kay, but why would anyone be following them?

"I know this has hit you hard," Simpson said, "but fair warning. If you interfere with our investigation I'm going straight to your lieutenant."

She gave him a pitying smile. She didn't intend on interfering. She intended to find Diane's killer. After another hour, IPRA cut her loose and she left the Area Three building. Her car was still in front of her brother's place, so she took a cab for the long ride up to Rogers Park. The whole night seemed like a dream. She got her car and drove back south toward her Lakeview high-rise. The bright moon hung over the lake. It looked swollen, overripe. She called her brother on the way. Louise answered.

"Kay, it's one in the morning." She sounded more curious than irritated.

"I have some bad news. Is Tom there?"

"Tom's passed out and won't be waking anytime soon. What happened?"

Kay heard Louise gasp as she told her of Diane's murder. "I don't have any more information than that. She's down at the morgue for an autopsy. They got the names of a couple of her relatives off her phone, so they'll take care of her when the body's released." She sounded cool, as if she were saying these words to someone she didn't know about a body she'd never seen. "I wanted to give you the heads-up. The detectives will want to talk to you both. They might be on their way now. Have Tom call me as soon as he wakes up."

"I'll do that. This is ghastly. Are you all right, Kay?"

"I'm fine," she said and hung up.

When she walked into her dark condo, she could see lights twinkling in the harbor below. Some early birds had brought their boats out of storage, and a party was going on in one of them. She stared out the window, her body rigid, though she was exhausted and felt sick to her stomach. She was afraid if she sat down she would be overwhelmed. She was not on friendly terms with deep feelings of any kind. They were rarely pleasant. Diane had been the rare exception.

The last time she'd been this rattled she was a second-year uniformed officer, and she'd been no hero that time either. She and her partner Michael Hanson had taken a call at 2300 hours to backup narcotics detectives serving a search warrant in Uptown. They'd pulled up to the building—a rundown six-flat with crumbling front stairs and boarded up windows in half of the apartments. The entire building was dark. Another squad pulled up and then an unmarked sedan carrying the detectives. Their lights and sirens were off.

A tall, gangly man got out of the sedan, as relaxed as if he were poolside with a margarita in hand. His partner got out of the driver's side and huffed his way to the front of the building, where the others were gathered. His gut flopped over his trousers. He lit a cigarette. Very old school, Kay thought. She looked toward the tall one.

He spoke quietly. "I'm Pendergast. That's Nichols." He jabbed his thumb toward his partner. "We've got a warrant and a fresh tip on a drug dealer named Kurt Becker."

The name didn't mean anything to Kay. She was itching to get underway, itching for action.

"We're going to the third floor," Pendergast continued. "Quietly. One of you get your battering ram."

Hanson ran back to their squad and picked up their ram, carrying it on his shoulder as if it were rolled up poster board. He was overbuilt, his uniform straining at the seams.

"I don't expect there to be other people inside. This is his place of business. He may or may not have a gun. Assume that he does." He studied his small crew and sent two to the back of the building. "Let's go up and get this done."

Pendergast led the way silently up the stairs, with Kay and Hanson following and Nichols bringing up the rear. Everyone drew their weapons at the top of the stairs, and Hanson got in place to use the battering ram.

Kay felt the adrenaline flood her system, as it did every time she was called to something dangerous. She loved it. It made her feel intensely alive. She didn't feel fear as much as hyperawareness. Pendergast gave the signal, and Hanson hit the door with a thunderous clap. Kay stepped in front of Pendergast as the door swung open and jumped into the apartment's living room, weapon raised in a two-handed grip. As she swung her arms from right to left, a man roared into the room, pointing a gun at her and screaming. She fired immediately. Her first shot missed and the second hit him in the stomach. Pendergast's shot went over the man's head. The police were generally terrible shots. She kept her weapon trained on him and could see it trembling at the end of her arms.

"Is this Becker, Detective?" Kay said. Her voice was tight.

"Yeah, that's the man." Pendergast looked behind him and barked. "You three clear the rest of the apartment. Nichols, call this in."

Kay and Pendergast approached the wounded man. He was alive, clutching his belly and struggling to sit up.

"My wife," Becker rasped. "She's in the bedroom." He pointed to the wall behind him. There was a bullet hole in the drywall about two feet from the ground. Kay felt the first flush of fear.

One of the other officers called from the back of the apartment. "Detective, I need you back here."

Nichols stayed with Becker as she and Pendergast walked a few steps into the hallway and turned into the bedroom adjacent to the living room. Someone had flipped on the bare light bulb overhead. Becker's wife lay on top of a bare mattress, blood streaming from a bullet hole in the side of her head. Her eyes were fixed and staring at the ceiling.

"Oh, fuck," Pendergast breathed.

Kay got to the bed in two strides and felt for a pulse, knowing full well there wouldn't be one. On the floor next to the bed was a glassine envelope with what looked like heroin along with a needle, spoon, tourniquet, and lighter. Kay looked at Pendergast but said nothing, her heart pounding so loud she was sure he could hear it.

The other officers completed their sweep of the apartment and found an open brick of cocaine and a scale and other supplies for breaking it into smaller packets. There were more packets of heroin in the wife's purse. A duffel bag was searched and rolls of cash were found tucked under a sweatshirt and jeans. They returned to the living room, where Pendergast put on gloves and picked up Becker's gun. It was unloaded.

Soon the EMT, additional police, the area lieutenant, and a couple of brass descended on the scene. IPRA showed up within minutes. Kay stood still amongst the chaos. Pendergast came over and put his hand on her shoulder and told her it was a clean hit. Hanson and Nichols said the same thing. But none of them had just killed an unarmed woman.

Now she shook the memory loose and moved into her kitchen. She drank two fingers of bourbon, and then two fingers more before throwing up in the sink and stumbling to her bedroom. She fell asleep on top of her bed covers, fully clothed.

❖

The Area Four detectives were housed on the second floor of 23rd District headquarters near Wrigley Field. The year before, an office furniture consultant had sold the brass on the idea the detectives would work most effectively if their space was designed like an insurance claims department. Cubicle desks ran in three parallel lines along the long axis of the room. They stopped at the south end, leaving enough open space for a conference room, the lieutenant's office, a coffee station, mailboxes, and a large white board listing all the open cases and who was assigned to them. There was nowhere for detectives to sit down together other than the conference room, and the lieutenant strictly regulated its use. Nowhere for them to shoot the shit and find out who had shown up with the worst hangover, whose kid had won what medal, who had been shafted by the lieutenant, and what was going on in each other's cases.

The lieutenant's office was in the southwest corner of the room, its glass walls giving him a direct view onto the open area. He knew who was drinking the most coffee, who was loitering with others in front of the mailboxes, who was coming and going from the room. He was mostly an easygoing guy, but his gaze still prevented detectives from any bull sessions like they had when the room was open and littered with desks.

Kay entered the room at the start of her shift and walked up the narrow aisle to her cubicle. She didn't glance to see if the lieutenant was in, didn't stop to check mail or get coffee. She threw her long coat over the partial wall of her tiny space and dropped in her chair. Adam's desk was across the aisle and one down from hers. He jumped up when he saw her pass and stood at the invisible door to her cubicle.

He reached over and patted her shoulder awkwardly. "Don't you want to take some time off?"

"I don't want time off. I want to get to work."

He grabbed a chair from the empty cubicle next door and sat in the aisle. He looked cautious, as if the enormity of Kay's story required a delicate diplomacy he wasn't capable of. "Do you want to talk about it?"

She looked at him as if he were insane. "All I did last night was talk about it. No more talking. Time for action, so buckle up."

Kay scribbled down some names on a piece of paper and handed it to Adam. "What I want is the contact information for these people. They're colleagues of Diane's in the painting department. I'm going to interview them." Her brother had been near tears when they'd talked earlier in the morning and he'd given her the information.

Adam looked at her warily. "It's not our case, Kay. I know you want to go after this guy, but we've got to work our own cases. You haven't even asked for an update on Nora Sanderson and she's your sister-in-law."

"Ex-sister-in-law. Extremely ex." She turned to her computer. It struck her that two people she knew were murdered within a couple of days of each other. Like a lot of cops, she wasn't a great believer in coincidence. She felt the fog clearing a little, her detective mind reasserting itself. The suspect in Nora's murder and the man who shot Diane were both wearing black sweatshirts, but they didn't look alike. And why did the man from the previous night disguise his voice unless she may have recognized it? Her gut started to ache.

She opened a database. "I find it hard to believe this guy was following Diane. She's a painter. Who wants a painter dead? And if he wanted one of us dead, why the ruse of a robbery? Why not shoot and run?"

"You think he was following you? Targeting you?"

"Yeah, I do. Think about how many people might have a beef with me. Lots. I'm going to find which of my arrests have been released from prison in the last six months. Make it a year. Then we're going to contact each one of them."

Adam leaned toward her and spoke in a loud whisper. "Kay, please. The lieutenant will kill us if he finds us working on this. Who's caught the case?"

"Simpson and Arroyo out of Area Three."

"Don't know 'em."

"They don't do much to distinguish themselves. I'm not leaving this in their hands." She continued to punch in search terms.

"What are we going to do about Nora Sanderson?"

Kay spared him a glance. "We work it, of course. There're more than eight hours in the day."

"So now you're saying we're going to work overtime to cover both cases?" He looked like he'd just been given extra laps at track practice.

"Off the clock, though. You won't get paid for it."

He tilted his chair backward and rubbed his face hard. "I don't know."

"Remember, you wanted to be treated as a full partner. I need backup. Someone murdered my—"

"Your what? I mean, she wasn't even your girlfriend."

She looked at him with narrowed eyes. "She would have been. She meant something to me." Diane would have been her lover; she knew that. It felt as if she'd gotten a quick glimpse of happiness before the door clanged shut on her. She doubted she'd get another chance at it.

She hit enter on the computer and a list of parolees scrolled in front of her. "Christ. They're seven names in the last year."

She looked at their mug shots. She remembered each of them, but found it hard to believe any would be angry enough at her to seek revenge. The arrests themselves might have been made as far back as six years ago, when she became a detective.

"Get me that contact information," she said. "I'm going out to interview some artists and ex-cons."

"Do you even want to hear about Nora Sanderson?"

Kay started printing off the list and then gave Adam her full attention. "Sure. Fill me in."

He opened a file and pulled out the artist's sketch of the man who left Pinky's with Nora. She looked it over for any resemblance to the man who shot Diane, but she couldn't find any. A dimple or scar, something it would be hard to disguise. She knew those skilled in disguise were brilliant at diverting the eye toward the most obvious features—a scraggly beard, sunglasses, a unibrow, long hair. With a little putty, the brow could be made heavier, a cleft chin either invisible or prominent. The combinations were endless.

"Not much help there," Kay said.

"It's not a total wash. I showed it to a couple of people on her trivia team. They both said it looked like the guy at the bar, so at least we know it's fairly accurate. They also said it was unusual but not unheard of for Nora to hook up with a guy."

"She was in her twenties," she said. "That's what they do."

"I got names of more of Nora's friends and interviewed them last night. Nothing points to boyfriend problems or any other motive. No one else spoke to the guy at the bar. During the game Nora sat at the table facing the bar and she made a beeline to our man as soon as it ended. Her friends didn't talk to her after that."

Kay tossed the sketch onto her desk. "So what do you want to do next on your case?"

"It's not my case, Kay. It's our case."

"Well, let's say the next move's up to you. What would you do?"

"We need to finish reading her diary. We need to get more from the bartender about who she was friendly with at Pinky's. We need to talk to forensics and go to the autopsy. There's a lot more."

Kay was staring at her printout, trying to map out where the seven ex-cons were living. Three were in the city, the rest in far-flung suburbs or downstate. "Excellent thinking. Go do that."

"On my own?"

"Take what's her name, the rookie. Elise? I think that's it. You can be her field training detective for the day. I think Wallace is off."

"But what'll the lieutenant say?"

"Tell him I'm still caught up in last night's shooting. Ask him for the help."

She folded her printout and stuck it in her pocket. When she stood, Adam was still in the chair, blocking her way. She placed a hand on his shoulder. "You need to act like you're running a murder case. You look like you want to kill yourself."

"Doesn't it strike you that you had a connection with both Diane and Nora Sanderson?"

She looked at him. "I noted it. Don't know if it means anything."

She grabbed her coat and brushed by him. The lieutenant's office was dark as she hurried past. She knew he'd want to see her about the shooting last night. She'd have to dodge him as long as possible.

When Kay crossed the parking lot, she saw rookie detective Elise Sokolov getting something out of the back of her car. When she straightened up and closed the trunk, she saw Kay and raised a hand in greeting. She was in her late twenties, a blonde with Slavic features, quite beautiful. She'd joined Area Four a couple of months earlier, but Kay had yet to talk with her, mainly because they'd been working different shifts. Elise held a shiny new briefcase and seemed a little embarrassed by it. Kay walked toward her on the way to her car.

"Good morning, Detective," Elise said.

Kay stopped. She felt a tug of sympathy for the new detective. She remembered how nervous and awkward she'd been when she was brand new. She stuck out her hand. "Good morning. I'm Kay Adler."

"Elise Sokolov. It's an honor meeting you."

Kay raised her eyebrows. "An honor?"

"Sure. I've already heard about what a great detective you are. The guys on overnights talk about you." Elise stood a couple of inches shorter than Kay and looked up at her with deep brown eyes. She seemed completely without guile, unusual in a cop.

"Someone was pulling your leg, no doubt."

"Would they do that?" A small frown creased her forehead.

Kay laughed. "Sounds like they're taking it easy on you. Just don't believe everything you hear while you're getting your feet wet."

Elise shifted her briefcase to her other hand. It was a heavy leather with the letters ELS monogrammed on the front. Kay wondered what she could possibly have in there. Elise took a deep breath. "This may be asking too much, but I was hoping I might get your advice from time to time. You have the highest closed case rate in the area and I want to learn from the best."

Kay didn't know whether to be flattered or annoyed, but she admired her straightforwardness. "Sure. For today at least you'll be working with Oleska on one of my cases. Your FTD is out sick."

"That's fantastic. Can I have your phone number then?"

Kay gave her the contact information, impatient now to get going. "I've got to run, but don't be shy about calling. Not that I think you would be."

Elise flushed, the red that blossomed on her face a stark contrast to her pale complexion. Kay tried not to laugh as she walked across the parking lot. Her personal car, a used Audi she'd bought at CarMax, was pointed toward Halsted Street. As she opened the door, she saw a Zip rental car drive slowly south, the driver leaning over toward the open passenger window, lifting his hand in greeting. It was Griffin Sanderson, ex-husband and prime exploiter of her tendency to blame herself for everything. He was grayer than when she'd last seen him, but his face was instantly recognizable. It had so often been jammed inches from her own, contorted with rage, spittle flying from his mouth as he yelled at her. She shivered as he drove by, giving her a hopeful smile, as if they'd just had a spat and he wanted to make up. They hadn't spoken since she left him sixteen years ago, though he'd called and sent dozens of texts and emails she didn't respond to. Eventually, they stopped and she thought she was well rid of him. She shouldn't have been surprised he was in town following his sister's murder, but she felt shock shoot through her body, followed by rage. Diane, a woman who'd made her heart sing, had been murdered only hours ago. That was where her focus belonged, not once again hijacked by her jealous ex-husband.

She got in her car and tried to shake off the sick feeling he left behind. She needed to get to work. First on her list of ex-cons was Edward Ferris, who'd been released from Joliet Correctional Center the month before after serving five years on a robbery charge. Kay and her partner back then, Jimmy McTamany, had caught him in a nearby flophouse after he'd dropped his key in front of the Dollar Store he'd broken into. It seemed like the dumbest store to rob, but that was Jimmy. The key tag said "Imperial Hotel," a name that belied the yellow brick, six-story building with torn window blinds and a metal gate at the door. They'd gotten his room number from the bored, porn addicted man at the front desk and knocked on Ferris's door. He'd opened right up, as if he were expecting a pizza. He hadn't seemed particularly upset to be arrested. She couldn't imagine him plotting revenge on her. He wasn't smart enough to track her movements, nor did he have enough motivation to try. But she needed to check it out.

She called Norma Merendez, Ferris's parole officer, a surprisingly easygoing woman given her enormous roster of hard case clients.

"Yeah, he's one of mine," Norma said when Kay got hold of her. Her voice sounded like a truck bed of rocks over a bumpy road. "And if you're looking for him, go to Twenty-sixth and California. He got picked up last night around nine."

"What for?" Kay said.

"Armed robbery in Wicker Park. He dropped his gun during the commission and the guy he was robbing beat the shit out of him."

"I'd laugh if it weren't so pathetic." Kay's heart had tripped to hear Ferris had committed armed robbery last night, but he was already in custody when she and Diane were attacked.

"Ferris is hopeless on the street. He has a higher chance of survival in prison than he does outside. I don't think he's sad to be going back."

Kay thanked her and crossed Ferris off her list. She started her car and drove out of the parking lot, anxious to get moving. She saw Elise and Adam heading toward a pool car in the back of the lot.

The next ex-con on her list was Terry Mitchell, released three months previously after serving six years on burglary charges. It was his second conviction. Kay had been instrumental in breaking up a burglary ring that was operating in the Gold Coast, land of upscale high-rises north of downtown. Mitchell had been the leader of a group of five men who managed to work their way past a shocking number of experienced doormen. Most owners were out during the daytime, and Mitchell and his gang picked their way into condos in their respective buildings. Pretty straightforward stuff. Still, Mitchell had enough brains to coordinate his staff of burglars, convert their hauls into cash, devise ways to get by the doormen, and pick a few locks himself. Maybe he hated her for bringing his empire down.

Mitchell's parole officer directed Kay to an apartment building in Uptown, a rough neighborhood sitting in the midst of prime lakefront land. An ex-con would blend in easily in the area populated by addicts, the mentally ill, and young people buying up condo conversions. Kay pulled up to a large courtyard building two blocks from the lake. It stood between the most depressing retirement home she'd ever seen and a methadone clinic. She found Mitchell's name scrawled by a cramped hand on the building intercom. It blared in her ear when she rang, followed by a loud voice asking who it was.

"Kay Adler. I'm a detective."

A pause. "I know who you are. What do you want?"

"You're not in trouble. I need to talk to you about something."

There was a longer pause. Kay pushed the buzzer again.

"Do I have a choice?" The voice squawked out of the box. Kay knew he had a choice whether to talk to her or not, but all the better if he didn't think he did.

"No choice, I'm afraid. Your PO sent me here."

The door clicked open with another blare of the buzzer and Kay climbed to the third floor, making up something marginally plausible to question him about. When she reached the top floor, Mitchell let her into a studio apartment. He wore pressed jeans, a neat button-down shirt, and very white sneakers. They weren't Converse sneakers, but Mitchell's build could be that of the man who shot Diane. The room was spotless. Kay glanced around and saw an expensive stereo set, a tiny old TV, and a neat pile of books on the coffee table.

"I'd ask you to sit down, Detective, but I trust this is going to be a short conversation."

She pulled out her notebook and a pen and made a show of opening it up to a new page. "I think we'd be more comfortable sitting down, but I promise to not take much of your time."

Mitchell shrugged and motioned her to a cheap armchair sitting perpendicular to his futon sofa. They sat.

"I'm curious to see what this is about," he said. "As far as I know, I haven't violated parole."

She leaned back and tried to look friendly. "As I said, you're not in any trouble, Mr. Mitchell. I'm simply doing a follow-up for a project my district has taken on. We're interested in knowing how ex-convicts do after they've returned to our area."

"You're kidding." Mitchell looked amused.

"Not kidding. I want a brief—very brief—summary of how your time inside was and what your prospects are now that you're out." She poised her pen above her notebook.

Mitchell smiled. "It's nice you take an interest, Detective, as strange as I find it. As you can see, I have a place to live. I'm employed as an oyster shucker at the new Mariano's grocery store, and my prospects are as good as any poor, minimum wage fool's are. What else would you like to know?"

"And your time inside? How was that?"

Mitchell burst out laughing. "Should I write my Yelp review? 'A quaint, medium security prison in a great Illinois location. Warden Hughes was fantastic! Every question I had was quickly answered by one of his helpful and courteous staff. The only complaint I have about my stay in Pontiac is that it was too short!'"

Kay looked at him blankly. She was convinced he wasn't her man. His height was about the same as the man who stood behind her, holding her by the collar. And he was smart enough to pull the murder off, but the motivation seemed insufficient.

"One last question, Mr. Mitchell. Where were you last night between nine and eleven?

Mitchell stopped smiling at his own joke and stood from the low-slung sofa. "I knew this was all bullshit. You think I've done something." He walked to the door and opened it. "You can leave now. I'm not saying another word."

She stayed where she was. "Actually, I don't think you've done anything, but you can completely eliminate yourself from my list by telling me where you were. This shouldn't be a problem for you."

He was gnawing at his lower lip. Kay worried it would split open any second. Eventually, he quieted his mouth and shrugged. "What the hell. I was at an AA meeting."

"What time was that?"

"The meeting was from nine until ten, and then I went out for a bite to eat with the others. There's a lot of people who can vouch for me."

"Then you won't mind giving me a couple of names so I can verify."

Mitchell shook his head. "No way. I can't break their anonymity."

"You'd rather go in for questioning than break someone's anonymity?"

Mitchell looked relaxed. "Absolutely. I didn't do anything. I'm not worried about any questioning."

She stood and joined Mitchell at the door. "I'll let that go for right now. I'm glad things are working out for you."

"Need I remind you I'm an oyster shucker."

She smiled. "Well, you're not in prison." She trotted down the stairs and out the door into the bright sunshine, slipped on sunglasses, and got into her car. Mitchell's alibi had the ring of truth to it, and she didn't have nearly enough to bring him in. For now, she was comfortable crossing him off her list. She checked her phone and saw messages from the lieutenant, her union rep, and her mother. She ignored the first two and called her mother back.

"What the hell is going on?" was her mother's greeting. Her voice was vibrating. "Your brother told me what happened. Were you going to call me? I want to hear everything."

It was no surprise to hear how excited Susan Adler was. Her exuberance had little to do with concern for Kay and everything to do with how shocking the event was. Her mother loved nothing more than a big story, something she could really chew over with her friends. She had a field day with 9/11. That was a story with real meat on its bones.

"I'm sure Tom filled you in on the basics, and it's all over the papers, you'll be happy to know."

"Well, it's unbelievable," her mother said. "Who was the woman who got shot? Was she your date?" Kay could hear the slightest hint of sarcasm in her voice. She gave lip service to accepting she was a lesbian, but Kay always felt she thought her relationships a little less than. Her mother honestly couldn't imagine life without a man.

"I don't have time now for the details, and I'm fine, thanks for asking," Kay said.

Her mother was silent for a second. "You always land on your feet, Kay. I don't worry about you. Now spill."

"I don't want to talk about it, Mom." She thought it might be nice to have her mother worry about her once in a while.

"I can't imagine why not. Don't you need to process this?" She sounded more cajoling than understanding. "I mean, this woman was shot to death right next to you. You must be in shock."

Kay stalled. She put her headphones on and pulled out on the street. She wanted to hang up, but she'd not hear the end of it if she did. "I can't talk right now."

"Promise me you'll call later. You have until two this afternoon. We're leaving for that cruise later today so I won't be reachable."

Her parents now spent every vacation on a Holland America boat, and her mother came away from each one with ten new friends. The number would be higher but for the people her father alienated. Kay was charged with looking after their house while they were away. "I'll try to call, Mom. I can't promise anything. Happy cruising." She hung up before her mother could say anything else. She'd only recently learned how to say no to her. Her pattern had always been to worry about her mother's mood, which meant she usually accommodated her various intrusions into her life. Her mother always made it clear she wasn't concerned about Kay, let alone her mood.

She steered toward the nearest Starbucks to get refueled and plan her next steps. So far she hadn't crossed paths with Simpson and Arroyo. She wondered if they'd even considered this line of inquiry into the ex-cons. Probably not. She felt absolutely justified in poaching their case. Her case. She was pretty sure her lieutenant wouldn't agree.

It was Friday afternoon, one of the first nice ones of the new spring, and cars jammed the neighborhood streets. Everyone was out, escaping work early, heading out of town. She felt her mood sink further as she sat in traffic, trying to keep her feelings at bay. She was sure there was some way she could have saved Diane. A nanosecond in which she moved the wrong way and allowed the bullet to hit her. No one would be able to convince her differently. One way or the other, she was responsible for her death.

CHAPTER THREE

From Uptown it was a short trip down Lake Shore Drive to the Art Institute, where she hoped to catch one or two of Diane's colleagues. She rolled her window down and let the chilly lake air in. Piles of stubborn, dirty snow held firm where the city's snowplows had created mountains of the stuff. Frigid rowers were in their boats on the Lincoln Park Lagoon. The lake itself sparkled, and as she drove farther south the great skyline of Chicago showed itself off. She guided her car around the curves of the Gold Coast and down by the city parks fronting the lake, west toward the Loop, and then down into the vast Monroe underground parking garage. She was glad to have a service weapon at her side as she made her way through the dark and somewhat sinister complex. She trotted up the stairs onto Michigan Avenue and popped up like a mole into the heart of the city. The Art Institute stood like a citadel on the east side of the street, its front stairs crowded with tourists. She walked to the Columbus Drive side of the building to enter the school.

Tom came to get her at the reception area and led her into a nearby conference room. He wore a somber suit and tie. He pulled Kay into a hug and sobbed, as if they'd been separated by war. For a moment she was annoyed by him calling attention to himself, as usual. Then she found herself holding back tears. She couldn't afford to cry, not now. She took him by the shoulders and pushed him away.

"Tom, get your act together." She held him stiff-armed as he hung his head and searched his pockets for tissue.

"How could this have happened, Kay?" he finally said. He may as well have said, "How could you let this happen?"

"I'm not here to rehash what happened last night. I'm trying to find the guy who killed Diane."

He sat at the table and blew his nose. "She was just with us. I can't believe it."

"I know. I was there."

"Tell me what happened."

"Only if you promise to call Mom and relay it to her. I can't tell you how much I'd love it if you'd do that for me."

She filled him in on the details of the murder, speaking in a monotone. He looked incredulous, as if she'd told him Diane had been eaten by cannibals. "You're a magnet for bizarre police drama," he said. She couldn't disagree.

He brought her up to the second floor, down a long hallway of painting studios, to a group of small faculty offices at the end. He tapped at the door of one and poked his head in.

"Charlie, I've got a police detective here to talk about Diane. She's my sister. Don't let her scare you."

Kay walked into Charlie's office as Tom returned down the hallway. A nervous young man sat at a small desk. She knew most people were uneasy around homicide detectives, the squeakiest of the clean included. They worried they'd say something stupid that would lead to all kinds of unspecified trouble. Charlie looked like he'd been to wardrobe and makeup for the part of a hipster art teacher. His hair was long and curly and bound at the top of his head in a fat knot. He wore a black T-shirt and skinny jeans. Kay checked for Doc Martens on his feet, but instead found black Converse Chucks, apparently the world's most popular shoe. His thin arms displayed full sleeve tattoos. He was probably late twenties. He stood and extended his hand and Kay introduced herself. They both sat.

"I hope there's something I can do to help," Charlie said. "I'm totally bummed about Diane." He cleared his throat.

"I'm gathering background on her. How well did you know Diane?"

Charlie shrugged. "She's only been here a short while, but we hung out. Her office is next-door. Was next-door, I mean."

"Do you know if anyone's been through her office yet?"

He looked at her curiously. "Not that I've seen. Aren't you supposed to know that?"

Kay ignored the question. She'd leave the office search to Arroyo and Simpson, assuming they'd be at the school sooner or later.

"Tell me about Diane," she said, anxious to hear her described, to fill in detail she'd never learn from her.

"I dug her. She was a lot older than me, but that didn't seem to matter. We hit it off, as it were. We had lunch together, grabbed a beer a couple times."

"What would you talk about?"

"Art most of the time. Personal stuff, too. I'm going through a breakup so I hit on her for advice. Called on her greater experience, so to speak."

"Did she talk about herself?" Kay said, not in the least interested in Charlie's breakup.

"Yeah. She opened up to me, which was cool. She was in a pretty good place, from the sound of it. Once in a while she'd mention the woman she was dating."

Her stomach dropped, as if she were in a plane hit by a strong pocket of turbulence. She'd not had much time to speculate on Diane and her life, but it never would have occurred to her she was dating someone else. Why would she go on a blind date with Kay if she was already seeing somebody? Was she that type of woman? The thought depressed her.

She wasn't sure how long she was silent, letting the news sink in. "Tell me more about this relationship of hers."

"Don't know much. She said they'd see each other for a while and then stop and then start up again. I think she's a lawyer. They'd started up again recently, and Diane said she didn't know if she could take it much longer."

"It? What it?" Kay said sharply.

"I don't know. Whatever it was that made them break up so much. That's about all she said about her."

"Did she ever express any fear or concern about this woman?"

Charlie paused. "No, I don't think so. She threw a lot of tantrums, but I don't think Diane thought she'd harm her."

"Do you know her name?"

"Shelly. Shelly what, I don't know. Do you really think she did it? Because I don't see it, if you don't mind me saying."

Kay didn't see it either. It was not Shelly who jumped them last night. She heard the clack of heels coming quickly down the hallway. Charlie peeked out the door as Kay turned her head.

"Oh, my God, it's her. Shelly." He looked alarmed.

"Has she ever been here before?"

"A couple times. She scares me, to be honest."

A woman came striding toward them, her expression like one you'd have when you're fighting with the cable company. She was in her early forties, wearing a bright red power suit and high heels. She was average in all ways except for the most glorious head of hair. A warm auburn, thick, brushed away from her face, touching her shoulders. Kay felt jealous for the hair alone. She stopped in front of Charlie's door and pointed at him.

"You knew Diane, correct?" She completely ignored Kay. Charlie looked at Kay before speaking.

"Correct. I was talking to Detective Adler about her."

Shelly swung her head sharply and appraised Kay up and down. Her eyes were like laser beams. She wasn't a woman to fuck with.

"Detective. I'm Shelly Fineman. Maybe you can tell me what's going on. All I know is what I heard on the news, which is a shit way of finding out your girlfriend's been murdered."

Kay winced at the word girlfriend. "I'm glad you're here. I'd like to ask you a few questions."

"I want answers, not questions," Shelly said. Charlie was standing stock-still, as if he were a rabbit stopped in his tracks. "And I intend to get them."

Kay turned to Charlie. "Do you think we could borrow your office for a few minutes? Is there something you can do elsewhere?"

Charlie quickly came around his desk and headed for the door. "No problem," he said as he scooted away.

"Why don't you have a seat?" Kay said as she moved to get the chair behind the desk. "I'll tell you what I know, which isn't much at this point." Shelly perched on the edge of the guest chair. "Diane was in the company of a woman, apparently returning to her car around ten last night. They were jumped before they could get there. Diane was shot, the woman is okay. She gave a vague description of the assailant and that's all." Kay was almost tempted to tell her she was the woman Diane was with, but it didn't seem the right tactic.

"What do you mean in the company of a woman?" Shelly said rather fiercely. "What woman?"

"We know they were coming back from a dinner party where they were both guests. The hosts say they seemed to hit it off pretty well." Kay couldn't help herself.

"What?" Shelly looked not so much shocked as furious. "Like on a date?"

"That's what the party hosts report. Do you have any idea who may have wanted Diane dead?"

This sobered Shelly a bit, as if realizing that she was about to curse out a dead woman. "Absolutely not. Diane was a gentle woman, very mellow. We were a case of opposites attract. Or at least I thought we were."

Kay could sympathize. "How long had you and Diane been seeing each other?"

Shelly opened her mouth as if to answer and then snapped it shut. "Are you asking me questions in an official capacity, Detective?"

"Of course."

"Then I elect to not answer them. I know well enough how the husband/wife, boyfriend/girlfriend are targeted by the police. I have no interest in you twisting my words."

Kay put her hands on the desk and leaned forward. "I find it interesting that a murder victim's girlfriend, as you claim to be, wouldn't do what she can to help us find her killer. We're gathering information. You can help."

She flipped her hair back with a practiced motion. "I'm a lawyer. I'm trained to protect clients, which in this case is myself. When I retain a criminal lawyer we can talk." She stood.

Kay leaned back. "As I say, your attitude is interesting. Calls attention to itself. You've managed to both not help this investigation and pique my curiosity."

"Whatever you say. I came here to find out what happened, and I guess I have." She walked out and tried to enter Diane's office next door. The door was locked.

"Who do I have to see about getting into the office? I'm sure there are things Diane would want me to take for safekeeping."

"You would need to talk to me, and I'm telling you there's no way you're getting in. It's considered part of an ongoing investigation and you're not authorized to be here."

"We'll see about that. I'll talk to the dean."

"You can talk to whoever you like. You're not going to get your way. I bet that's hard for you." Shelly shot her daggers and turned to leave. "You'll be hearing from me. We'll need you to come in to answer some questions. You're welcome to bring an attorney."

Shelly retreated down the hall, her heels like a blacksmith's hammer on the tile floor. Kay let her get to the stairs at the end of the hall before following her at a more leisurely pace. She was gone by the time Kay reached the ground floor lobby. Sun poured through the giant windows and she saw Simpson and Arroyo enter the lobby as she walked through. Unfortunate timing. Simpson was wearing a plaid shirt and capacious blue jeans, with a windbreaker and a White Sox ball cap on his head. Figures he was a Sox fan. Arroyo was sharply dressed in a suit. Both saw her and headed her way.

"What is wrong with you, Adler? Do you want to get suspended?" Simpson said. He didn't sound hostile.

"Not particularly." She was taller than Arroyo, dwarfed by Simpson. She tried to convey nonchalance, hoping to keep Simpson cooled down.

"What are you doing here?" Arroyo asked.

"My brother works here. He teaches painting. He's upstairs if you'd like to talk to him."

Arroyo looked at Simpson. "We probably should. He can give us some other names."

"That's bullshit. You're here for the same reason we are—getting background on the victim."

"Is that such a terrible thing?" Kay said.

Simpson pulled his phone out of his jacket pocket and hit a number on speed dial. "I'm calling our lieutenant. You're not poaching our case." He walked a few steps away and talked into the phone. Kay looked at Arroyo.

"You'll want to talk to a painting teacher here named Charlie. My brother can direct you. I also just met the victim's girlfriend, Shelly Fineman. She's a lawyer and refused to answer questions. Maybe you'll have more luck with her."

"Thanks, Kay. I'll try to get Simpson to be more cooperative, but you know you're not going to be able to work on this. You're involved."

"We'll see." She left the school and walked back to the parking garage, unsure of what step to take next. There was a new voice mail from Lieutenant Sharpe. Time to go face the music before she got suspended.

❖

Lieutenant Jack Sharpe was a former defensive linebacker at the University of Illinois. Now in his forties, he managed to stay at his fighting weight through a grueling schedule of workouts. If you couldn't find him in his office, you could always find him in the station's fitness center.

Kay walked into the fug of the gym, her nose crinkling in protest. There were five cops working out, including Lieutenant Sharpe, who was lifting a tremendously heavy barbell. Kay approached when he lowered the weights and reached for his water bottle.

"You wanted to see me, Lieutenant?"

He turned his head toward her and scrunched his brow. "Adler! I wondered when you'd show up."

"Your message said it was urgent, sir."

Sharpe put the barbell on its rack. "Walk with me."

She followed as he headed for the water cooler in a far corner of the gym. The other police were out of eavesdropping range. "First of all," he said, "I want to say I'm sorry about what happened last night. You should have called me. I'd have gladly given you some personal time."

"There's no need, sir. I'd rather work."

"I haven't seen much evidence of you actually working today. Do you remember what I like to say, Adler?"

As if she could forget.

"Teamwork." He looked at Kay enthusiastically.

"Yes, sir."

"Teamwork is everything. We're part of a team here, the Area Four team, and we need everyone pulling together to close our cases and make our stats shine." He pulled his soaked T-shirt away from his body and fanned himself. Kay prayed he'd be brief.

"Now, the detectives in Area Three are on another team. I got a call a little while ago from their lieutenant saying you've been trying to investigate their case."

"I think of it as my case, Lieutenant."

"There's where you're wrong. It's not your case when you're one of the victims."

She watched him as he drank more water and unconsciously reached for his crotch to readjust himself. "The thing is, Adler. If you're trying to play for the other team, you're not pulling your weight on your own team."

"Yes, sir," she said. He nodded approvingly.

"You're too important to the team to have you off on your own. If you keep working the murder from last night, you can be suspended, and we don't want that. Go help your partner on your own case. Remember, teamwork." He clapped his hand on her shoulder.

Kay escaped and took the stairs up to the detective's room on the second floor. She knew she'd gotten off easy. The question now was how much further she wanted to push it. She walked by the coffee machine where Adam was pouring himself a cup and crooked her finger for him to follow. Elise came into the room and she motioned to her too. She threw her coat over the wall of her cubicle and settled into her chair before turning to them. Adam seemed wary, while Elise was eager. They both looked so young.

"Did you talk to the lieutenant?" Adam said.

"Yes, we had a nice chat." She motioned for them to pull up a couple of chairs. "Now. What's the latest on Nora Sanderson?"

Adam and Elise looked at each other. He nodded for her to go ahead.

"We talked with Nora's mother and got the names of more of her friends. She was a wreck. I'm not sure she's able to think clearly now about anything."

"That's okay. I'll talk to her again later. I don't think she's going to know much about her daughter's sexual habits."

"Right," Adam said. "So we went to see Nora's best friend Jenny. She was pretty distraught too. She found out about the murder when she called Nora's mom to try to find her. It was unusual for her and Nora not to talk every day."

"The last time she'd seen Nora was when they went to a movie last weekend," Elise said. She spoke with ease and confidence, not like a rookie at all.

"Did she recognize the man in the sketch?"

"No, unfortunately," Elise said. "She said Nora would occasionally pick up men in bars when she'd had too much to drink, and she always felt bad about it the next day. She wasn't that surprised to hear Nora had brought a man back to her apartment. She hadn't had a steady boyfriend for at least a year."

"Did you get the name of the ex-boyfriend?"

"We checked him out," Adam said. "He's an actor in one of the rinky-dink theater companies on the north side. He was onstage and then out to dinner the night Nora was killed."

"Follow up with the mother and friends to see if her ex has been showing up lately. It sounds like a solid alibi, but you never know."

"Got it." Elise jotted in her notebook.

"Try to find out from the bartender at Pinky's whether there was anyone else at the bar who might have seen our guy or overheard him talking with Nora. And give me the forensics reports. I want to know what the blood says."

She scanned the fingerprint analysis and saw the only prints found were Nora's and a few others in the living room, kitchen, and bathroom. They were probably irrelevant. She didn't believe the killer had moved beyond where the body lay near the door. If he had, he would have left a trail of blood throughout the apartment. Forensics had picked up some trace evidence, along with a small square piece of paper found by the door. It said "Inspected by No. 18." Fibers were attached to it. If they found the same fibers somewhere else it would be helpful. For now, they told her nothing.

The blood spatter report was straightforward. The spray of blood on the floor and walls was consistent with a slashing injury over a major artery. The drip pattern showed the suspect, who would have been covered in blood, had turned away from the victim and left the apartment. Dripping blood made a trail out the door, leaving footprints on the floor and carpeted landing. Those trailed off after a few steps.

Kay turned the page to read more about the footprints and froze. The experts were able to come up with the style of shoe worn by Nora's killer. Converse sneakers, the same Chuck Taylor style Diane's killer wore. Holy Mother. It was the same man who killed Diane. She didn't doubt it.

"What's wrong?" Adam said. He was staring at Kay as she sat motionless in her chair.

"We've got the same sneaker at both scenes. I saw red Chucks on the man who jumped us last night. What did the other witnesses at Pinky's say about what that guy was wearing?"

They both started flipping through their notebooks. Elise stopped before Adam did. "One of her trivia teammates thought he was wearing low top red Converse. She noticed them when she came to the bar for a drink and checked out the guy Nora was flirting with."

"Fucking A," Kay breathed. "And both killers were wearing black sweatshirts. I'm going to the lieutenant."

"But how could they be the same? The guy you saw was medium build and the one who left with Nora was thin."

"The guy I saw wore baggy clothes. It's possible he was thinner than he looked." She slipped between their chairs and started to walk away before stopping and looking back. "You can come with."

They scrambled up and followed her. Lieutenant Sharpe was just back from the gym, his hair wet from his shower, leaning back in his chair drinking Gatorade. A giant canister of protein powder stood on the corner of his desk. He waved them in.

"Back already? What do you need?"

She entered the office and left Elise and Adam standing at the door. "I need bodies and I need that case transferred to me. I just found a link between Diane's murder and the Nora Sanderson case."

The lieutenant raised his eyebrows. "What kind of link?"

"It's solid. The man who killed Nora Sanderson and the one I saw last night wore the same color sweatshirt and the same type of sneaker."

"What type?"

"Converse. The old basketball ones."

"Chuck Taylors," Adam said.

"A witness at Pinky's says our suspect's were red," Kay said. "Forensics confirmed they were Converse. The shoes I saw on the guy last night were red Converse. Can't be coincidence, right? How likely is it that this would happen with two people I know within forty-eight hours? The only hitch is the description of the man at Pinky's is different than the man I saw."

"So you think he's wearing disguises?" He drank more Gatorade.

"I don't think there's any other explanation. Lieutenant, this is the first bit of useful evidence turned up in either of the cases. We can't ignore it. And we can't have two completely separate investigations. We're going to miss too much. Arroyo and Simpson are already blocking me out."

She could hear Adam shuffling behind her. He was probably hurt she wasn't including him in the conversation. She pointed her thumb at them. "I want these two with me."

"That's your team?" Sharpe asked. He leaned forward and folded his hands on his desk. "Isn't Sokolov a rookie?"

"Yes, sir, but she's sharp. I can act as her FTD. She'll learn a lot." She saw a slight frown on Adam's face.

"Okay. What else?"

"I need bodies to start calling shoe stores. The shoes I saw looked new. The report on the other pair said they were new also. I'll need them for other leads as well. Give me two more."

Sharpe was looking up at Kay with a smile. "And you also want me to get the case transferred to you? That's not going to happen. Officially, you're working the Nora Sanderson case. I'm going out on a limb even doing that."

"Understood, sir. Perhaps the detectives from Area Three could at least share information with us?"

"I'll call Benson over at Three and see if we can cooperate. And you'll have to make do with the two on your team. I'm not convinced we have multiple murders."

Kay guessed this was the arrangement she'd have to live with. The thought of cooperating with Arroyo and Simpson, especially Simpson, was galling, but she'd make it work.

"Thank you, sir. I'll wait to hear the status from you."

Sharpe picked up the phone as Kay led her small posse back to her desk.

"Jesus, Kay. The shoe thing is huge," Adam said.

"It's a huge tease right now." She plopped into her chair. Adam and Elise moved as if to sit down also. "Don't sit. Adam, I want you to figure out an approach to finding where the shoes were bought and get on it. Elise, you get back with your witness who identified the shoes at the bar and nail her down on it. Take a statement. Get in touch with everyone else who was there and see what they say. And talk to the bartender about the guy's voice. We need to know what he sounded like." She turned toward her desk. "Go."

Elise quickly left. Adam lingered. "Kay…"

"No. Don't start. Don't even think about it. There's no time or space for your feelings, Oleska."

"I was going to say we have to get someone looking into your ex-husband. He's a legitimate suspect, don't you think?"

The thought made her shoulders sag. "For killing his sister? I don't know. Let me deal with that."

When Adam left, she blew out a breath and put her head in her hands. There seemed no doubt that the two cases were linked, and the link was not only the Converse sneakers and sweatshirt but herself, too. The killer was taunting her. Wearing the same clothes at two different crime scenes was amateurish, but he was smarter than that. He wore different disguises and he did it to tease her, to make her play catch-up when he had an impossibly long head start.

The only thing that was certain was that Diane and Nora would be alive if it weren't for her. She felt as guilty as if she'd done the murders herself.

❖

It was nearly midnight when Kay pushed her way through the revolving door of her high-rise. Gerald, the shockingly old doorman, sat at his desk and stared at Kay from slitted eyes. His features drooped alarmingly, as if the force of gravity had defeated the resistance of his facial bones. She didn't know why he hadn't retired, or been forced to retire. It wasn't because the owners in the building loved him. He was notoriously ill-tempered. His normal expression was a scowl.

"Not so fast, missus. I've got a couple more envelopes for you. You running numbers up there?" His voice sounded like gravel being raked.

She approached the desk. "That's right. If you ever want into the craps game, knock on my door four times." The lines grew deeper in his face. He didn't have a terrific sense of humor.

"Smarty-pants," he said. Kay would have laughed if she'd had the energy. He shoved a letter-sized white envelope and a larger manila envelope across the desk. Her breathing hitched as she saw Griffin's handwriting on the smaller of the two. She recognized its sharp angles. Her name was typed on the second envelope, with no indication who it was from. She took them upstairs and locked her door for the night. She was exhausted. She needed a drink. She needed to get out of the tailored trousers and button-down shirt. The clothes seemed to be grasping her and she felt claustrophobic.

When she'd changed into T-shirt and shorts, she lay propped up on the sofa with a tumbler of Four Roses and stared at the envelopes. She had no desire to read what Griffin had to say, but she ripped it open to get it over with. The sixteen years since their divorce had been almost enough to forget him. Now that time seemed to have collapsed, as if she'd never passed through it.

Kay—

I knew you were working at the old Town Hall station, but I didn't expect to see you there when I drove by this morning. Don't worry, I'm not stalking you. I'm not like that. I'm a different man. I hope you'll allow me to apologize for my past behavior when I see you at Nora's wake. It runs from noon until eight on Sunday, but I'll be there the whole time. Isn't it time we let go of the past?

A dread she remembered well fell over her like a cloak. His calm and reasonable words were so often followed—sooner or later—by pure vitriol. He would fly into a rage over the most banal things she said or did. There was no way for her to anticipate and avoid his wrath when anything could provoke it. She hunched her shoulders as the scene of his last tantrum came back to her, the one that finally caused her to flee the house and not return.

They'd been married a year. They were still living in Normal, where Griffin was an assistant professor at ISU and Kay was taking a graduate class the summer after she'd gotten her bachelor's. It was the first week of class and she'd joined a group of students for coffee with their adjunct professor. When she got home before dinner and told Griffin where she'd been, he politely asked what they'd talked about. She was pleased that he seemed genuinely interested and chatted on about the book they were reading in class—*Sister Carrie*—while she pulled pots and pans out to start dinner. He stepped aside as she took food out of the refrigerator and leaned back against it as soon as she closed the door. She could feel his gaze following her. She'd always loved how he looked at her as if she were something exquisite, but that wasn't what she felt from him now. It was harder to read what was going on behind his bright green eyes. She'd made the mistake several times of mistaking interest for rage—rage that came out of nowhere and seemed to be unattached to anything she'd said or done. Rage that made her terrified.

"It was a great discussion. I had fun," she said.

"Tell me about your teacher. He sounds amusing."

She started washing vegetables in the sink, her back to Griffin. "Oh, he's totally amusing, which is what makes these coffees so fun. Everyone likes him." She didn't think he could object when she was in a group.

"How old is he?" His voice remained conversational.

She glanced over her shoulders. "I'm not sure. Probably around your age." She turned back and starting tearing up lettuce for a salad.

"Maybe he's a little like me, then," he said. "It wasn't that long ago I was your teacher."

She hesitated. When she glanced at him again, his eyes were hooded. He made her think of a cobra about to strike. "No, he's not like you at all. You're much more a presence in your field. More of a presence, period. I thought of you in an entirely different way when I was your student."

"Oh, I doubt that very much. I'm certain you were looking for the same kind of fun from him that you got from me, weren't you, Kay?" He was using his teacher voice, the one that demanded agreement with everything he said.

She threw things into the salad bowl, trying to pretend there wasn't anything wrong, hoping he'd snap out of it. He sometimes did. He pushed himself away from the fridge and took two steps toward her. His voice trembled with barely contained fury. "Are you seducing him the way you seduced me?"

She kept her back to him. "Of course not. There were four other people there."

Griffin grabbed a skillet and slammed it on top of the range so hard it dented the cheap burner. She flinched. She knew he saw it and fed off it.

"Will you fool him the way you did me? Covering up what a stupid whore you are?" He grabbed the skillet again and brought it down on the countertop, chipping the Formica, screaming at the top of his lungs. "Did you fuck him in the café bathroom?"

She'd backed up so she was leaning against the kitchen door. Something clicked. Something told her things were never going to get better. Griffin would never change. As he flung the skillet across the room, Kay slipped out the door and starting running as fast as she could to her friend Alice's studio. And this time she didn't come back.

And now he says he wants to apologize? She wasn't fooled. He wanted something she didn't want to give. She'd told him she was a lesbian. She'd discovered it herself the year after she left Griffin, when she'd met a woman and all the pieces fell into place. But he'd never acknowledged it. She took a deep breath and threw the note back on the coffee table. She needed to go to Nora's wake, but seeing him was a big price to pay for it. And why approach her now? Because he happened to be in town for his sister's funeral? Or was he in town for something else?

The other envelope contained a single sheet of white copy paper. The large, bold type leaped off the page at her.

I know everything about you. Where you live, where you work, who you know. What fun this has been, and there's more to come. Sit tight.

She dropped the paper onto the coffee table as if it were on fire. The killer was letting her know that Diane and Nora's killer were one and the same person. It wasn't paranoia on her part. And now he was baiting her, promising more death to lay at her feet. She scrambled into some blue jeans and raced downstairs.

Gerald's midnight shift replacement was helping him push the revolving door as he left for the night. Kay went through a side door and met him outside.

"Jesus Christ on a crutch. What's the matter with you?" He stood in front of the door, bent at the waist and drowning in a long woolen coat.

"Gerald, were you at the desk when those envelopes were delivered? It's important."

"Everything's always important to you people."

"I'm talking to you as a cop now. This is official business. Were you here or not?"

He gummed his toothless mouth as if working his way up to words. "Yes, I was here. The first came from a guy who kept trying to talk to me. I don't want anyone talking to me." That would be Griffin.

"I know. What about the other envelope?"

"That one came in not too long ago."

"And?" Kay was clinging to whatever last bit of patience she could summon. "What was the person like who delivered it?"

He closed his eyes as if conjuring up a picture. "Tall fellow. Wore a ball cap way down on his head. He had a ponytail."

"What color hair?"

"Couldn't tell you. Dark."

"Do you remember anything else about his face?"

He sighed as if expelling the last breath in his body. "The only thing I saw was a bandage across his nose. Must have broke it."

"Was it like a Band-Aid across the bridge of his nose or a big bandage covering his nose?"

"Big. It covered most of his face."

"Was he heavy or thin?"

"Thin, I'd say."

Kay was scribbling in her notebook. "What was he wearing?"

"Cripes, I don't know. Clothes."

"Did he have a jacket on?" She expected him to cut her off at any moment.

"Sweatshirt, I think. And I guess he had blue jeans on. I only saw him a second."

"Did you see what shoes he was wearing?"

"No, I didn't see his goddamn shoes. I'm going now."

Kay opened her phone to the two artist's sketches. "Did he look like either of these men?"

He screwed his face up tighter and peered at the small screen, shaking his head. "I don't want any trouble." He looked over at a car idling in the circular drive. "That's it, I'm going."

She put her hand on his arm. "Is there any way the same man could have delivered both envelopes?" She didn't believe Griffin would have killed his sister, but she had to look at all angles.

"Not unless he got his nose broken between deliveries."

"So other than that they could have been the same man?"

He stared at her with watery eyes. "I'm lucky I can tell it's a man standing in front of me. Other than the bandage over the nose, I couldn't tell you a thing."

He shambled over to his ride. Her heart was beating fast as she rode the elevator up. She'd still had hope she'd been wrong about her being the real target of the killer. Now there was no doubt.

She arranged for a forensics technician to pick up the envelope. By the time she got to bed she felt wired. She stared at the ceiling, waiting for the release of sleep. It didn't come easily.

CHAPTER FOUR

K ay sat at the Area's conference table with Simpson, Arroyo, and Lieutenant Sharpe. The two Area Three detectives had been urged to cooperate with Area Four on Diane's murder case while its possible connection to the Nora Sanderson case was being explored. The small room was crowded with boxes of documents and a large, blank white board. The table was littered with Starbucks cups and empty pastry wrappers. Kay had called in the files on every case she'd worked on since becoming a detective and intended to read through them. The room was windowless and smelled musty from the documents.

All eyes were on a copy of the message Kay had received the evening before. The original was downtown at the forensics lab. She'd be surprised if they found anything on it other than her own fingerprints.

"If this is from our killer," Sharpe said, "it confirms what you suspected from the footprints. He's behind both cases." He looked at Kay. "You're only here because of the Nora Sanderson case. If this connection with Diane means you can't be objective in that investigation, than you're off it altogether." Sharpe was dressed in a crisply ironed white uniform shirt, his bars shiny on his mountainous shoulders. There'd soon be pressure from above to solve the linked cases, and Sharpe had dropped his easygoing demeanor. His stats were in jeopardy.

"That won't be a problem, Lieutenant," Kay said.

He picked up the paper and waved it in the air. "So what about this? Let's hear some thoughts."

"I'm the real link between them," Kay said.

"I'd say we've established that," Simpson said. He was still chewing a pastry and small puffs of powdered sugar flew in the air as he spoke.

"So what does it mean?" Arroyo said. "He's talking about more to come. Do we need to tail Kay twenty-four seven?"

"I have no problem with that if that's what it takes, but it's not like I have to be present for him to strike."

"We don't know shit," Sharpe said. "Go find out more. I want a report at the end of the day. Call me at home."

He left the conference room without another word. Arroyo and Simpson stared at her.

"So what's next?" Simpson said. "We have Adam on the wild goose chase about the shoes. What else are we doing?"

She put the copy of the message into the thickening case file. "I finished reading the diary yesterday. Nora picked someone else up at Pinky's early in the year, but either she didn't know his name or didn't bother to record it in her diary, so there's no follow-up. We've got more names of her friends we're pursuing. I've got Elise on that, but we could use more help."

"We can do that," Arroyo said.

"We need to go through these old case files of mine. If we're thinking this might be someone I arrested, we might be able to find him in those. We don't know what he looks like other than he's tall, probably slender. Maybe we'll get lucky."

Simpson wiped his hands on his jeans. "Sure. I'll stay here and get started on that." Kay was mystified by the personality shifts everyone seemed to have undergone. Sharpe was no longer chummy, and Simpson and Arroyo were no longer antagonistic, perhaps because their own case, Diane's murder, was at a dead end. The connections with the Nora Sanderson case were the only lead they had.

Arroyo busied himself collecting cups and wrappers. "How about this ex-husband of yours? Are we going to talk about him?"

Kay stared at her hands. There was no avoiding this. She was already unsettled by Griffin's note and seeing him drive by the station. It'd taken her a long time to cast off whatever spell he had on her. She was a different woman now, invulnerable to him, though everything about that time made her feel uneasy and full of shame.

"I don't know that there's anything to talk about. I haven't seen him for sixteen years. He's completely out of my life."

"Consider it background," Simpson said. "We want to know more about Nora, so it makes sense to talk to her brother. Do you know where we can find him?"

Adam came in the room and took a seat, as if he knew Kay was talking about her private life. No one was privy to much of that.

"I have no idea where he is. I'll ask his mother when I talk to her later."

"He'll be at the wake, won't he?" Arroyo said.

"I would think that's why he's here." She moved her chair back and stood.

Simpson waved his hand. "I knew she wouldn't tell us shit."

Kay paused. "Griffin was a very angry man. That's why I divorced him. Whether he's capable of murder is your guess as well as mine."

She walked out the door, unsure what she said was true. She didn't know what Griffin was capable of. He'd been threatening before—why would she think he no longer was? She needed to talk to his mother. She left Area Four and returned to the Jefferson Park bungalow. Theresa answered the doorbell within seconds, as if she'd been poised on the living room couch, waiting for it to ring. She opened the screen door for Kay to enter. Her eyes were red, and the bags under them far more pronounced than when she'd seen her Thursday. She'd not gotten to know Theresa well during the time she was married to her son. He was generally dismissive of his family. They'd been living in Normal at the time. But Kay remembered her as spirited and friendly, a very different version of the woman before her.

They sat within arm's distance of each other on the couch. "How are you holding up?" Kay asked.

"There's no describing what I'm feeling. I won't even try." She looked down at the hands clenched in her lap. Kay reached over and squeezed them gently. Then she pulled back and got her notebook out of her coat pocket.

"Theresa, I know you've talked to detectives a couple of times already, but I'd like to go over a few things again."

"I want to help," she said, trying for a smile that ended up a grimace.

"We haven't told you yet that we have a suspect. It seems likely Nora brought the man home with her on Tuesday night. Witnesses at Pinky's say she went to the bar after the trivia game was over and talked to a man there for quite some time. They were seen leaving together."

"You're saying Nora picked up the man who killed her?" Her tone was even, as if she were confirming delivery of a new dishwasher.

"That's our working theory. We had a sketch artist draw his likeness. I'd like you to take a look." She handed her phone to Theresa, who glanced at it before handing it back.

"Never seen him before."

"Are you sure? You only looked for a second."

"I saw enough. I don't know him."

"So he wasn't a boyfriend of Nora's?"

Theresa looked at Kay. "She didn't have a boyfriend and she seemed to like it that way."

"Does it surprise you she'd bring a stranger home?"

Theresa took a breath. "It's not shocking. It's not smart, but she was young. They're not always smart."

"Is that something she'd tell you about?"

She smiled, a genuine one this time. "Nora and I talked about everything in the world except her sex life. Or mine, for that matter."

"Was there anything else going on in Nora's life?"

Theresa hesitated. "Would you care for something to drink, Kay?"

"No, thank you. There is something else, isn't there?"

Another pause. "I didn't want to bring Griffin up, not with the history you have with him. But, yes, there was some trouble between Nora and Griffin."

"Don't concern yourself with that. This is official police business. Griffin's already been in contact with me."

"He's in town?"

"I saw him yesterday when he drove past my work and waved at me. Then he sent a message to me at my condominium. He's not been in touch with you?"

"No, but I'd left him a message about Nora's death. And the funeral home said he called to ask about the service. But we haven't talked." Theresa stood and walked toward the back of the house. "I'm having a beer." She got a can and sat at the kitchen table, pointing Kay into a chair. "There's a lot that's happened after you left Griffin." Kay remained silent, not knowing if Theresa had been angry with her for leaving her son. She cracked open the beer and took a long drink.

"I don't blame you for leaving him. His behavior has always been erratic, since he was a little boy. After you left he went a little crazy. He started drinking heavily. He was spending money he didn't have. We visited him at the university before he lost his job, and there was a new car in the driveway, a whole house full of new furniture, and he'd redone his kitchen. He started visiting us more, but every time he came over, he got angry. We seldom knew why. Then one day he showed up with a new wife, a college student who'd fallen for him. You remember what it was like. He could turn on the charm machine and nearly always get what he wanted."

Kay knew exactly what she meant. She'd been an undergraduate when she met him and he dazzled her. The first adult who'd made her believe she was something special. She drank it in like she was dying of thirst.

"Things turned bad quickly. Sandra—the new wife—called me when she could and she didn't hold back. She said Griffin wasn't hitting her, but she always felt he was about to. He terrorized her in a number of ways. He flew into uncontrollable rages, he accused her of cheating every time she saw someone outside the house. He followed her, tried to control everything about her life. It was so bad one night that she called the police and they called an ambulance. Not for her. She was shaken, but fine. They took Griffin in for evaluation at the emergency room. He was delusional, and anyone could see it. Sandra used that as the pretext for getting him committed to the psychiatric wing."

Kay was shifting around in her chair. "I knew there was something seriously wrong with him."

"The diagnosis was borderline personality disorder. They say there's no cure for it." They were silent for a bit. Having a diagnosis of mental illness should have made Kay more sympathetic toward Griffin. It did not.

"What about Nora?" Kay asked.

Theresa drank more beer. "You have to understand how he disrupted our lives for years. He couldn't maintain relationships and yelled at us for the terrible upbringing he had. He couldn't keep a job and was constantly asking us for money. We bailed him out of jail at least twice."

"What for?"

"DUIs. He'd developed a serious drinking problem within a year or so of you leaving. He didn't show up for his father's funeral, though I'd let him know he'd died. A week ago, he reached out to Nora to ask for money and she basically told him to shove it."

Kay raised her eyebrows. "How did he react to that?"

"He left a few nasty voice mails. The worst she'd ever heard from him. She thought he might be delusional again."

Kay wrote down Griffin's number. "Do you know where he lives?"

"No idea. I believe he moves around a lot."

"We didn't find those voice mails on Nora's phone, but she could have deleted them."

Theresa stopped the beer can on its way to her mouth. The color drained from her face. "What if the man at Pinky's wasn't someone trying to pick her up, but was Griffin instead?"

"Could he have fooled her by wearing a disguise?" Kay said. "Look at the photo again." She handed her the phone and Theresa studied the sketch. "Is there any way that could be your son?"

She shook her head. "If this is Griffin, you could have fooled me, and Nora too."

"It might be a very good disguise. His body is the same build as Griffin's." Kay stood. "Do you think Griffin could murder his own sister?"

Theresa spoke in a whisper. "God help me, but I do."

Kay retrieved her coat and walked quickly to the door. She turned to give Theresa a hug and found the woman sobbing in her arms. It seemed like hours before Kay gently pushed Theresa away, but it was probably closer to a minute.

Theresa scrubbed her face and looked through her fingers at Kay. "I'm so sorry for losing it like that."

"You're so brave to try to help us. I'll let you know everything we find out."

She left the house and trotted to her car. The collateral effect of murder, the tearing apart of the loved one's world, the depth of despair and grief that created a feeling so horrible it was impossible to describe. She wanted justice not just for Nora and Diane, but for everyone whose lives they touched.

What was the probability Griffin murdered Nora and Diane? Wouldn't she know her own ex-husband? As she'd stood next to Diane facing their assailant, she'd gotten a good look. His face had been mostly hidden by his hood and beard, but what she saw didn't closely resemble Griffin. The nose was too long and his lips too full, but that could be the effect of a little putty. She couldn't see his eyes, and it was impossible to see what his build was like because of his baggy clothes. The last time Kay had seen Griffin he was lean like the man described in Nora's murder. Could her ex-husband take these two lives? If so, she was responsible. Griffin was trying to harm her. They'd be alive if it weren't for Kay.

She called Adam on her way to Area Four. "I want you to put a BOLO out for Griffin Sanderson. Use the description in the file and also post the two artist's sketches. I believe the killer is disguising himself. Maybe we'll get lucky and he'll use the same one twice. Got that?"

"Right. We're already looking for your ex-husband. What should we do if we find him?"

"Bring him in for questioning. He's a legitimate suspect. I'll fill you in when I see you."

"That would be good."

"I saw him yesterday. He drove by Area Four in a Zip car, one of those that have a big Z on the door. See what you can find out from them. I'll be in the area in a few minutes."

She briefed the team in the conference room on Griffin's mental illness, which made him more of a suspect. She got out of the room as quickly as she could. She'd rather be looking for Griffin than talking about him. She knew she'd see him at the wake. If he was the killer, he was very confident he wouldn't be recognized. She sat at her desk and held her head in her hands. She was tired. Her sleep the previous two nights had been fitful, even after taking Ambien. She needed to get away and come back to the case with fresh eyes. She needed a drink. She called her best friend Alice to meet her at Big Chicks later and then drove to her parents' house to get the mail and feed the fish.

Kay's old neighborhood was lined with large, solid frame houses, old and new. The streets were broad and trees towered overhead. Their house had been in the Adler family for several generations and it'd been a grand Victorian in its day. Now its spindled wraparound porch needed a coat of paint, its driveway was full of broken concrete. Before leaving home for college, Kay had lived in the maid's quarters, which had its own back stairs, very useful when Kay came home late as a teenager. Not that she'd have gotten into trouble. Her parents barely knew she was out and certainly didn't note the time she got in.

Her favorite part of the house was the creepy attic. It held treasures from a long line of Adlers. Ancient wedding dresses and parcels of letters tied with silk ribbon. Strange baby dolls with porcelain faces and penetrating eyes. An old musket. In one big wooden trunk there was a mishmash of costumes, mostly of historical figures—a Lincoln top hat and beard (her favorite), George Washington's pig-tailed white wig, Ulysses Grant's uniform. She and Tom spent hours dressing up and conquering things.

Her mother complained about the creaky house, but there was never any serious talk about leaving. As confusing as her childhood had been, the house seemed like the one stable, stalwart thing. Like igneous rock, it didn't shift beneath her. She had to be on her toes so much of the time to navigate the varying moods in the family. She became expert at reading tones of voice and facial expression, able to anticipate a blowup before it happened.

She parked in the drive and entered by the side door. The Adlers' next-door neighbor was pulling dead stuff out of her garden. She waved to Kay with her gloved hand and got back to work. She was relieved she wouldn't have to make small talk with Mrs. Aberdeen, who'd been known to flap her jaw well past Kay's limit of patience. Inside the house a couple of lamps were lit in the front parlor. Her father set up timers when they were out of town and somehow always managed to have the lamps light up during the day and turn off at night. She went to the front door to collect the mail, which included catalogs from Harry & David and Coldwater Creek and the new issue of *National Geographic*, a magazine her parents had subscribed to for decades and never read.

She fed the fish in her father's elaborate aquarium. He kept it squeaky clean, stared at it regularly, and named all the fish. She had very strict instructions on how to feed them. In the kitchen she looked in the fridge for spoiling food, but it was practically empty, cleared out for the vacation. If nothing else, her parents were fastidious.

❖

Kay sat waiting for Alice at Big Chicks, a gay bar in Uptown where they often met for a drink. As usual, the place was ninety-eight percent men. She and Alice were the two percent. Alice climbed onto the stool next to her and threw her bag onto the bar. You wouldn't call it a purse. It was more like a saddlebag. She leaned over to give Kay a hug and pulled back with a concerned look on her face. She'd been texting Alice to keep her up to date on all that'd been happening. They'd been very long texts. It was second nature for her to reach out to Alice. They'd been best friends since college, where they'd roomed together all four years—Kay reveling in parties and life away from her parents, Alice staying holed up in the pottery studio, suffering through a long coming out process.

Alice sat sideways to the bar, her bent arm holding her head up. She'd come directly from her studio and wore a clay splattered Pink Floyd T-shirt and jeans with holes in them. There was a daub of clay on her bare knee. Her long dark hair was braided into pigtails.

"Are you okay?" she said.

"I'm holding up. The drink feels good." Kay picked up her bourbon and finished it in one swallow. Alice ordered beer.

"Tell me everything" she said.

The bartender was a hairy man wearing a kilt. He scowled when Kay motioned for another round.

"Who first, Diane or Griffin?" Kay said.

"I'm so sorry about Diane. Truly." Alice reached over and gave Kay's hand a squeeze. "Have you made any progress finding who did it?"

Kay took a mouthful of the Four Roses. She didn't much care whether she got drunk or not. It might be nice to take a little vacation from reality. Surely she deserved that much? She told Alice about Griffin's mental illness, which surprised her as much as a sunset would.

"I tried to tell you there was something wrong with him. I hated the way he looked at you, as if you were a prized horse—valued, but completely under his control. That was the worst time in our friendship. I thought I'd lost you."

Alice's phone pinged and she picked it up to check a text message. "It's Mary. She's says to not hold dinner, as if I was planning to whip up a home cooked meal for her. When has that ever happened?"

"How is Mary?" Kay liked Alice's wife. She was kind and completely understanding of Alice's art career. She was working on a novel and they led fairly separate lives. It seemed like the perfect kind of relationship to her. To have someone but not be always intertwined with her.

"No, back to your thing. Tell me about Diane."

She felt a sting behind her left eye. "She was wonderful." She fiddled with the coasters in front of her.

"And...?"

She shrugged. "I dug her. We were really attracted to each other. It was obvious from the moment we met. I was already fantasizing about a relationship with her."

"That's awful. I'm so sorry," Alice said.

Kay took another drink. She was starting to feel it. "I'm such a jerk," she said softly.

Alice leaned her head closer. "Why?"

"I found out the day after she was killed that she was in a relationship with another woman, though it sounded like a rocky one. It took the wind out of my sails."

Alice stared at her. "That's not right. I don't like deceptive people."

"But surely there're lesbians who date more than one woman at a time?"

"Honey, we're almost constitutionally incapable of it."

"I know it's stupid, but I felt like my whole fantasy was a joke."

"Maybe not. You have no idea what might have happened had she lived. Maybe she would have dumped the girlfriend to be with you. I would."

"You'd dump Mary to be with me?"

Alice smiled. "I was speaking figuratively. It doesn't sound like they were in a committed relationship. If you felt a real buzz with her, that meant something."

"I don't know. My track record with women is, as you know, abysmal. I'm in my late thirties and I've had only one relationship lasting more than a year, and that was a disaster."

"I wish we didn't have to bring that asshole up, but I suppose it's not a surprise he's here for his sister's funeral. What are you going to say when you see him?" Alice said.

"As little as possible. It's never been a problem for him to dominate a conversation. In this case, I want to know what I can about where he's been and when he got in town."

Alice upended her beer bottle and finished it off. Kay signaled the bartender before she put the bottle down. "Not for me. I'm going to try to work more tonight."

"See, I need someone like Mary in my life. You spend as much time with your pots as I do with investigations, and you don't catch hell for it."

"I catch a little hell for it." Alice smiled. "I try to be reasonable."

Kay drank more bourbon. "I still feel shame about Griffin."

Alice looked at her in surprise. "Why would you feel shame? There's nothing you did that was wrong."

Kay shook her head. "I didn't leave when he started showing his true colors. I stayed with him like a classic abused wife."

"I'd show more respect for the classic abused wife, if I were you. I was there, remember? I saw how charming he was in the beginning, how it lit you up in a way I'd never seen before. Be gentle with yourself."

Kay thought climate change would be halted before she'd ever be gentle with herself. "I was a different woman then," she said. "If that happened to me today I'd punch him."

Alice slid off her seat and took Kay by the elbow. "That would never happen today. You're a much stronger version of yourself. Let's get something to eat. I'll drive you home later."

"Why drive me home? I'm fine."

"Darling, you've had two double bourbons in the time I've had one beer, and I don't believe you're finished for the night. You're not driving."

Kay ordered another drink and knocked it back before following Alice out the door. A half block away was Little Vietnam, a scruffy couple of blocks stuffed with Asian restaurants and markets. At Hai Yen she drank beer while Alice chattered about her work, Mary, topics having nothing to do with murder. It was as soothing as a hot bath.

❖

Kay climbed her way up from a deep sleep and slapped the phone on her nightstand. The sharp trill of its ringing felt like an ice pick in her ear. The call went into voice mail before she could aim her finger well enough to connect it. She went back to sleep, her mouth parched and her tongue swollen.

Again, the blasted ringing. She grabbed the phone with one eye open and answered the call.

"What?" she rasped.

"Detective Kay Adler?" a sturdy male voice said.

"Yeah." Kay scooted up and leaned against the headboard.

"This is Captain Carter of the fire department. I'm sorry to tell you this, but your parents' house is on fire."

"What?" Kay snapped fully awake.

"Neighbors told me your parents are away and gave us your name as a family member."

"How bad is it?"

Carter paused. "It's pretty bad. I'd get down here if I were you."

"On my way." Kay threw the covers off and scrambled for clothes, phone, and wallet before flying out the door. She couldn't tell if she was hung over or still drunk. Her brain was trying to catch up to the news. Then she remembered she didn't have her car. It was like a fucking conspiracy. She called Flash Cab while she was in the elevator and waited restlessly in the lobby until it arrived. The doorman was asleep at his desk and didn't stir. The cab dropped her off at Big Chicks. It was past closing time, but she could see there was an after party going on in the dim interior. If it hadn't been for Alice, she might have been sitting there herself.

She trotted to her car and gunned her Audi to her parents' house. There were so many emergency vehicles parked in the street she had to perch her car at the very end of the block. She could see flames licking up into the night sky. She felt like throwing up, her stomach sour from last night's drinks and the sight in front of her. She ran to the scene. Many of her parent's neighbors were watching from behind a barrier and she skirted past them to the cluster of department brass standing back from the fire. The house was completely engulfed in flame. Firefighters were blasting water on it and the houses on either side to prevent it from spreading. She saw the Nelsons huddled in front of their house next door, nervously watching. Mrs. Aberdeen stared blankly from her yard on the other side. Kay sent up thanks that her parents were on their cruise. She didn't want to think about what their fate might have been had they been home asleep.

She approached a white-shirted chief standing with a megaphone in his hand and a radio clipped to his shoulder. He shot her a look like she'd snuck through the perimeter.

"I'm Kay Adler," she said, showing her identification. "This is my parents' house."

The chief's expression softened and he motioned her to stand next to him. It was cacophonous around them, and he raised his voice to be heard over the blasts of water and the shouts of the firefighters. "The house is completely gone, I'm afraid."

"Yeah, that seems obvious," Kay said. "Any idea what started it?"

"We won't have a clue until we can examine the scene. The fire was well on its way when we got here. The arson investigator's over there, if you want to talk to him." He pointed to a tall, incredibly handsome man standing apart from the others.

"But you suspect arson?" Kay looked at him with hands on her hips, daring him to evade her question.

"Talk to him." He shrugged. "When will you tell your parents about this? I understand they're on a cruise."

"I'm not ruining their cruise. I'll tell them when they get back. You can funnel anything through me."

The radio crackled on his shoulder, and he twisted his head away from her to answer. She walked toward the investigator, who was interviewing Mrs. Nelson. Kay stood at the outer range of earshot, behind Mr. Handsome.

"I'm Officer O'Banyan," he said, his tone gentle. Mrs. Nelson looked in thrall to him, her eyes locked onto his. "Can you tell me what the fire looked like when you first saw it?"

"The noise woke me up. I heard glass shattering and could smell smoke. Our bedroom window was open." She stopped. She looked shy.

"And...?" he prompted her. "What did you see?"

"I looked out and saw flames shooting out of the Adlers' windows. I don't really know how much of the house was involved at that point. I called nine one one and then woke my husband and ran for the kids. We've been out here ever since."

He jotted down a couple of things in his notebook. "Do you remember what the flames looked like? What color they were?"

Mrs. Nelson screwed up her face as if she'd reached the hardest question on an exam. "Gee, let me think." He watched her with an understanding smile. Kay didn't think his smile was helping her stay focused. "The flame was yellow. I mean really yellow, like a lemon. And the smoke was white, but I saw some black puffs starting up by the side kitchen door."

"Did you see anyone outside?"

"No. No one. But I only looked for a second. I wanted to get us out of the house."

O'Banyan talked with her some more before she rejoined her family. Kay stepped forward and tapped him on the shoulder.

"Kay Adler. Detective. This is my parents' house."

He gave her a sympathetic look that seemed to be sincere. He was becoming annoying. "I'm very sorry."

"Was this arson?" Kay said.

He smiled down at her. He was at least six foot three inches of perfectly sculpted body. "I understand you want to know, Detective. Not only is this your parents' house, but it's in your nature to want to know how and why. But it's way too early to comment on whether this was arson."

She didn't appreciate his assumption about her nature. He couldn't begin to understand her nature.

"Did Mrs. Nelson tell you anything useful? What's all that about the color of the flames?" She was growing anxious, a thread of fear working its way up from her belly to lodge in her chest.

"Nothing solid. We'll have to wait until the fire's completely out and the scene cleared before I can determine cause and origin. The detective assigned just left."

"I'll get in touch. What about the flame?"

"I'm telling you this because you're police and I trust you to know speculation from fact. The yellow flame and white smoke indicates accelerant was used to start the fire, probably gasoline."

"So it was arson."

He didn't change expression. "Do you know if the doors would have been locked?"

"Yes, of course they were locked. I was here in the afternoon and locked them myself."

"Good. We'll be able to tell if they were jimmied." They stood silently for a moment. Kay couldn't think of more questions. Her brain was in meltdown.

"When will you be able to start?" she said.

"I'm guessing we'll get the go ahead by midmorning."

"I'll be here."

O'Banyan frowned. "I don't particularly want you here. I'm happy to go over what we find when we have a reasonable picture of what happened."

"I appreciate that," Kay said, "but I'll still be here tomorrow morning." She walked away from him to the other side of the house and stared at the fire from inside the barricade. Flames were still flaring up, but the fire was on its way to extinction. It was a complete loss. No more attic with the Lincoln costume and trunks full of photos and family mementoes. The old frame house was simply not there anymore. Several neighbors came up to her to commiserate, and Kay responded by standing rigidly and nodding her head. Any word out of her mouth would be followed by tears, and crying was not an option. What her neighbors didn't know, would never know, was that Kay caused the fire as sure as the gasoline did. She was being targeted again, she had no doubt. Did the arsonist intend for her parents to die in the fire? Who had a motive so strong, a hatred so deep, that he'd kill her parents? Was Griffin that far gone?

Chapter Five

K ay mindlessly ate her yogurt. She was hungry, but she couldn't taste the food. She was experiencing some kind of sensory shutdown, self-limiting to small doses of input. It was survivor mode, for how else to cope with the fact that people were losing their lives because of her? She put her half eaten breakfast on the coffee table and turned back to the lake view out her window.

It was a beautiful spring day. The lake stretched out below her, as blue as she'd ever seen it. Runners and bikers crowded the lakefront path, the harbor was busy with people working on their boats, the tennis courts were full. She now had to consider what might be revealed about her life each time she walked out the door, because it was clear someone was following her. For whatever reason, the man wasn't interested in killing her. Only in tormenting her.

And there was the lesser problem of what she would do with her parents once they came back from their cruise. The thought of them moving in with her made her shoulders hunch up to her ears. But until this was cleared up, or at least until she found them a secure place to live, she didn't see any alternative. For the moment, they were homeless and didn't know it. Her condo was about to become a bunker for displaced and oppressed Adlers.

She looked at the time on her phone. It was past ten, late enough to go to the house and see what the arson investigator could tell her. She didn't doubt it was arson. The question was whether she could tie it to Diane and Nora's murderer. She put her spoon and bowl in the dishwasher and took out the garbage. She'd already spent the morning cleaning and scrubbing in a self-soothing frenzy. She also called her teammates to let them know about the fire. Elise offered to meet her at the scene, though there was no need for it.

When Kay pulled up in front of the remains of the house, she sat in the car and stared. Her hangover wasn't bad, but her chest felt like someone was sitting on it. She rubbed both eyes with the heel of her hands. She tried to imagine how her parents would feel when she told them, when they saw what used to be their home. But that was still days away. She had to get to them before their cab from O'Hare arrived home. She didn't think there was a worse way for them to learn their house was gone than driving up and seeing it. Her mother would be hysterical, her histrionics having a base in reality for once. Her father would swell up with anger and look for someone to blame, and he didn't have far to look. Kay consulted her moral compass—did she have to tell her parents the arsonist was really targeting her? That moral compass was spinning as if she were moving around in a magnetic field.

Maybe she would find some things of value in the rubble of the house. Like the little bit of jewelry her mother had, the brass monkey door stop that had been in the family forever, the fireplace tools. What else would survive such a hot fire? Her throat tightened as she remembered decades of family recipes stuffed into a folder, now nothing more than ash. So many irreplaceable things. She couldn't afford to start crying.

She saw O'Banyan and three other men working around the perimeter of the house. O'Banyan was in the back, crouched in what used to be the kitchen, moving some sort of device slowly along the floor near the back wall. She got out of the car and walked slowly toward him.

"I thought I'd check in with you," she said.

O'Banyan stood and smiled down at her. "I expected as much."

"Well? Have you found any evidence of arson?"

He held the device in front of him. It looked like a handheld vacuum. "The door locks appear to have been interfered with, which points toward arson, of course. Now we're working to identify the accelerant used. The gauge on the vapor analyzer jumped, which indicates one was used here in the kitchen. It looks like there are two points of origin. Parker found the same thing along the front wall in the living room. He probably set that fire first and then the one here. He would have exited out the back."

"So how does this get translated into evidence?" she said.

"We'll be taking samples from all over, especially at these points of origin. The gas chromatograph will give us the conclusive results, which will probably be that the vapor is from gasoline. Maybe we'll come across what he used to start the fire—a lighter, a match."

"A match?"

"Sure. A match head can survive fire, which probably seems like a paradox. I can go into the science of it—"

Kay held up a hand. "No, please. I believe you." She took a step back from him. He had crept within her personal space. Why did people do that? She snuck a look at his left hand and saw a wedding band. "Anything else?"

O'Banyan put his analyzer down and reached into his pocket. "There's something that may be nothing." He brought out a plastic bag with a tiny piece of fabric inside. "I found this down by the garage, where the rose bushes are? The thorns snagged someone's clothing. Maybe it's the arsonist's."

He handed the bag to her and Kay held her breath. The fabric was black. It could be any kind of fabric, but it looked like a bit of a sweatshirt. "Please leave the chain of evidence clean on that. We'll need it for comparison testing. It may be a tie-in with a couple of homicide cases I'm working."

His eyes widened. "The detective assigned to this should be here any minute. You'll want to explain that to him."

Kay caught sight of Elise climbing out of a dented Toyota Tercel, parked behind her car. "I'll have Detective Sokolov do the honors."

She turned away from O'Banyan and walked toward the street to intercept Elise. She was dressed in a track suit with parallel stripes running down the sleeves and legs. Her running shoes were bright white. She looked slightly out of date, unhip. She walked up to Kay with a solemn look on her face.

"I'm so sorry, Detective. Thank God your parents weren't home." She looked up at Kay with her doleful brown eyes. She couldn't fault Elise's eagerness to help. She didn't have to come in today, but here she was. She still had a bit of the panting dog in her, anxious to please, but Kay could see her becoming a good detective. When she didn't respond, Elise carried on. "We haven't been able to locate Griffin Sanderson yet. He hasn't used the credit card he used to rent the car since he returned it. He's not at his mother's. We can start calling hotels."

Kay shook her head. "That's a low percentage use of time. I'm sure I'll see him later today at the wake."

"We did get his jacket. He has two DUIs in Illinois, and a forged check charge."

"Did he serve time?" Kay said. She was surprised at the course Griffin's life had taken. He'd always been so sensitive to anything reflecting badly on him.

"None. I talked to his probation officer who said he'd served his terms without incident." Kay stared at what used to be her home and didn't respond. "How long ago were you married to Griffin?"

Kay looked at her sharply. "You're not getting anything out of me that isn't relevant to this case." She reluctantly accepted that time frame might be relevant. "We got married when I was twenty-two, about sixteen years ago. I haven't seen him in all that time, so this is as much a surprise to me as it is to you." She settled her gaze on O'Banyan as he continued taking readings. "I want you to brief the detective assigned to this arson investigation. The arson investigator found some fibers that are a possible match with the black sweatshirt."

Elise was busy staring at O'Banyan also. "Is that the one I should talk to?" She didn't take her eyes off him.

"No. The detective isn't here yet."

"Ooh la la," Elise said, giving Kay a sidelong look.

"I thought you had a boyfriend?"

"I do. He's my fiancé, actually. But I've got eyes in my head. That guy is hot."

Kay stared at her. "Try to keep your pants on, will you? We have work to do."

Elise laughed and walked toward O'Banyan. Kay got in her car and drove off. She wanted to drink. She considered herself a social drinker, but right now she was an antisocial drinker. She wanted to hole up in her condo and draw the blinds. She wanted to get buzzed enough that the anvil on her chest would lift and the extremes of her anger and dread would be blunted. She promised herself a trip down that rabbit hole before the day was over.

She drove to Area Four and reached her desk without seeing any of the detectives on her team. She reread the report on the trace evidence found at the Nora Sanderson murder scene. There were enough fibers clinging to the inspection tab found there for the lab to test for a match with the fibers from the rose bush. She was skeptical they were the same. The sweatshirt worn during Nora's murder would be drenched in blood. Even laundered, it was a piece of evidence against him. He seemed unconcerned about it, as if the evidence left behind was meant to frustrate Kay.

She made a pot of coffee at the break station. While it was brewing she went to the conference room. Adam was there bent over a stack of paper.

Kay rapped softly on the door. "You came in on a Sunday," she said.

Adam looked up with a resigned smile. "We got the last of the interviews done on all of Nora's friends and family. I wanted to look the statements over with fresh eyes." He leaned back in his chair and stretched his arms over his head. He looked tired.

"What do they tell you?" Kay said.

"They tell me fuck all. No one we talked to had any beef with Nora except her brother. I still think that's farfetched, don't you? I mean, you know the guy. Would he kill his own sister?"

She shrugged. "I have no idea. Turns out he was crazier than I knew. It's possible."

"I should go with you to the wake."

Kay hesitated. She'd have to be civil to Griffin to get him to answer questions, and every cell in her body rebelled at the thought. She'd much rather humiliate him as he'd so often humiliated her. Her acting skills would be stretched to their limit, and she was loathe to have Adam witness her making nice with the creep. But she needed his extra set of ears.

She agreed and sat in a chair with her hands flat on the table. "Nothing's come up about Diane that points to any conflict. There's nothing we can find in her background, except her girlfriend, and I've eliminated her. She was truly surprised to hear Diane was on a date the night she died." She stood. "The arson investigator found some torn fabric that might be from a black sweatshirt. Who knows, maybe they'll find a footprint from a Converse sneaker."

"Maybe you should step off the Nora Sanderson case. The brass is going to yank you off sooner or later. And Sharpe will get his ear torn off for allowing it."

Kay looked at him grimly. "If everyone keeps a low profile the brass might not figure it out at all."

She went to the coffee station and brought two cups back to the conference room. She sat next to the mountain of case files. "This is going nowhere too. I don't see anyone from my past arrests who would have sufficient motive. Why risk their parole by terrorizing me?"

"How about from when you were in uniform?" Adam said.

Kay raised her mug to her lips to blow on the hot coffee and thought of her years in uniform. She'd put handcuffs on plenty of people, a lot of them ended up in prison, but what sort of motivation would they need to come back to her years later and start murdering people?

She jerked out of her chair. "Oh, shit. I forgot about Kurt Becker."

"Who's he?"

"He's from a long time ago, my second year on the job." She looked at Adam. "I killed his wife."

His eyes widened. "In the line of duty?"

"Sort of. She was collateral. She shouldn't have been shot."

"Tell me the story," he said a little too eagerly.

"Forget the details. The important thing is he was crazy about his wife and I killed her. I heard he went a little nuts after his arrest, that he couldn't accept she was dead. That might be motive enough to get back at me."

"Sounds promising."

She sipped her coffee and sat back down. "He doesn't look anything like either artist's sketch, but he's using disguises. He has roughly the same build, from what I can remember."

Elise walked in the room. Before she could open her mouth Kay said, "I have an assignment for you. Find the file on a Kurt Becker. He was arrested about fourteen years ago. If records doesn't have it, find out where it is and bring it to me. It's important."

Elise opened her mouth again, but Kay cut her off. "Double-time on this. Go."

"Yes, ma'am."

"Oh, Christ, don't call me ma'am." Kay sprang up and headed back to her desk, with Adam right behind. "Let's find out where he is." She punched up the state database that kept tabs on every prisoner's parole status, whether they'd been released or were still in, and their rap sheet.

"It shows he got out on early release from Pontiac about sixteen months ago. Shit."

Adam bent over her shoulder and pointed at the screen. "And he broke parole last December. Hasn't been seen since."

"Oh my fucking God," Kay breathed.

"Let's track his PO down. We can talk to him today, right now," Adam said.

Kay turned to look at him. "Find him. I'm going to try to reach the detectives who were on the scene of the Becker shooting with me."

Adam went to his desk and Kay went into the online directory of CPD employees. She remembered Pendergast, the detective directing the operation. He'd gotten in trouble for not waiting for more backup. Maybe if he had she wouldn't have killed Becker's wife, though it was futile trying to cast off blame. Her gun, her bullet.

Pendergast wasn't in the directory, which probably meant he retired. She found him in a different directory and put in the call.

"Hello," a man said. Kay could hear a Bulls game in the background.

"Is this John Pendergast?"

"Speaking." He sounded friendly, unlike the suspicious tone she had whenever answering an unknown number.

"This is Detective Kay Adler out of Area Four. I'm wondering if you can help me with something." The basketball noise ceased. She could feel adrenaline starting to move through her system, lighting up pathways as it went.

"What can I do for you, Detective?"

"I'm calling about an incident that occurred a long time ago, when I was in uniform and you were a detective out of Area Four. It was a drug bust. The guy's name was Becker."

"Ah. I think I remember who you are."

"I'm the one who shot Becker and killed his wife with a bullet that went through the wall. I don't know if that counts as memorable in your book."

"That could have as easily been me. It was a freak occurrence."

Kay shrugged that off. "I'm wondering if I can meet you for coffee to talk about it. Becker's active again, and I'm trying to get a handle on him."

Pendergast paused for a moment, probably thinking of his beer and easy chair. "Of course, anything I can do to help. Where and when?"

Kay arranged their meeting for an hour later at a Starbucks in Edgebrook, where Pendergast lived. Edgebrook was another enclave of cops and city workers on the outer edge of the Chicago's northwest side. She'd need to leave shortly to get there in time. As she rose from her chair she saw Adam headed her way, with Elise not far behind.

"Report," she said, staring at them grimly while feeling mildly ridiculous. That's what the captains on Star Trek were always barking.

Adam passed over a piece of paper. "Here's the parole officer's name, number, and address. I haven't reached out to him yet."

"Good. Elise?" She looked down at the rookie, who seemed wary.

"The file you want is in central storage. We won't be able to pick it up until the morning."

"Crap. Okay. I want both of you to go see this parole officer and find out what he knows about Kurt Becker's whereabouts. Every detail."

"Kay, don't you think we should know the story of how you killed his wife?" Adam said.

He was right. They were both eager to help, willing to work and do whatever it takes. Her own embarrassment wasn't enough reason to not tell them of that night. She filled them in, fiddling with a Bic pen and shifting back and forth in her chair. Adam remained stone-faced. Elise's eyes grew larger as she listened, no doubt whatever hero worship she'd had for Kay now gone. Without another word, they left on their assignment and Kay headed out to meet Pendergast. On the way she took a call from O'Banyan, who told her she'd be able to enter the remains of her parents house the following morning. Christ, she'd almost forgotten the fire. It felt like fireworks kept going off in her brain, each brilliant explosion obliterating the one before. Diane, Nora Sanderson, the fire, Kurt Becker. She couldn't address one thing before another hit. Her boat was in danger of being swamped.

She walked into the Starbucks and recognized Pendergast immediately. Every detail about the night she killed Dina Becker came back to life. His red hair was flecked with gray, but he didn't look much older than he had when she saw him fourteen years ago. She wasn't as memorable for him. He didn't recognize her until she sat at the table he'd snagged among a row occupied by people wearing headphones and staring at their laptops. It was fairly safe they wouldn't listen in on their conversation. Pendergast reached out his large bony hand and grasped hers firmly.

"Good to see you, Detective," he said, smiling widely. He pushed a cup of black coffee across the table. "I guessed you took yours black."

"You guessed right. Please call me Kay."

"Call me Jack. No more Detective in front of my name."

"You retired?" She shrugged out of her coat and took a sip of the scalding coffee.

"Yep. Unwillingly. They show you the door when you hit sixty-three. I'd rather be working."

She nodded. "I have a complicated story to tell you, but you'll understand why I'm interested in Becker when I'm done." She took her time filling him in on everything that'd happened since Nora Sanderson's death, including the new revelation that Becker had skipped his parole. Pendergast had no reaction on his face.

"I was a uniform back then," Kay said, "so I didn't get any background on him, any news of what happened to him after his arrest, other than he was torn up about his wife. I was told he was thinking of filing a civil suit against me, but that came to nothing. I don't know absolutely that he's behind this, but we don't have anything better to go on."

He took a slow sip of coffee and wrinkled his nose, like he'd had one too many cups. "What do you want to know from me? Haven't you gotten the case file?"

She opened her notebook. "We've ordered it. But I'd want to talk to you anyway. I want what you know about Becker as a person. What was he like? How did he operate?"

"That's asking me to go back pretty far, but it was one of those cases that stand out. You don't quickly forget them. I hope you know that we all supported you back then. Any one of us could have fired that shot. It was your misfortune. It was not your fault."

"I missed the target. That's on me."

"You missed a running target in a chaotic scene. Hell, I missed him by a mile. It happens all the time," he said.

Kay waved him away. "Whatever you can remember will be helpful."

"Becker was an interesting guy. He was a cocaine wholesaler who'd been in business a few years. I spent a lot of time interviewing him, but whatever I forget about here you can find in the case file."

He drank coffee and looked out the window as if daydreaming. His glasses were slightly askew.

"He got started in high school up in Winnetka. His parents were well-to-do. He got tagged once for holding a couple of ounces of weed, but nothing came of that. High-priced attorney and a white kid. Poof—charges dropped. In college, he expanded his marijuana business. I remember this part clearly because he was bragging on it. As if it would help his case.

"What set Becker apart from other dealers was his business acumen. He understood the importance of organization and systems. He kept personnel files on his sales staff, as he called them. He used QuickBooks for his accounting. His books would pass any audit, were any of it legal. He understood the need to maintain business relationships. He regularly gave his retailers bonuses and he wined and dined his suppliers. Guys liked working for him and selling to him. He had quotas for his sales staff and they easily beat them. He had a steady supply of high quality product. His business boomed.

"Once he got out of college and established himself in the city, he moved away from pot and into cocaine. The product was easier to handle and the profit margins greater. He was good at what he did, I'll give him that."

He'd described someone who could easily conduct a detailed, complex campaign like the one being waged against her.

"He came to our attention in the usual way. About a month before his arrest, one of his street sellers was tagged and gave up Becker in exchange for probation. We got a warrant for his West Loop loft, but couldn't find a single thing to incriminate him. He must have off-loaded the product. I suspect he had an office somewhere, like any businessman."

They were silent for a while. Kay finished making some notes. "You remember a lot."

"Like I said, he was an unusual man."

"Will you give me your version of what happened the night we entered his place? The night his wife was shot. By me."

"A person draped in guilt is not someone people want to be around, Kay. You're going to have to find a way to forgive yourself."

"I don't know how to do that," she said softly.

"I'd say therapy, though I never thought I'd hear those words cross my lips."

"Yeah, it's been suggested before. I'll think about it."

Pendergast nodded, apparently satisfied with her response. "We'd gotten a fresh tip from a CI where Becker could be found, and we knew he'd recently taken a big shipment of coke. My partner and I grabbed up a warrant and headed straight over there, calling for backup on the way. We got you and three others. As you know he was holed up in a shitty Uptown apartment, not a place fitting a man of his means. I thought he'd have a nicer workplace. We rammed the door open and entered. Somehow you slipped in ahead of us, so you were the first person who saw Becker enter with a gun. You know the rest."

"I do. When were you able to interview him?"

"He had surgery that night and we were in his room the next afternoon. He was torn up about his wife. He demanded to know who shot her and was threatening action against the department. It was like he didn't recognize he was under arrest and no longer in charge of his life. He alternated between sobbing and snarling. Then, as we questioned him, he started talking about his business. I don't know why he didn't call for an attorney. He went on as if he were sharing industry secrets at a trade show for drug dealers. He was supremely confident, a smooth talker. Then he'd realize where he was and that his wife was dead and he'd start sobbing again. He was a mess."

"How about his mental state?" she said.

"He was all over the place, but whether that means he was mentally ill, I don't know. Maybe there's something in the file about a psych evaluation."

Pendergast glanced at his watch. "I need to get back home. The grandkids are coming over."

"Of course." Kay smiled at him. "You've been a tremendous help. One last thing—could you give me the name of the other detective present that night?"

"Sure. That was Tommy Nichols. He was my partner for at least ten years. But he's down in Arizona now. Couldn't take the weather up here." He picked up his phone and scrolled. Kay took down the contact information. "He'll love to talk to you about this. I did too. I miss the job."

She walked out with him to the parking lot and watched him drive away. When she got back to Area Four she saw Adam at the coffee station chatting with Jamie Sidwell, an experienced homicide detective transferred the year before from Area Two. They were contemporaries—same age, same academy class, both made detective the same year. They should have been good friends, but they weren't. She asked Adam to come with her and didn't acknowledge Sidwell, who turned her back on her. She was close to six feet tall, athletic build, short salt-and-pepper hair, and watchful green eyes. She was good-looking in that way confident, self-possessed people often are. The studied way they ignored each other was standard, ever since they'd worked on a case together the year before, shortly after Jamie had joined Area Four. Kay's partner had been out on vacation and Jamie's partner was sick. The two were thrown together on a homicide in West Lakeview.

The body was that of a female gang member. West Lakeview was not gang territory, unless you counted the packs of young mothers pushing strollers in and out of Starbucks, their base of operations. But street level gangs were generally in neighborhoods farther from the lake. The dead girl was no more than sixteen, probably younger. She lay faceup on the sidewalk, a bullet in her chest.

Kay and Jamie were cautious with each other. They'd never worked together and were feeling each other out. They stood next to the body, in the middle of a perimeter set up by the uniforms. Kay knelt down and Jamie followed.

"She's not wearing a jacket. A T-shirt and shorts aren't enough for this weather," Kay said.

"Right. So she was killed indoors somewhere and dumped here, is that what you're thinking?" Jamie said.

Kay nodded and bent over the body to see the girl's tattoos. There was a Chinese character on the left side of her neck, a tat so common it was banal. On the right side were a sun and moon. More interesting were the tattoos across the fingers of her left hand. They spelled out "Nita." On the inside of her arm near the elbow was QLK, which she guessed stood for the Queens of the Latin Kings.

"Well, Nita, let's see if you have any ID on you," she said. She reached her gloved hand into the front pocket of her shorts. They were about an inch deep—girl pockets. There was no sign of a purse.

"I'll get hold of the gang unit and see what they say about the Queens, whether they're making forays up here," Jamie said.

"No need. I've got contacts who can give us the lowdown."

Jamie looked across the body at Kay. Her eyes had narrowed. "And you think I don't have contacts?"

She shrugged. "It didn't sound like it to me."

"I have contacts."

"Okay, great. Call them."

Jamie's lips were pressed together, as if she were holding something in. She reached for Nita's hand and gently tried to bend the fingers. They were stiff. "Rigor's in place, so she's been dead at least a couple hours. It's eight thirty now."

"Probably much longer," Kay said. "You can see the lividity along her calves." She stood and looked around her with her hands on her hips, assessing the scene. "Why don't you wait here in case something comes up from the door-to-doors?"

Jamie stared at her. "Why don't you? Or better yet, why don't we both process the scene the way we're supposed to?"

"No need for that. I'll go ahead and get in touch with my contacts. You can finish processing the scene."

"What's with you, Adler? No one put you in charge."

Kay was used to taking control of a scene. She didn't appreciate the push back. "We need to divvy up assignments, right? Or do you want to do everything together? We can do that, if you'd like."

"What I'd like is to not have an asshole for a partner."

She laughed. "Believe me, we aren't partners." She wondered what it was about Jamie that put her teeth on edge. She felt off-balanced, challenged, as if she were dealing with a better version of herself.

Jamie blew out her breath. "Forget it. I can't think of anything I'd least rather do than work next to you." The ME came on the scene and they went their separate ways. Kay kept in touch with her to let her know what she was doing, but they'd obviously gotten off on the wrong foot. Jamie remained frostily polite, and Kay continued to be annoyed by her composure. They had a suspect by the end of the day and that was all she cared about. Despite the chill in the air, she thought they'd been effective, and Jamie clearly knew what she was doing. A search was underway for the suspect when Kay returned to Area Four.

An hour or so after she'd gotten back, Kay bumped into Alonso Martinez, an old-timer with one ambition only—to make it to his upcoming retirement. He worked a lot of weekends and

Kay rarely saw him. He stopped her in the hallway and she turned to him, surprised.

"What is it, Martinez?"

He came up close to her and she smelled the stale scent of smoking. He pulled her to the side of the hallway and spoke *sotto voce*. "I thought you should know that Sidwell is saying some shit about you."

Kay looked at him. "I'm not interested in your gossip."

"It's not gossip. She said it directly to me not fifteen minutes ago."

"What the hell did she say?"

Martinez looked nervous. "She said you're a hot shot and not a team player." He stepped back a little, in case Kay exploded.

"What? Jesus H. Christ. Does she want to hold hands or something? I was perfectly cooperative today. What else did she say?"

"Nothing, really. She asked me what I thought of you."

"What did you tell her?"

"About what?"

"About me. I might as well know what everyone's saying." She was curious and anxious at the same time. She was stung by what Jamie had said.

"I told her you're our best detective. What else would I say?" He grinned. "I tried to set her straight, but she didn't look convinced."

Martinez walked back into the detective's room while Kay continued to the washroom. Who the hell did Jamie think she was? It's not like she was a pillar of cooperation herself. She felt agitated, taken aback that Jamie felt so negatively about her.

In the year since then, they'd maintained a cool distance from one another. Now Jamie was hovering around on a Sunday. She didn't like it. Once she was back at her desk she turned to Adam. "What did Sidwell want?"

"Nothing." He was aware of their feud though he didn't understand its origins. "She was just chatting."

"What's she doing here on a Sunday?"

"She's got the shift. The bigger question is what are we still doing here on a Sunday?" he said.

"We discovered a lead in the case, remember? Now we have to find him. Should we call everyone else in?"

Adam frowned. "I wouldn't. Let's figure out what we're going to do and what you're going to say to the lieutenant."

Kay looked up at him as he stood next to her cubicle. "Okay. What did Becker's parole office say?"

Adam pulled up a chair and took out his notebook. "Carlton Osborn. Nice guy. Apparently, Becker was a model prisoner and finished up his sentence in Pontiac Medium Security. Released early in March of last year. His parole was going fine, though Osborn was riding him about getting a job. Becker was living in an apartment up in Roger's Park."

"Roger's Park? That's where Diane and I were."

"I know. Anyway, he doesn't seem to need money. His father died while he was in prison and he inherited a bundle. Still, ex-cons are encouraged to get jobs. But why get a shitty job when you don't have to work at all?"

"I think I'd still work even if I won the lottery or something," Kay said.

"Yeah, but this isn't a shitty job."

"Sometimes it really is." She smiled grimly. "What else?"

"Becker was in monthly touch with Osborn until December, when he didn't check in. They couldn't find him anywhere. Osborn interviewed the people Becker hung with in prison, but no one copped to any knowledge of him planning to break parole. An arrest warrant went out for him, but so far nothing." He closed his notebook.

"If the disguise theory is true, they won't find him. Obviously, he has a new identity."

"Maybe it's based on one of his disguises," Adam said.

Kay looked thoughtful. "I have a CI who knows most of the forgers here. I'll get in contact." Adam was right. She needed a game plan for how to locate Kurt Becker. It was late in the day, time for Nora's wake. She told Adam to meet her at Theresa Sanderson's house. When she got into her Audi, she dialed the number Pendergast had given her for his partner. Tommy Nichols picked up on the first ring. She drove north on Broadway with the phone to her ear. After they made their introductions, she jumped to her questions. Nichols didn't know the same level of detail Pendergast did, which didn't surprise her. He'd seemed so much the lesser cop. But he was expansive about the time he spent with Becker in the hospital.

"I spent a lot of time with him that first day after his surgery. He was really torn up about his wife, though I know you know that. I only say it because he wouldn't stop talking about her."

"What did he say?" She heard a cigarette being lit and some ice cubes clinking in a glass. The joys of retirement.

"It was mostly about how life wasn't worth living without her, blah, blah, but at one point he mentioned a kid."

"Oh, shit. What kid?"

"The wife's kid. Apparently, she had a daughter from a different man. I think he said she was about fourteen, but I wouldn't swear to it. The wife must have been older than Becker."

"Thank God the girl wasn't in the apartment with them."

"No kidding," he said, inhaling loudly. "The kid spent regular time with her father, but Becker kept saying he would adopt her. From prison, like that was an idea that was going to work."

"I wonder what happened to her? Do you remember a name for the daughter and her father?"

"Sorry. You've got all I know. Good luck tracking him down, the bastard."

Kay disconnected. Maybe when she got the file the next day she'd find out the child's name and where she'd gone. With the father, probably. If she could find the girl, who'd be an adult now, she might lead them to Becker.

❖

Adam was waiting for Kay on the sidewalk in front of Theresa Sanderson's home. When she joined him she could hear the noise of the crowd inside through the open front door.

"Seems Nora had a lot more friends than I was aware of," Adam said.

Kay touched his elbow as she continued toward the house. "Her father worked for Mayor Daley. Pretty high up, at least when I knew the family. I'm pretty sure his cronies are in there, fulfilling their duty at the drinks table."

Adam looked impressed. "Wow. Would that be the old Mayor Daley or the young one?"

"The young one retired a few years ago. He wasn't so young." She led the way into the house. The overly furnished living room was stuffed with people. Some women sat scrunched up together on the long couch, bending their necks upward to see the men standing over them. Adam recognized a group of Nora's friends. The rest of the room was filled with upper middle-aged men huddled together, drinks in hand, erupting in laughter. Kay led the way into the adjoining dining room, where a similar but larger crowd hovered around the food and drinks tables. Kay pushed her way through, hoping to find Theresa before running into Griffin. She turned to Adam.

"For whatever reason, Griffin is being friendly to me, and I have to use that to get him to answer questions. Don't mistake what I say for anything like affection for the man." She looked in his eye. "I can tell you, since you're my partner, that I hate him and would as soon ram the butt end of my weapon into his balls as give him the time of day. So play along."

Adam looked pleased. "I'll follow your lead, boss."

She scanned the room but didn't see any sign of Griffin, though she did see Theresa backed into a corner of the room, grasping a glass of wine as she looked up at the tall, burly man facing her. Her face was pinched, as if the conversation was causing her pain. Kay waved to get her attention and saw the relief on her face when she saw her. She ducked around the man and joined Kay and Adam.

"Kay, I'm so glad you're here. Thanks for rescuing me."

"Who was that guy? He looked like he was lecturing you."

Theresa waved her hand as if swatting a fly. "He was Daley's chief of staff. An overbearing prick, excuse my language. Naturally, my husband adored him."

Kay smiled. She'd not understood why Theresa stayed with her thoroughly unpleasant husband, especially when it was clear she didn't even like him. "It looks like there are a ton of his cronies here. They take the loyalty thing a little far, don't they? I mean, your husband's been dead over a year."

Theresa glanced around her. "It's absurd. I always felt like we were in the Mafia. Some of these guys are retired, some have slid into Rahm's administration. They're exhausting me."

"How are you holding up?"

"I think I look like I'm doing better than I actually am. Some of Nora's friends are here, which is nice."

As Kay introduced Adam she saw Griffin entering the room from the kitchen. He had a glass of whiskey in his hand and his arm around an older man who was loudly laughing at something Griffin said. They stopped and shook hands. Griffin then moved on to another man at the drinks table, clapping him on the back and leaning in to say something. He behaved as if he were at a political banquet instead of his sister's wake. It didn't take long for him to look up and around and see Kay standing across the room from him. He was at their side in a moment. Close up, she could see Griffin's dark blue suit needed to be cleaned and a collar button was missing from his dress shirt. His tie had a stain. The man she knew had been fastidious and clothes conscious. He was also around six foot and slender, just as their suspect was. Before he could say anything, Kay looked at him with a strained smile. "I'm catching up with your mother, expressing my condolences about Nora. You must be devastated."

Griffin ignored his mother and composed his face into an expression of grief. Kay almost laughed. "Of course. Still, I'm so happy you're here." He couldn't keep the eagerness at bay.

Theresa was shuffling uncomfortably. "I'm going over to talk to Nora's friends. Thanks for being here, Kay." She left quickly, and still Griffin ignored her, as if she hadn't physically been there.

"Griffin, this is my partner, Adam Oleska." Griffin looked at Adam with a blank face, but held out his hand.

"Is that partner as in you two are in a relationship?" He knew perfectly well she was a lesbian.

Kay wished she could say yes. "Adam is a homicide detective. We're teamed up together."

A smile spread across Griffin's face. "Homicide! I keep forgetting that Nora was murdered and there's a murderer to be found." Kay couldn't quite imagine how a brother could forget his sister had been murdered, especially at her wake.

"Well, that's why we're here, of course." She saw the disappointed look on Griffin's face.

"I thought my note had enticed you here. I've wanted to see you for a long time, Kay. I have a lot to say." He turned to Adam. "Would you give us a few minutes?"

Adam looked at Kay, and when she nodded, he walked toward the food table. She put her hands on her hips. "Let's keep this brief. Unlike you, I have very little to say."

He took her elbow and steered her toward a first floor bedroom opposite the dining room. The hair on the back of her neck rose, a muscle memory of his hands on her. She stopped and held her ground. "We're fine right here."'

"Don't be like that," he cajoled her. "My old bedroom is just there. It'll be more quiet, private."

"For just a minute, then."

"I'll talk fast." He took her elbow again and it was all she could do to not rip it out of his hand. The small bedroom was furnished with a twin bed and a desk. She stood in the middle of the room and faced him.

"I don't understand what you want to talk to me about," Kay said. "I think it was pretty clear what I thought of you when I left. It hasn't changed much with time." She couldn't help herself.

He raised his two hands in the air, as if placating a child. "That was a long time ago, and I've changed. I want to apologize for being…such an angry man. I behaved very badly, but I've gotten help. I won't go into all the details, but my problems started here, in the house I grew up in."

She supposed this was his version of taking responsibility for his actions—blame the parents. She kept quiet.

"I loved you so much that everything made me afraid you would leave me, until finally you did. I couldn't stop trying to control you. I had no regulating mechanism." This sounded like therapy talk to her. "It's so ironic. The very things you do to avoid being abandoned are the things that drive your lover away." Kay shut her eyes at the word lover.

They stared at each other for a moment. "Is that it?" Kay said.

He looked at her hopefully. "Do you accept my apology? Please, Kay. It'll help me forgive myself."

He disgusted her, but he didn't strike her as the murderer of Diane and Nora. He didn't betray any anger in his cajoling approach. But on the other hand, he was crazy.

"Let's just say there's nothing you did in the past or could do now that would affect me. As far as I'm concerned, you never existed."

His eyes clouded and he took a deep breath. "I've never stopped thinking about you. I did exist for you, Kay. I was your husband, your lover. For the most part, what we had was good."

Borderline personality disorder must include a refined ability to delude yourself. "What do you want from me?" she asked.

"To be friends, of course. Are you in a relationship now?" Kay's brow furrowed. "I want to be respectful of that. Just friendship, that's all I want."

"Before I tell you what I think of that, can I ask you a question?"

"Of course." He touched her shoulder reassuringly.

"I haven't mentioned yet that I'm the lead detective in the investigation into your sister's death. I'd like to ask you a few questions about her." She saw him look alarmed. "Just as I asked your mother. It's all standard background, but I could really use your cooperation."

He regarded her for a moment, like she was a chess game and he held a rook hovering above the board. "Certainly. Any way I can help." He still hadn't said anything about the loss of Nora.

"Good. I'm going to call Adam in here and we'll get this done right now."

"Really? I thought this could wait until we have coffee or a meal together."

She walked to the door and leaned her head out. Adam was looking her way and she waved him over. She turned back to Griffin. "Time sensitive. This won't take long."

Adam joined them and they stood in a triangle. He took his notebook out.

"Can you tell me how your relationship was with your sister?" Kay said.

"With Nora? We hardly had a relationship at all, but it was pleasant enough. We were never terribly close because of the age difference." He looked composed.

"So what your mother told me about a recent disagreement is false?"

His eyes snapped shut for a moment. "I don't know what she told you. The only thing with my sister is I asked her to loan me a little money and she couldn't. It's not like I was mad at her for it."

"What did you need the money for?" Adam said.

"I don't know the relevance," he said.

"Humor me, then," Kay said.

Griffin was shifting from one foot to the other. "I don't like to say this, but I'm between jobs and was a little short on cash."

"Okay. When did you arrive in Chicago?"

"I got here a week ago." Before the murder. "I'd been living in southeastern Wisconsin and decided to relocate."

Kay and Adam stared at him. "Did you talk to Nora when you got into town?"

"No."

"Your mother?"

"Nope, didn't call her either."

"So what brought you to Chicago?" Adam said.

Griffin was looking only at Kay. "I needed to see you." He stood calmly with his hands behind his back.

"What day was that?"

"A week ago today. I'm staying at an Airbnb in Lakeview."

Adam and Kay looked at each other. That put Griffin in town at the time of Nora's murder, and they knew he had already lied to them about his argument with Nora.

"I hope you'll remember when I ask this next question that it's strictly part of a standard interview. Will you tell us where you were on Tuesday evening, April seventh, let's say from six p.m. through the next morning?"

Griffin smiled. "Can't you see what a different man I am, Kay? What's the likelihood I wouldn't have blown up at that question the way I used to be? I'll answer. I have nothing to hide. It's not a very satisfactory answer though. I spent the evening at the library on Belmont near Broadway, working on a job search, and then I returned to my room about eight. I didn't leave again until morning."

"Will the owner of wherever you're staying be able to vouch for that?"

Apparently, this was amusing as well. Griffin's smile widened. "I doubt it. He was running out when I came in, said he was on his way to Halsted Street and I should make sure the front door was locked before I turned in. I have no idea when he returned."

Kay watched Adam finish scribbling in his notebook. "We won't take up anymore of your time, but I would like your address and phone number, and your promise you'll let us know if you plan to leave town."

"Of course." He gave Adam the information. "And now, tell me when you and I can get together. I still have a lot to tell you about my journey since we parted. I think you'll find it interesting." He ignored Adam and looked at Kay.

"Let's see. How to answer that." Kay looked at the floor before raising her eyes to Griffin's. "If my choice was between falling into a pit of three thousand mating snakes or spending another minute with you, I'd take the snakes." She turned abruptly and walked to the door, but not before she saw the shock in his eyes. "Come on, Adam."

They worked their way through the crowd, out the door, and stood in front of Kay's car. "Man, that's a lot to process," Adam said. "Intense."

"The only thing I want processed is Griffin Sanderson as a suspect in Nora's murder. Get on his alibi, his movements, whatever you can find out on the street and online." She got in the car.

"Where are you going?" Adam said.

"Home to take a very, very long shower. See you tomorrow."

CHAPTER SIX

W here's Elise?" Kay was standing at the door to the conference room looking at Arroyo, Simpson, and Adam seated around the table. It was Monday morning and she had a mild hangover. She'd fallen asleep on her couch after several drinks, but the damage was minimal.

"She's bringing the Becker file back from records," Adam said.

She remained standing as she briefed her team about her interview with Griffin Sanderson. She felt Kurt Becker was a stronger suspect, but she wouldn't rule Griffin out. There was no evidence yet that he didn't do it.

"Sanderson feels like the right guy to me," Simpson said. "He's the same body type, he was here the night of the murder, and he had a double motive—anger at his sister for not lending him money and some unfinished business with you."

"He's definitely a possible, but so far we have nothing we can bring him in with."

"He feels right to me, too," Adam said. "I talked to the Airbnb guy last night and he was out until two in the morning the night of Nora's murder. He can't provide Sanderson with an alibi. It's more of a gut feeling he's the one."

"Before you convict Sanderson, we need to track Becker down. His motivation feels stronger to me, though both have held on to their issues with me for a very long time."

"So let's find him. Where do you want to start?" Adam said.

"We have to track down the stepdaughter and her father. I need that fucking case file. In the meantime, get back on the phone with Becker's PO and get his file. Get Becker's file from Corrections, too. He was at Pontiac max first, and then they moved him into the medium security unit. Let's see what we can find there. Simpson, you and Arroyo cover that." Simpson shrugged as if he didn't care what he had to do, as long as it wasn't too challenging.

Kay was taking a seat when Lieutenant Sharpe came in. He looked crankier than ever.

"Give me an update," he said.

Kay filled him in and watched as his expression changed from grim to hopeful to grim again. He stared at her for a long while. She had no idea what he was thinking, but she had to keep herself from squirming. She wanted to work. She wanted first crack at finding Becker's stepdaughter, but she was getting a bad feeling. Sharpe let out a breath and left the room, crossing to his office on the other side. She saw Jamie Sidwell waiting by his door. She went weeks sometimes without seeing her, and here was twice in two days. She didn't like it. Adam left on his assignment as Arroyo came in with some coffee. She uncapped hers eagerly. Her mouth was still dry and she didn't feel rested. She hadn't felt rested in days.

"What do you want us to do?" Arroyo said.

"Simpson will fill you in. We need to get answers fast. We don't get much time between strikes."

She was getting up to return to her desk when Elise came in with her big briefcase. She put it on the table.

"Please tell me you have that file."

Elise smiled. "This is the soonest I could get my hands on it." She dropped a thick file on the table. "What do you want me to do next?"

Kay grabbed the file and started out the door. "Don't know yet. Let me read this first." She walked as fast as she could without running and opened the file at her desk. Thin paper was piled high on the right side, held together by a clasp running through two holes punched at the top of each page. On the left side were manila envelopes stapled to the cardboard file cover, with photographs of the crime scene tucked inside. She started on the right side and flipped through until she got to the statements on Dina Becker's death. All said the same thing. Becker had a gun, shots were fired, and no one knew there was anyone on the other side of the wall. It wouldn't make any difference if they did. Becker pointed a gun at them, end of story. She wished she could accept the accidental death as easily as other police. She could understand Becker nurturing his anger, plotting his revenge.

She didn't find any reference to the daughter until she came to the incident report written by Pendergast. Nowhere else had she found any reference to the dead woman's daughter. Becker had given them the name of Dina's mother as someone who should be notified of her death. Her contact information in Ohio was buried amidst scraps of paper. She wrote it down in her notebook and sprang from her chair. She strode to Sharpe's office, relieved that Sidwell was nowhere in sight. The lieutenant was tapping away on his phone, probably entering stats from his morning workout. She stood at the door.

"Lieutenant, I think we've found something very promising. We're trying to find out about Becker's stepdaughter, and I've come up with the name of her grandmother. I'd like permission to travel to Ohio to interview her."

Kay's heart was beating fast with excitement. Here was a genuine lead, maybe their best shot. Sharpe waved her in.

"Sit," he said. She sat on the edge of the chair. "I need to talk to you, and you're not going to like it."

"Oh, fuck." She knew what it was. She'd been half expecting it.

He looked at Kay as if he felt sorry for her. "I've got it from above and there's nothing I can do. You're off this investigation. Completely."

"They can't do that, Lieutenant. Who better to investigate these cases than me?" She tried to keep it from sounding like she was pleading, but she was prepared to beg. She knew it was ludicrous to have her on a case where she was the target.

"It doesn't matter. You're off the team. You're not even on the bench. If I hear of you doing anything *ex officio*, you're looking at suspension, without pay."

"What about the rest of the team?" At least she could get updates from them.

"They all stay, for now. I'm adding one more." She didn't want to hear what was coming. Sharpe looked almost apologetic. "Detective Sidwell's going to lead the team, starting immediately."

The rubber band snapped. "This is bullshit. Sidwell knows nothing about this case. You're removing the best asset you have. It's shortsighted."

"Be careful, Detective." He gave her a stern look. "If Sidwell needs you for anything, she'll let you know. But don't challenge me on this, Kay. I'm following orders. This is on the captain's radar. The press hasn't picked up on it yet, but as soon as they realize one killer is responsible for two separate murders and possibly a fire, they'll be all over it. It won't escape their notice you have personal involvement in this."

She stared at the Illini pennant behind Sharpe's desk. She couldn't look him in the eye. She felt like she'd been stripped naked, vulnerable and humiliated. Without official access to information, she had no way to find out where Becker was. More people she loved could be hurt or killed. She wanted to scream.

"Kay," he said gently. "You'll be okay. This is for the best."

"It's definitely not for the best."

Sharpe paused for a moment. "I need you to brief Sidwell. Can you do that?"

"Yes, sir," she said through gritted teeth.

She left his office and walked back to her cubicle. She slammed the desk with the palm of her hand. She'd brief Sidwell, but not before talking to Dina Becker's mother in Ohio. She wouldn't go quietly. She made the call.

"Is this Miriam Shields?"

"Speaking. Who's calling?" Miriam's voice sounded wary, suspicious of a sales pitch.

"This is Detective Kay Adler from the Chicago Police Department. I'm calling about your daughter, Dina Becker."

Silence. Then an audible breath. "She died many years ago. What could this be about?"

"We're trying to locate her husband, Kurt Becker. I'm hoping you can help us."

"What do you mean locate him? I thought he was in prison."

Kay explained Becker's disappearance while on parole, but didn't mention he was murdering people. What purpose would it serve to upset her more? "I need the locations of your granddaughter and your daughter's first husband." She crossed her fingers.

"I can give you their names, but I have no idea where either is. I never knew my granddaughter. Dina and I had been estranged for many years before her death."

"Can you tell me why?"

Another hesitation. "Dina married Anthony Baran when she was eighteen. That's reason number one. He was ten years older than her, and worse, he was a drug dealer. He got her addicted to heroin. He was a bastard, but she was crazy about him."

"Why did they divorce?"

"I think his heroin addiction was too out of control for her to handle when she finally tried to get off drugs. Anthony couldn't hold down a job, he stole from her, the whole thing. Plus I think he was hitting her. He was arrested for possession and given a short sentence, maybe two years. She was pregnant when she met Kurt. She divorced Anthony while he was in prison and married Kurt as soon as she could. He was even worse. He was selling drugs too and she relapsed."

"But the estrangement? How did that start?"

"It's nothing I'm proud of. Once Dina died I saw what a mistake I'd made. She died thinking I didn't love her, but I did. All of the problems were due to drugs. There was always chaos when she came to visit. She'd yell and scream at me. We found cash missing. I swore I'd have nothing to do with her as long as she was involved in any way with drugs. I wanted to scare her. She stopped talking to me and wouldn't reconcile, even when I reached out to her. She couldn't stay clean."

"This rift lasted even after her daughter was born?" Kay said.

"Yes. Dina sent me a birth announcement and photo when the baby was born. Her name was Erin. Her note told me to not bother getting in touch."

"And Erin has her father's last name?"

"As far as I know," Miriam said.

"Do you have any photos of Erin as she grew up? Any photos of Becker or Anthony Baran?"

"None. She was completely out of my life."

"I'd like you to send me the baby photo of Erin," Kay said.

There was a pause. "I'm not sure I have it anymore," she said quietly. "I've moved several times. You know how it is."

She did. Her mother had gone through a massive decluttering and thrown out Kay's report cards, artwork, athletic awards. Her exact words had been: "I threw away your old stuff and a bunch of S&H Green Stamps. Can't use any of it anymore."

Miriam agreed to look for the photo and they rang off. Kay scribbled in her notebook and thought of Jamie waiting at her desk for her to brief her. She was itching to start tracing Erin and Anthony Baran. Her desk phone rang.

"Adler."

It was Lieutenant Sharpe. "Get your ass over to Sidwell's. She's waiting." He hung up. Christ. Sidwell actually complained about having to wait a few minutes. Not a good sign. She left her notebook behind and marched over to Jamie's cubicle. She was leaning back in her chair, phone to her ear and a smile on her face. When she saw Kay her smile faded fast. She put her feet on the ground and got off the phone.

"Conference room in five minutes," Kay said, before turning to walk away. She could see Jamie was annoyed. She walked back to her desk and composed herself. It wouldn't help to go into the meeting angry. She wanted to know what was going on with the investigation, and Jamie could stymie that easily. She walked to the empty conference room and took a seat farthest from the door and waited. It seemed forever before Jamie strolled in, but it had been no more than a few minutes. She took the opposite seat from her, as far away as possible. She wore a well cut dark gray suit with a blue boat neck blouse and carried a leather portfolio.

"You've gotten the news from Sharpe," she said, not so much a question as an opening gambit.

"Yes, a few minutes ago. He also told me you were quite impatient to get briefed, so here I am."

Kay sat motionless, her hands folded on the table in front of her. She felt resentment in every pore. Jamie getting handed a nice juicy case that Kay had done all the work on, taking away her only weapon against the man terrorizing her. She was known as a good detective, but no one was a good substitute in this case. She tried to shift her attitude, but for now, her resentment held firm.

Jamie opened her portfolio and took up her pen. Kay wondered whether she had money. Her clothes looked expensive. And while she was at it, she glanced at her left hand for a ring. There was none. She'd never heard any gossip, but she wondered if she was gay. She was getting a clear vibe she was, but she'd been wrong before.

"I'm sorry about what you've been going through," Jamie said. "It sounds like a nightmare."

"And yet it gives me the perfect position from which to find the killer. The best insight. You must see that."

"They're not my rules, Kay. You knew they'd yank you off." She spoke softly, as if to a skittish horse.

"It's ridiculous," she said, her tone bitter despite her best intentions. She looked down at her hands and reminded herself to not alienate her.

"Are you going to make this hard for me? Do I have to get my briefing from your partner?" She was no longer gentle, her tone challenging.

Kay pointed at the two files sitting on the middle of the table. "That's what we have on Diane Hansen and Nora Sanderson's murders. I believe the fire at my parents' house is also connected, but there's even less evidence of that. You'll find what you need in the files."

Jamie laughed. "You're still not much of a team player, are you?"

She glared at her, furious because she was right. She was being an ass. "Tell me what you want."

"What do you think? Everything. I need you to summarize what's happened, what's in the files. Be as subjective as you like. I need to be briefed on your team. I need to know where you were going to take the investigation next."

"All right."

"And I need to understand why this Becker guy would be after you. I want that story."

Having to tell the story of Dina Becker's death to Jamie was torture, like standing naked in front of your high school class. She breathed deep and prepared to start talking when Adam poked his head in the conference room door.

"I've got the PO's file on Becker," he said to Kay. He looked at Jamie and nodded.

"Adam, Sidwell's the new head of the task force. I won't be working on it anymore."

Adam's face fell, which made her want to hug him. She felt better seeing his disappointment. If nothing else, she could use him as an informer.

Jamie turned to him. "I'll need to see everything you've got after I'm done with Detective Adler. Where are the other detectives?"

Adam looked at Kay. "Out on assignment. Except for Elise. She's in with the lieutenant now." He left as if he couldn't get out of there fast enough.

Jamie looked at her. "Can we begin now?" Kay admired her ability to maintain a perfectly neutral expression. Kay's initial reaction to something could be read across a room. She'd go broke playing poker.

She spent the next hour bringing Jamie up to speed, including her history with Becker and the possibility her ex-husband was the killer. She tried to be thorough and polite, but she kept the conversation she'd just had with Dina Becker's mother to herself. It would take Jamie a while to ramp up to where she was in the investigation. She intended to continue working it no matter what anyone said.

"Have you contacted the FBI?" Jamie said.

"That's up to the lieutenant, but no, we haven't. I'd rather not, if we can avoid it."

"It's not your call anymore, is it?" She lowered her gaze to the table, closed her portfolio, and fished her phone out of her jacket pocket. "I think that's it for now, Detective."

Kay rose quickly and left the room. She'd done her duty. As she passed the lieutenant's office, Sharpe waved her in.

"You get it done?" he asked. He was pulling his duffel bag toward him, getting ready for his midday workout. She imagined only football players and Jackson Sharpe did two-a-days. It couldn't be good for him.

"Yeah. She's briefed. Now what am I supposed to do?"

"You're back on rotation. And I've got a new partner for you until Oleska is free. I'm making you Sokolov's training detective. You seem to see something in her."

Kay frowned. "I do. But I didn't want to officially be her FTD. I'm not right for that."

He looked up at her. "You're the right fit if I say you are. Remember, you volunteered."

"I'm not doing anything right now. I'm going to Diane's memorial service."

"Fine. Get out of my sight."

Kay left, pouring herself some rancid coffee before going to her desk. Diane's service started downtown in an hour, and she'd worn a dark suit for the occasion. She punched up her computer and went to work trying to find Erin Baran. She called up the Accurint web page and entered the password. Her life as a detective had improved when this database service became available. Instead of combing through a dozen separate databases on vehicle and driver's license information or real estate records and voter registration, or a dozen other trails, Accurint provided one-stop shopping. And because it was so valuable, it seemed available only half the time. The department's subscription was expensive, and the city often missed making payments, cutting off their access, usually when Kay needed it most. Today it popped into action and she entered Erin's name into the search field.

The only record appearing in her profile was a birth certificate from Cook County. There was no criminal record, no report of assets other than a passbook savings account from the mid 2000s. Erin had never registered to vote or reported herself the victim of a crime. The only people connections uncovered were with her parents, Dina and Anthony Baran, who were listed on her birth certificate. She'd look up Anthony after the memorial service.

She grabbed her coat and left the building. It was warmer out, but raining. She snapped her collar up and walked through the parking lot to her car. She saw Arroyo and Simpson drive out on their way to Pontiac. Her orders were still being carried out, but not for long. How could she trust anyone else to do the job she would do to find Becker or pin down Griffin? Who else had the motivation? She knew Jamie had a good reputation. Maybe as good as her own. But she didn't have that something extra. She didn't have skin in the game.

❖

The memorial service was in the Three Arts building on Dearborn, a residential street with stately old graystone buildings. It had long been an elite area of the city, a surprisingly quiet and uncongested few blocks in the Gold Coast. Kay found parking and joined a few people passing through the grand entrance into the lobby. She climbed the stairs to the large auditorium on the second floor and saw Tom and Louise waiting at the top. Louise reached for her hand.

"How're you holding up?" she asked. She was wearing black, but not in a funereal sense. It could have been another day in New York or Paris, stylish without calling attention to itself. Tom looked ill at ease in comparison, his suit coat a little tight, his shoes a little scuffed.

"Is Diane's family here?" Kay asked.

"They're in the front row," Tom said.

She led the way into the half filled room and sat as far from Diane's family as she could. She dreaded talking to her parents. She'd reached out after Diane's death, letting them know she was available to talk about the night Diane died. Hearing a firsthand account of the murder had to be done on their timetable. It seemed like weeks had passed since Diane was shot, when it was only four days. Time seemed to hold none of its normal meaning to her.

After a faltering eulogy by Diane's older brother, a stream of people came to the dais to speak about her. All the detailed remembrances painted a picture of a woman entirely too good for her.

When the service ended, she made her way into the line waiting to speak to Diane's parents. The knots in her stomach were getting knots as she inched forward. After an interminable amount of time, she stood before them. They looked at her with questioning eyes. Mrs. Hansen was a tall, reedy woman dressed in an elegant black pantsuit and high heels. Not a single gray hair showed in her shoulder length bob. Her eyes showed signs that work had been done on them, though they were tired and red from crying. Mr. Hansen stood stolidly by her side.

Kay offered her hand to Mrs. Hansen. "I'm Kay Adler. I was with Diane the night she died."

She gripped Kay's hand and didn't let go. "Thank you for coming. We're so sorry for what you've been through." She glanced at her husband. "Aren't we, Charlie?"

Charlie grunted. He looked like he was barely holding himself together and any attempt at speech would unhinge him. Kay was nonplussed. She hadn't expected kindness.

"We were going to contact you sooner," she continued, "but between the shock and the preparations for the memorial service, it didn't happen."

"Of course, I understand," Kay said. "If there's any way I can be of help, please tell me."

Mrs. Hansen finally let go of her hand and looked at the long line behind her. "We want to hear exactly what happened that night, but frankly, I don't think we're up to it yet."

Kay reached in her bag for a card and pressed it in her hand. "Whenever you're ready." She moved out of the line and wondered if it would be better or worse for the Hansens to know Diane's murder was because of her. Maybe the thought of random street crime would be easier to live with.

Tom and Louise asked her to lunch, but she begged off. There was no one she wanted to be with, perhaps most of all her brother. She'd told him about the fire at the family home and he was naturally full of questions about it. Unsurprisingly, he didn't offer to help out in any way. He was masterful in sidestepping anything he found unpleasant. She promised to call him and quickly left the building. By the time she reached her car, she'd plunged into a horrible mood. Despair over Diane's parents' loss, Theresa Sanderson's loss, her inability to find the man responsible. When her phone rang, she answered reluctantly. It was Elise.

"What do you want that can't wait until I'm back at my desk?"

"Did you know the lieutenant has partnered us up? I'm very excited." She sounded eager.

"That couldn't wait?"

"We caught a case. I thought that was worth a phone call."

Crap. She didn't feel up to it. "What's the story?"

"I'm on my way to Roscoe Village. A husband came home early from work and found his wife's body." She rattled off an address. "Can you head there now?"

Kay was exiting Lake Shore Drive at Belmont to return to Area Four. She continued west past Boystown toward the scene, a mile and a half away. It could take five minutes or twenty, depending on the traffic. "On my way. Do you have any more info?"

"That's what I have. I want to say how excited I am to be working with you as my FTD."

Elise was no doubt expecting something more from Kay than being hung up on, but she wasn't capable of it. Every part of her life seemed terrifying and beyond her control. She didn't want to break in a new partner, let alone worry about the quality of her training. She'd much rather use Elise as a mole to report to her on what was going on with Sidwell's investigation. It didn't surprise her that Sharpe had been quick about putting Kay onto something new, hoping to keep her occupied. Fifteen minutes later, she turned north on Leavitt and pulled in behind Elise's Toyota in front of a small-step ranch house, dwarfed by massive new construction homes on either side. The crime scene perimeter had been taped off, and at least a dozen official cars of one sort or another were massed in front, blocking street traffic. She clipped her star to the pocket of her jacket and got out of the Audi.

Elise was waiting for her on the walkway to the house, officers jostling her as they moved in and out. She needed to lighten up with the rookie. It wasn't her fault Kay hated everyone right now. It wasn't her fault she was a rookie and didn't know what she was doing. Kay signed the logbook handed to her by a young officer and walked past Elise to the front door.

"What do we have?"

Elise followed close behind. She carried a small Moleskine notebook and a pen.

"I haven't been inside yet, Detective. I only know what I told you on the phone."

"Two things. If we're going to work together, you need to call me Kay. It's simpler. Secondly, when you arrive at the scene of a homicide, you find the officer in charge and start getting the facts. No reason to wait for your partner." They'd stopped on the front steps. Elise nodded and looked around, hoping to locate a lead officer. Officer Carey came out the front door of the house, carrying his clipboard.

"Hi, Ed. Looks like we caught another one together." Kay stood with her hands in her coat pockets.

"Detective Adler. Always a pleasure to work with you." She had no idea if he was sincere. "Let's get you booted up and you can go on inside." He handed her a box of paper booties. She pulled her own latex gloves from her pocket.

"What's it look like?"

"Woman, mid thirties, GSW to the head, dead as a doornail. I don't think she knew what hit her. She's in the kitchen where there's a side entrance to the house. No sign of forced entry. The front door was unlocked, which it shouldn't have been, according to the husband."

"Maybe the perp ran out the front door as the husband came in the side?"

"All I know is he's the one who found her."

Carey followed them into the small foyer which held a coat closet and an unframed poster of Paris tacked to the wall. He lowered his voice. "He says he came home sick from work and found her dead. He's in the basement rec room, crying his eyes out. We have someone down there with him."

"Hmm. A good actor, perhaps?"

Carey smiled. "That's always possible. But he actually does seem sick. The EMT examined him and he's running a hundred-and-two-degree fever."

"What are their names?"

"Jim and Brooke Cameron." He led the way down the short hallway toward the kitchen. It was dark with wood paneling and family photos hung haphazardly on both sides, opening onto a surprisingly large kitchen spanning the width of the house in back. A window over the sink looked out on a minuscule city backyard. The appliances were old and tired looking, the countertops chipped Formica. Either they hadn't yet gotten around to working on their house or the Camerons had low standards.

Brooke lay on the floor between the dishwasher and stove. The room smelled like badly burnt toast. She saw the charred pieces in the toaster. A carton of eggs was on the counter. Kay kneeled by the body and motioned Elise to the other side. Brooke was on her side with her right arm cradling her head and her left arm draped over her stomach. It looked like she was taking a nap. She wore tight jeans and a ruffly top Kay would consider dressy. Why wear it on a day off work? She'd never understand. She was blond, her hair caught up with a clasp on top of her head. There was a look of curiosity frozen on her face, which could mean she didn't know her assailant or she knew him and he was acting out of character.

"Officer Carey, where are we on photographs?"

"I think forensics is arriving now."

Kay looked at Elise. "We can't move the body yet, but we have a pretty good idea what happened."

"There's a bullet hole in the middle of her forehead. Not much question what killed her," Elise said.

"We'll let the ME determine that. What can this wound tell us now? Kneel down so you can get a good look."

Elise knelt across from Kay and looked closely at the wound. "I'm not sure what it says."

"You see how there are tiny red marks around the wound, like a tattoo? That happens when the weapon is fired from close range, say six inches to a couple feet."

Elise looked up at her. "Which would make sense if the victim answered the side door and the killer fired immediately."

Carey was standing across the room by a small table and two chairs. "I haven't told you yet about the hole in the screen door."

Kay gave him a withering look. She and Elise got up and looked at a small hole about head height in the door. "That seems pretty straightforward. Hopefully, we'll find someone in the canvass who heard something."

"Unless he used a silencer," Elise said. "A gunshot in the middle of the afternoon in this neighborhood would make someone call nine one one, don't you think?"

Kay considered her for a moment. "I agree." She saw Elise hold back a smile, as if she'd scored well on a test. Two forensic techs walked into the room. "Let's get out of the way and talk to the husband." Before they left the room, she looked at Carey. "Put every officer you can knocking on doors. I want to know if anyone heard or saw anything."

"I'll call my sergeant for more bodies," he said, reaching for his radio.

Kay and Elise found the basement stairs and headed down, coming into a large, uncluttered recreation room with a giant TV and a leatherette couch in front of it. The other end of the room held workout equipment. Jim Cameron was sitting on the couch staring at the blank screen. An officer stood near the basement exit to the backyard.

Cameron was pale skinned with dark, sleek hair worn shoulder length. He had a strong brow and enviable bone structure. Kay would consider him handsome except for the fact he probably murdered his wife. She introduced herself and Elise and they perched on either side of him.

"Take me through your day, from the time you woke up until you returned here and found your wife," Kay said.

He wiped his eyes with wadded tissue. Kay believed the husband was usually guilty in cases like these, but she had to acknowledge this man was an exceptional actor if that was the case. His despair seemed genuine. She pushed the box of tissue on the coffee table closer to him. "Take your time."

Cameron tried to compose himself. "I'm sorry. I'm barely functioning here. I can't believe this is happening." He looked from Elise to Kay. "Can I have some water?"

Elise left the room and they waited until she got back with the water. He took a long drink.

"My wife and I woke up at six thirty, as usual. Well, she woke up. I kept dozing. She came down here to work out as she always does, even though she was taking today off."

"Why was she off work?" Kay said.

"She said she had a bunch of errands because she's been out of town so much," he said, pausing to blow his nose.

"What does she do?"

"She's a paralegal. She works on big litigation cases at a law firm. One of the huge ones—Spitzer Calden. She got back from New Jersey Friday."

"What was out there?"

"They're doing a big document production, or something like that. They've been out there for weeks." He swallowed a gulp of air. "I'm such a bastard."

"Why do you say that?" Elise said.

He stared at his hands. "I tuned out whenever she talked about her job. It was so boring. And she talked about it all the time. She was under a lot of stress."

"Did she tell you when she was going out on those errands?"

"No. I don't even know what the errands were." He looked ashamed at his failings as a spouse. If she were to stick the polygraph wires onto him right then, she was pretty sure he'd pass. He hung his head. "Oh, God, her parents. I'm going to have to tell her parents. They'll kill me."

Kay tried to catch his gaze. "Why would they want to do that? Are you responsible for her death?"

"What? No. God, no. I adore Brooke. Adored. Her parents don't like me much. I don't know why, but it was that way from the start. We didn't see them often."

"Are they here in Chicago?"

"No, thankfully. They live in San Diego."

"What's your line of work, Mr. Cameron?"

"I teach high school math at Ogden."

"I understand you came home early today. Tell me about that."

He finished off his water and daubed his eyes again with tissue. "I left the school around two thirty. It really wasn't that much earlier than the normal end of my workday, but I was feeling really punk, like a flu was coming on. When I got home I parked in our driveway. Brooke always puts her car in the garage, so I didn't know if she was home or not. The moment I came through the door I saw her on the floor."

"And you checked for signs of life?" Kay said.

"Of course. But it was pretty obvious she was gone. Her eyes were open." Cameron fell into another round of sobbing and Kay put a hand on his shoulder.

"We're going to need a lot more information from you, but for now you can rest here. We'll get back with you in a little bit." They went to find Officer Carey. He was chatting with another officer in front of the house.

"How's the search going?"

"It appears it was a robbery, or at least made to look like one. The bureau drawers in the master bedroom have all been dumped, and her jewelry case is mostly empty. We'll have to get an inventory from the husband. The study is a little more interesting. It looks like our man was looking for something specific in there."

"Take me."

They followed Carey down the hall to the bedrooms. One of them was being used as a study. IKEA bookshelves and storage racks lined the walls of the tiny space. Sitting in front of the window was a desk made of a wooden door placed atop two file cabinets. The file drawers were flung open, and in one drawer there was a neat gap amid the file folders, as if someone had yanked out a handful.

"That would fit with someone fleeing the scene. I think they'd rearrange the files to not give away what they were looking for," Kay said.

Forensics techs entered the room to do their thing. Kay led Elise and Carey into the master bedroom, not much bigger than the study but with a tiny bathroom attached. Clothes were piled on the floor by the dresser, where the drawers had been pulled out and dumped. A jewel box sat on top of it, its contents spilled on the surface. She knew enough to see what was there was inexpensive.

An officer poked his head in the room. "Detective, there's a neighbor here who'd like to talk to you. She showed up on her own—we're just getting the door-to-doors started."

Kay peered at his name badge. He looked about twelve years old. "Thank you, Officer Fraser. We'll be right out." They left the room and headed for the front of the house again. When they stepped outside she saw an impatient woman standing next to Fraser, holding a little girl by the hand. Fraser made the introductions.

"Detective, this is Lori Ballou. She lives next door." He pointed at the sparkling new house on the north side of the Camerons. The new plantings in the front yard looked like they'd just been delivered by the nursery.

Lori shifted her weight back and forth. "I don't have much time. I need to get Madison to a play date." She looked down at the fidgeting child, who had a ferocious look on her face. "We'll go soon, sweetheart."

"What did you want to tell me?" Kay said, not liking the woman already.

"As you can see, we've recently moved in next door. Unfortunately, the window in my kitchen looks right out on the side drive here. I already know too much about my new neighbors."

"And?"

"I was making our lunch at about one today when I saw a man knock on their kitchen door. I turned away because Maddy started crying. She gets that way when she's hungry. When I looked back a couple minutes later, he was gone."

Elise had her notebook out and was scribbling furiously. "Can you describe him for us?" she said.

"Let's see. Shortish. He didn't look over five seven or so. Dressed in a gray suit. Super short hair, like a buzz cut. I didn't see the front of him, so I can't tell you what he looks like."

"What was his build like?"

"Fireplug, I'd say. Very thick but not fat."

Kay felt relief wash over her. This couldn't be Becker or Griffin. How refreshing.

"Did you see what he drove? Was he parked in the driveway?"

"The driveway was empty. The Camerons keep their car in the garage. It's only a one-car garage." Kay could see the massive garage in the back of the Ballous' property. It could hold three cars easily.

"Did you hear anything that sounded like a gunshot? Any noise at all?"

Lori shook her head. "No. Nothing. I completely forgot about the man until the police arrived. Will they be blocking the street much longer? None of this looks very good for the neighborhood. Anyway, I thought I needed to let you know." She let go of Madison's hand and the child immediately dropped to the ground on her haunches. She looked like she could blow any second. "I take it someone's dead?"

Kay noted it had taken Lori this long to ask that question. "Yes, I'm afraid so. It was Mrs. Cameron."

"That's too bad, though I didn't know her at all. I wonder if this means he'll sell the house? I know there're a lot of developers who'd snap it up." She looked a little wistful before bending down and picking up the girl. "I have to go."

Kay stared at her. She wasn't in shock. Her world was filled with venal and hard-hearted people. She took a breath before responding. "Thank you for letting us know, Ms. Ballou. One of our detectives will come take a detailed statement from you. Elise, will you get her contact info please?" She turned abruptly around and went back into the house. She gave Carey the description of the man who'd come to the door and he radioed to the officers conducting the neighborhood canvass. Kay walked back into the kitchen. The ME was standing next to the body.

"We have a witness who puts the assailant here at one o'clock," Kay said.

"Nice to see you, too, Kay." Georgia Withers stood and looked at her with a smile. She took off her latex gloves and threw them into a canvas bag.

Kay smiled back. She'd worked with Georgia for years and was always glad when she was the assistant ME called out to one of her cases. She was in her forties, somewhere between lean and spreading, and she seemed more at home with herself than anyone Kay knew, a warm, cheerful woman who could talk about the dead for hours. She loved testifying in the courtroom, and everyone believed her when she did. She didn't want to alienate Georgia. Half the time she wanted to date her.

"Sorry. I left my manners at home this morning."

"Don't apologize," Georgia said. She stepped closer to Kay and put a hand on her shoulder. "I did the autopsy on Diane Hansen. I heard the story. I'm so very sorry, Kay."

Oh, crap. She felt a sting behind her eyes as tears welled up. Why the hell was it that nice people made her cry? In a moment of true bravery, she didn't turn away from Georgia. She let her see her tears. She could feel her face color. "Thanks." That was all she could manage.

Georgia stepped away and pointed at the body, as if understanding Kay couldn't handle anymore. "One o'clock fits with body temperature. It looks like a close range shot to the middle of the forehead."

"That'll do the trick. If it didn't seem so unlikely, I'd suspect a mob hit," Kay said.

"We'll do the postmortem, but I don't anticipate any surprises. Time and cause of death seem clear. Who did it is your bailiwick." Georgia slung her bag over her shoulder. "Any time you want to talk, I'm more than happy to. It's time we shared a bourbon together anyway."

"It definitely is. I'll be in touch, how about that?"

Georgia laughed. "Uh-huh. Be good to yourself, girl."

She left as Elise came in. Kay turned to her. "Don't put your notebook away, Elise. I want you to interview the husband again. Let's see what he says before getting his official statement down. Take him back through the day to check for inconsistencies. Ask him how their marriage was. Then press him for names of the victim's friends and co-workers. Maybe they'll know something. The man in the suit makes me think this is a professional hit."

Elise looked eager. "What are you going to do?"

"I'm heading back to the area. I'll see you there as soon as you're done."

Kay gunned her Audi east on Belmont and got back to Area Four in minutes. She still had to look up Anthony Baran in Accurint. She wondered how far ahead of Sidwell she was.

❖

Kay logged out of Accurint and finished making some notes. She'd hoped both Erin and Anthony Baran would be served up on a database platter, but they weren't even on the menu. There was more on Anthony than Erin, thanks to his criminal record. He'd served two years before Dina Becker's death and then four years starting when Erin was eighteen, both for possession. The later sentence was at Pontiac medium security. She wondered if he'd crossed paths with Kurt Becker. Interesting.

The search also revealed that Baran had died of a drug overdose shortly after being released. That might have made his daughter closer to Kurt Becker, her remaining parental figure, if you could call any of them parental figures. She printed off a copy of his driver's license. The photo showed a man in his late forties, his long gray hair held back in a ponytail, his face pitted by old acne scars. His weak chin was covered by a spotty goatee. The address on his license was in Albany Park, where there was plenty of cheap apartments and plenty of gang activity as well.

She knew she couldn't hang on to this information. Jamie didn't even know Dina Becker had a daughter. She hadn't put it in the case file before turning it over to her. She'd even kept it from her team when she saw them that morning. She got up and walked down her aisle of cubicles to make her way over to Jamie's desk, but when she got to the open area at the end she saw her team gathering in the conference room. They were laughing, shaking hands with Jamie. She felt sick. As she turned to return to her desk, Adam rushed in, heading for the conference room.

"Kay," he said, as if surprised she was in Area Four at all. "I want to talk to you about getting yanked off the case. It's screwed up, I know. But I'm late to Sidwell's meeting." He glanced at his watch.

"Hey, I'm not holding you up. Go ahead."

He was anxious. He looked at his watch again. "I'm worried she's not going to be done by six. I have therapy."

Kay looked at him blankly. "I'm sure she will be. It's only four thirty now. How much could she have to say? If it gets late, you can always ask to be excused, right?"

"Oh, please. Like I'm going to tell her I'm in therapy." He scooted away and she watched as he took the last chair in the room. Arroyo, Simpson, and the lieutenant sat in the others. Jamie turned and caught Kay looking. She smiled and nodded to her, apparently willing to forget any animus between them. Her smile was lopsided and cute. Kay was embarrassed, as if she'd been caught staring into someone's living room window. She had her own case to work and she needed to get on with it. She got her coffee and went back to her desk. Elise came in a few minutes later and pulled up a chair.

"I gotta say, I don't think the husband killed Brooke Cameron," she said.

"What makes you say that? You know in the vast majority of cases the killer is the spouse or another relative." She tried acting like an FTD.

"Sure. That's well established. But there's something about him that tells me he's innocent. He's genuinely torn up about her death. He said they had a happy marriage."

"Which doesn't mean he's not the killer."

Elise opened her notebook. "I called the principal of the school, who confirmed he went home sick around two thirty."

"Which still doesn't mean he's innocent. We know he didn't pull the trigger, but lots of spouses use contract killers. They can't bring themselves to kill the person they've been sleeping with for years."

Elise frowned. "It's only my instinct."

Kay took a sip of the coffee and pushed it away. It was undrinkable. "It happens to be my instinct as well, but we need to work in fact. I want you to start gathering everything you can on Jim Cameron—his work history, his friends, his colleagues, his hobbies. There's a side to him we didn't see today, whether that makes him guilty or not. Then report to me. That should keep you busy for a while." Elise looked anxiously at her watch. "Christ, do you have to go to therapy, too?"

"What?" Elise looked confused.

"This is a hot homicide. Did you think we were off shift?"

"It's my fiancé's birthday is all. I was supposed to take him out to dinner."

"Get used to it. You're not a real detective until you've lost your first relationship to the job. Think of it as a rite of passage." Elise looked alarmed and Kay laughed. "Get done what you can before your date and then take off. As soon as your dinner's over I want you to talk to some of Cameron's people."

"Are you sure it's okay? I don't want to take advantage."

"Advantage of what? My good nature? I wouldn't lose any sleep over that." She shooed her away. "Give me the names you got from Cameron of his wife's co-workers. I'll start there."

Elise gave her a page from her notebook and left in a hurry. Kay did a quick search on the law firm Brooke worked for and then headed out the door herself. She glanced at the conference room. All eyes were on Jamie, who sat relaxed in her chair. She used her hands a lot while she talked. Kay turned away before she got caught looking again and left the room.

Spitzer Calden was located in the heart of the Loop at Monroe and Dearborn, in between the state and federal courthouses. Their web page described a huge law firm, with four hundred lawyers in Chicago and hundreds more in offices worldwide. The partner Brooke worked for, Ed Chalmers, specialized in mass tort and product liability litigation, whatever that was. She took the elevator up to the forty-fourth floor. The firm's reception area was stark with wood and chrome. Four leather chairs were grouped together in a waiting area, fresh copies of the *Times* and *Wall Street Journal* were lined up on the coffee table. Two men in catering jackets passed through the lobby. She identified herself and asked the receptionist for Brooke's supervisor. She wanted to get the skinny on Brooke from her co-workers before she talked to Chalmers. The receptionist gave her a brilliant smile before making the call. A few minutes later, a harried woman wearing a pink business suit came into reception and looked inquiringly at Kay.

"I'm Rebecca Nowicki, the legal assistant manager. Caitlin said you're a police detective?" She nodded toward the reception desk, where the woman with the smile sat. She was middle-aged, gorgeous, and magnetic.

"That's right." She showed her star. "Is there somewhere we can talk privately?"

"Of course, Detective. Though I can't imagine why you're here."

Kay followed her down a long hallway, where private offices lined the exterior wall and secretarial desks the interior. Rebecca turned into a private office and closed the door behind Kay, who took a chair in front of the desk, facing a startling view of the Chicago skyline.

"I'm afraid I'm here with some very bad news," Kay said.

Rebecca looked puzzled. She wore a cross necklace and dangly unicorn earrings. They swayed as she cocked her head to the side. "What could that be?"

"Brooke Cameron was found dead this afternoon. She was murdered."

Rebecca gasped. She threw herself back in her chair. She was speechless.

"I'm sorry for your loss. Had she worked for you a long time?" Kay said.

It took a while, but eventually Rebecca responded. "She'd been here over fifteen years, I think. Long before I was her manager. I don't understand how this could have happened. Who would want Brooke dead?"

"It's my job to find out, so I need to ask you some questions."

Rebecca leaned forward with her elbows on her desk. "Of course."

"How would you describe Brooke? As a person and an employee?

"We weren't close, so I couldn't tell you much about her personal life. I know she's married and I know she works a ton of hours. How much that impacted her home life, I have no idea. She was probably the best legal assistant we have."

"What was her work here? Tell me what she did during the day."

"She was a senior litigation legal assistant, which basically means she helped get court cases ready for trial. There are an endless number of tasks involved, some menial, some very complex. Brooke worked mostly on things that drew on her experience and used clerks for the more mundane tasks."

This threw only the thinnest light on the subject. "Was there a particular case she was on?"

"She'd been working almost exclusively on a huge products case. They're in the middle of discovery now, so she'd been traveling to our client's headquarters in New Jersey for a document production. She and some of the younger associates read through files in our client's offices and pick which are responsive to the request made by the plaintiff."

"What was the case about?" Kay said.

Rebecca looked at the pen poised over Kay's notebook. "I'm afraid I'm not free to talk about the firm's business. Anything more detailed and we'd have to take it to the partner."

Kay closed her notebook with an snap. "Fine. Take me to the partner. It's Chalmers, right? And the client's Eliann?"

"How do you know that?"

"Brooke's husband, of course. What is Eliann? I see their name all over the place, but I have no idea what they make or do."

"I think they do many things. You'll have to ask Mr. Chalmers about that."

Kay pointed at her phone. "Would you give him a call now?" Rebecca had become nervous. She jumped up from her chair. "He's down the hall from me. I'll go see if he's available."

When Kay was alone in the office she pulled out her phone. The screen was packed with texts and other notifications. One text was from her mother, checking in from Montego Bay. She couldn't think how to respond to that. There was a missed call from Griffin, but no voice mail. He was not letting things go.

Another voice mail was from Jamie, left a few minutes before, suggesting they get together so she could get more of Kay's input on the Becker case. That was a surprise and a little disarming. She hadn't expected her to voluntarily include her. She sent a text saying she'd be in touch as soon as she was free. She didn't add that she had some information to share with her.

Rebecca opened the office door and leaned in. "Mr. Chalmers is available if you'd like to come with me." Kay followed her a short distance down the hall and into an enormous corner office. Light poured through the east and north windows, the sun now out in a cloudless sky, lowering in the late afternoon. Chalmers rose from his chair and came around the desk, holding his hand out to Kay. He was a big man, tall and broad, with graying hair in a Caesar cut. His oxford shirt showed some wrinkles from his day, but his clothes were clearly expensive. She looked into his eyes as she shook and immediately distrusted what she saw. His mouth was turned down and his brow furrowed, but there was no real concern in his eyes. Only appraisal.

"I'm devastated to hear about Brooke, Detective." He pointed to a couch and easy chair arranged in one end of the room. "Let's sit over here and be comfortable."

Kay angled for the chair and took out her notebook as she sat. She'd not yet removed her coat. "I'm in the process of getting background information on Brooke and I'm hoping you can help me with that."

He looked relaxed, one arm draped along the back of the sofa. "Can I offer you anything to drink?"

"No, thank you."

"I can tell you this. Brooke was an incredible legal assistant. She should have been a lawyer and I told her that. I often gave her assignments I'd normally have associates do. But I don't know a thing about her private life. Like a lot of us here, she might not have had much of one. I had a brief conversation with her husband at a Christmas party, but that's about it."

His phone buzzed and he took it out of his shirt pocket to look.

"Can I ask that you put your phone away for now? I won't take up much of your time." Kay's tone was even but firm. A fleeting look of annoyance crossed his face as he put it back in his pocket.

"Of course. I know you have a job to do."

"It sounds like you worked closely with Brooke."

"I did. I'd say she was my go-to person. She knew how to get things done." He looked down at his watch. "Do you have any idea who might have done this?"

"As I said, we're gathering preliminary information. Both you and Rebecca have indicated Brooke worked a lot of hours. Was that mostly on the case involving Eliann?"

His eyes snapped to hers at the sound of his client's name. "How do you know about that?"

"It's our business to find things out, Mr. Chalmers." She watched him closely as he shifted position. "I'd like you to tell me what the case was about."

"I'm sorry I can't help you there. You'll understand that I'm not at liberty to discuss my client."

Doctors and lawyers. It was always this way. They guarded information about their patients and clients like mama bears. When that got in the way of finding a killer, Kay saw no conflict in what was more important. In this case, she wondered if Chalmers was hiding something behind his claim to attorney-client privilege.

"If there's a lawsuit pending against your client, isn't this information already available to the public?"

Chalmers looked more assured, almost amused. "Then I invite you to do your research, Detective."

"So why can't you summarize for me what it's about?"

He put his hands on his knees and stood from the deep sofa. He looked down on Kay. "A lawyer's reputation is largely dependent on his discretion. I wish I could be more forthcoming, but I assure you there's nothing in this piece of litigation that would provide motive to murder Brooke. That's ludicrous. Aren't you looking at the husband? He seemed like a nice guy, but you never can tell, right?" He said this heartily, as if he were telling a joke on the golf course.

"All I'm asking for is a general idea of what Brooke was spending so much time on," she said.

"I'm afraid I've said all I can. I hope I've been of some help." His tone was patronizing. Kay could feel her anger snap on like a closet light.

She left his office and poked her head into Rebecca's. "Can you bring me to some of Brooke's co-workers?" She glanced down at her notebook. "Particularly Andrea Chen and Bill Hertzig?"

Rebecca picked up the phone and made a couple of calls. "I think they've both left for the day."

She looked at the time again. It was getting close to six. "Then give me their cell numbers, please." She waited impatiently as Rebecca wrote the numbers down. "Thanks for your help. I'll be in touch again."

Rebecca didn't look too happy about that. She walked her back to reception and left her by the elevators. She saw the receptionist watching her keenly and wondered what she might know. She would have to come back here, but with the possible exception of seeing the receptionist again, she wasn't looking forward to it. The place seemed secretive and creepy, like a Freemason lodge.

Kay walked into Area Four. The evening shift had arrived, and a few detectives were huddled around the coffee station.

Lieutenant Sharpe's office was dark. She glanced at the conference room and saw Jamie with her head bent over some papers. Her profile reminded her of a college literature professor Kay had a wild crush on. The serious, intelligent face read sex appeal to her. If only she'd understood what the crush meant, she might not have been drawn into Griffin's world. The professor barely knew she was alive. Griffin made her feel she was the only person in the world.

Jamie saw her and waved her in, a cautious smile on her face.

"Kay, I was hoping to see you before I left. I'm wondering if you could join me for a chat. I want to fill you in on what's going on."

She was taking the high road, trying to include her in the case. She didn't have to do that, and now Kay felt petty for not having shared her news earlier. She entered the room and sat on the opposite side of the table. Jamie looked fresh, as if it was the beginning of shift, her tailored pants still had their crisp crease, her shirt looked like it was straight out of the dry-cleaner bag. There wasn't a hair out of place on her short, layered cut.

"Would you mind sitting closer?" she said. "There're a few reports I want to go over with you." She indicated the chair next to her and Kay moved over, trying to keep her face as neutral as possible. She felt anxious at how Jamie would react.

"Before we get to any of that, I need to tell you about some information that hadn't made its way into the file yet," Kay said.

Jamie sat back. "Oh?"

"I talked yesterday with one of the detectives on the scene the night Kurt Becker's wife was shot."

"Was that Pendergast? I saw his report in the Becker file," she said.

"No, it was Pendergast's partner and he had something interesting. Something that didn't show up in the old file or anywhere else, as far as I know." Kay paused for a long moment.

"I'm ready to hear it," she said.

"Becker's wife, Dina, had a fourteen-year-old daughter at the time she was killed. The father was Anthony Baran, her first husband. The daughter's name is Erin Baran. I have no way of knowing how close Erin was to her stepfather Kurt, but it would be good if we could find her."

Jamie closed her eyes. Kay imagined she was counting to ten. "When did you find this out? Or maybe the better question is why haven't you told me before this?"

"I started to look into both Erin and Anthony this morning. When I still had this case."

Jamie looked at the time on her phone. "It's seven o'clock. That's a whole day without that information."

Kay tried to keep from squirming. "A lot happened today. I'm telling you now."

"That's fucked up, Adler. This is the only genuine lead we have for finding Becker, as far as I see."

She shrugged. "I can brief you on what I've found out so far."

She sighed and opened her portfolio. "I knew you wouldn't like getting pulled from this case. I didn't know you'd try to sabotage me."

Kay felt a flash of anger. "That's ridiculous. It's my people who are being attacked. My parents, for God's sake. I'm not trying to sabotage you."

She didn't look at all convinced. "If you try to run a shadow investigation on me, I will report you. Count on it."

The air was staticky. She knew they were both trying to modulate their voices. Trying not to break out in a fight. "You've made it clear you have no trouble complaining about me to the lieutenant," she said.

"What are you talking about? I haven't had time to complain about you yet."

"Don't bullshit me. The lieutenant called me this morning because you complained I hadn't come over to brief you quickly enough."

Jamie looked confused. "I did not. I had to leave the area after I got the assignment from him. When I got back he asked me if you'd briefed me yet and I said no. I don't dislike you that much." She stared at Kay, waiting for her response.

Fuck. She kept losing points. And what did she mean she didn't dislike her that much? That sort of hurt, even though the relationship between them had long been antagonistic. "Do you want me to tell you about the Barans or not?"

Jamie picked up her pen and waited. She briefed her on her phone call to Dina Becker's mother, on the search results from Accurint. "I'll write it up for you," Kay concluded.

"That would be appreciated." She put her hands on the table and pushed herself up, as if she were discharging energy. Kay stayed seated.

"Kurt Becker's going to be hard to find," she said. "He's been planning this campaign a long time. Changing his identity, using disguises. His vendetta is very serious. Finding Erin is key."

"Yes," Jamie said.

"That's it? What are you going to do to track her down?"

Jamie opened the conference room door and held it there. "I'm not going to report to you, that's certain."

"Come on. I can help you with this."

She looked impatient. "Look, we're both experienced detectives. Don't you think I'll do whatever you'd do to find her? You're going to have to let this go or you're going to end up suspended."

Kay's temples were throbbing. "Will you at least give me updates? This is important to me."

Jamie looked at her a moment. "I understand the shitty position you're in."

"Is that a yes or no?"

"It's a maybe. That's the most I'm willing to do."

Kay got up and walked through the door without looking at her. She hoped she hadn't seen the frustration on her face. When she got to her desk she threw herself into her chair and rubbed her face with her hands. She had to get out of there. She threw the printouts she had on Erin and Anthony Baran into a file folder.

She'd write it up at home and give it all to Jamie in the morning, when she might be able to stand seeing her again. Area Four didn't feel like her place any longer.

She glanced at the conference room on her way out and saw Jamie leaning back in her chair with her feet on the table, reading another report. She was almost at the exit when Griffin burst through the door and nearly ran into her. She dropped her file in surprise.

"How dare you?" he roared. He pulled himself up short, his skinny chest puffed out, his legs spread wide. She recognized the intense and wild look in his eyes. There was no spittle around his mouth—he was working up to it. His anger was visibly escalating. She backed up to get out of arm's reach of him. He glanced at the papers on the floor and kicked them.

"What the hell?" Kay said. She knew she was dealing with a mentally ill man, but that didn't make the urge to punch him any more resistible. Instead, she put her hands up in a placating gesture. "I don't know what the matter is, but you need to dial it down right now."

Despite his red face and pinched lips, she could see him take a deep breath and relax his stance somewhat. "How dare you send your pretty boy detective partner to take my statement? You're harassing me, using your police powers to get back at me. Admit it." The volume was down, but his tone of voice was acidic. She thought about what a different place she was in now compared to when they were married. She'd been jobless, directionless, unsure of herself, dependent financially, afraid, brainwashed. Now she was none of those things, but his presence was still unnerving.

Before Kay could reply, Jamie came out of the conference room and stood by her side. "Is there something I can help you with, Detective Adler?" She spoke in an even tone, keeping her eye on Griffin. Kay was loathe to have her know this crazy, spiteful man was her ex-husband, but she had no choice.

"This is Griffin Sanderson. You may recognize the name."

"Ah," Jamie said. "Well, Mr. Sanderson, you seem to be taking an aggressive stance against a police officer, and my advice, which you'd be smart to take, is that you leave now."

Kay was irritated to have her come in and control the situation, but it's what she would have said if she wasn't so rattled. "She's right," she said. "You have no business being here." There'd been some kind of major fuckup downstairs to allow him to get up to Area Four.

"I cooperated with you at the wake. I answered all your insulting questions. And then you have the gall to send an underling, as if you couldn't be bothered yourself, to further insult me with more questions. Ones designed to make me seem like a suspect." His gaze was like a laser beam on Kay.

"I told you it was all routine procedure. I can't help what you make it up to mean," she said.

"That's bullshit," he barked. Spittle shot through the air. "After all I've done to make amends for the end of our marriage, all the overtures I've made with the best intentions, you still can't let it go." He took a step toward her and Jamie immediately stepped between them.

"How should we get rid of him, Kay? Should I shoot him?" She saw the glint in Jamie's eye.

"I don't think we're quite there, but keep your gun handy." She turned back to Griffin.

"What will it take for you to leave me alone?" she said.

He looked confused at the question. "I don't know what you mean."

"For you to stop contacting me. Once and for all. Because if it's an apology you want, I'm happy to say I'm sorry." Happy was the opposite of what she felt about it.

Griffin looked a little deflated. "Well, I guess that's something."

"And in return you will have no contact with me, other than in an official capacity, I'm off limits to you."

He looked pityingly at her, his anger replaced with the sort of empathetic voice a therapist might use. "Oh, Kay. It's almost sad the way you're avoiding what's so clear to me. It's time for us to get back together. Too much time has gone by, wasted. You'll see that, I know you will."

Her resolve disappeared and she grabbed Griffin by the collar of his sweatshirt and pulled him close, her head ready to explode with frustration. Before she could take a swing, Jamie reached over and held Kay by the arm.

"He's not worth it," she said. Kay gave her a furious look, but released the collar. "Why don't we call a couple of uniformed officers up here and have them escort him out? I can stay here until they arrive." She looked at Kay as if she were standing on a window ledge on the twentieth floor. "Don't let him get to you."

If there was a limit to how much Kay could take, she was precariously close to it. She spun on her heel and marched back to her desk before Griffin or Jamie could see her unravel. She sat down and wrapped her arms around herself and closed her eyes. She couldn't feel anything, as if all her systems had been taken offline. She remained frozen to her chair, staring at the wall in front of her, when she heard someone approaching. Jamie appeared and leaned against the entrance to her cubicle. Kay was mortified. She'd have preferred anyone else to have witnessed that scene.

"You have a stalker," Jamie said matter-of-factly.

She continued to stare at the wall. "Do ex-husbands count as stalkers?"

"In this case, certainly."

She looked up at her. "I don't know what to think."

"Does this make you suspect him more?" Jamie's hands were in her pockets, her legs crossed at the ankle.

"I don't know why he now wants to reconcile with me. Would he come to Chicago to either murder his sister or attend her funeral and then say to himself, 'While I'm here I think I'll see if Kay wants to get back together?'"

"You know him better than anyone," she said.

She started to gather her things. "I think he's unstable enough. And if he's the killer, then Diane, his sister, and my parents make more sense as victims, though Becker still feels more likely. But it doesn't matter what I think, does it?"

"I had a stalker once. I'll have to tell you about her."

"I'm sure it's a good story." She tried to imagine herself and Jamie sitting around swapping stories and found it quite easy to see. The image included a mahogany bar, padded stools, a bartender with a generous pour, and a near empty tavern. And if Jamie wasn't gay, Kay's radar was broken beyond repair.

Jamie smiled. "But not now. I'm heading home. Good night, Kay."

She watched her walk down the aisle away from her. She had a long, relaxed stride. Why was she being so nice to her? She waited five minutes for her to leave before she headed home herself.

❖

Kay threw her coat, keys, wallet, file folder, and phone onto the dining room table, which was seldom used for dining. She never entertained, didn't know how to cook, and always ate her takeout or microwaved meals in front of the television. She put the paper bag containing her drunken noodles on the coffee table and went to change clothes.

She tossed her black suit on the dry-cleaning pile in her closet. It made her think of Diane's memorial, which seemed like it happened a year ago rather than that afternoon. Her feelings for Diane had evolved into those she felt for any murder victim. She wanted justice for her, she would fight for her, but her focus now was on finding the killer, not losing a would-be lover. The memory of a three-hour fantasy romance was hard to sustain.

She pulled on her favorite sweats and slid into worn out woolen slippers. She could feel the tension in her shoulders start to ease. She slumped on the couch, turned the TV on, and watched an episode of a show she'd been following. It was a brief respite from her own troubles when she could concentrate on those of a group of women in prison. She paused the show long enough to take her plate to the kitchen and return with the bottle of Four Roses and a glass.

By the time the show ended she'd had two drinks, though they hadn't been poured with the measuring eye of a bartender. Two big drinks. She wanted more and that was a new feeling. A disturbing one. She'd certainly drunk more than this, many times. When she got together with other cops she got drunk. That was the purpose of the get-together. It wasn't a need. When she was in other social settings she drank the minimum and didn't give it another thought. But lately she felt herself reaching for the bottle because she needed to feel numb for a while. And who could blame her? If anyone had had the last four days she had, they'd be pounding them back too.

And even that would be fine if it weren't for her father, who was drunk from the time she was born until he abruptly quit the day she left for college. It was as if the reason he drank had been removed, like a thorn from a lion's paw. Since then, he'd been on a twenty-year dry drunk—all the anger and bitterness still there with nowhere to put it. She often thought her mother wouldn't be unhappy if he started drinking again. She pushed the bottle away. If there was one thing she was clear on it was not wanting to be anything remotely like her father.

There was work to do. She looked at her phone and decided to first make her way through the rest of the voice mails and text messages she'd been ignoring all afternoon. Officer Carey reported on the neighborhood canvass around the Camerons' house. The next-door neighbors on either side had both been home, both stay-at-home moms. Neither had heard a shot or any noise at all from the house. Only Lori Ballou had seen the man at the side door. Most people on the block were away at their jobs.

The second voice mail was from forensics. They'd found a probable match between the fibers found at the Nora Sanderson murder scene and those at her parents' property. No surprise there. The killer was either deliberately giving them clues linking the crimes together or he was sloppy. Kay didn't believe he was sloppy. It was something she had to report to Jamie, and better sooner than later. She made the call and prayed it would go into voice mail. No such luck.

"Is that you, Adler?" She didn't sound unfriendly. "I'm surprised to hear from you."

Kay sat up straighter and moved the computer and file folders off her lap. "I've gotten a report from forensics on those fibers found on the rose bush at my parents' house."

"Right. Whether they matched the fibers from the Sanderson murder scene."

Jamie was on top of things. She knew it was good that she was, but also slightly irritating. "They got a positive match— both from the same lot of the same knit used in most sweatshirts. Becker, or whoever our man is, wore the same black sweatshirt when he murdered Diane and Nora."

"Thanks for letting me know. It makes the sneaker match a less tenuous link."

They were silent for a moment. "Are you in your car?" Kay said.

"Yep, heading home. I've got you on speaker."

"But no one else is in the car, right?"

Jamie laughed. "We're quite alone." Silence again. "Is there anything else?"

Kay was listening for tone of voice—impatience, irritation, dismissal. They weren't there. All she heard was weariness. Maybe they could get back on even footing. "I'm sure they emailed the report to me. I'll get that and the Accurint information on the Barans to you in the morning."

"I appreciate it. Good night, Detective."

The call was disconnected before Kay could respond. She stared at her phone and wondered about her. She hadn't brought up the incident with Griffin, which she could've used to tease her. She didn't sound mad anymore about Kay's late delivery of news about Becker's stepdaughter. It's possible she wasn't thinking about Kay at all. If she tried to be a team player, maybe Jamie would let her in on the sly, keep her up to date, use her as a resource. But she wasn't counting on it.

Then she wondered where Jamie lived. She pulled up the police directory on her computer. She lived three high-rises down from hers on Lake Shore Drive. Why hadn't she seen her in the neighborhood? Partly because she didn't stroll around it like most people. She was always working. Partly because Jamie had worked different hours than her until recently. Her building's condos were much more expensive than the ones in her own. Maybe she had family money?

She clicked out of the website and looked at her phone again. The last voice mail was from O'Banyan telling her the fire scene had been fully processed and she could have their insurance company start on the claim. She hadn't even thought of the insurance. There'd been no room for it in her brain, overstuffed as it was with fear and guilt and a simmering anger. What if there was a company regulation that the claim needed to be filed within so many hours of the event? There was no way to know who her parents' insurance company was with every record in their house now in ashes. She glanced at the text her mother sent earlier saying they were having a wonderful time. That was followed by another text a few hours later asking why Kay hadn't texted back. Should she tell them about the fire? She didn't know the right answer. She felt like she was falling down a gravelly hill, unable to gain purchase and stop the descent. She reached for the bottle and poured one more before sleeping like the dead.

Chapter Seven

K ay woke early with a slight headache and a mouth so dry she couldn't lick her lips. She guzzled water while her coffee brewed and then set up her laptop on the dining room table. There was a ton of work to do. She quickly wrote up a report on her conversations with former detective Nichols and Dina Becker's mother. She placed it in a folder with the Accurint information on Erin and Anthony Baran and drove to the office, determined to stay involved with the investigation but not be an ass about it. She also had the Cameron case, which needed immediate attention.

Jamie was in the conference room. Kay casually walked in and tossed the folder in front of her. "There's the information I promised you," she said. She was leaning back in her chair with a cup of Intelligensia coffee in hand. She wore a well cut dark blue suit, with a blue silk tee and black boots. The boots had heels you could run in, but the truth was detectives were seldom called upon to run. She smiled up at Kay and lowered her feet to the floor.

"Thanks. Do you have some time for me? I need to hear more about your ex-husband."

She looked out the conference room window and saw Elise heading for her desk. She'd rather eat glass than tell Jamie about her marriage. She didn't want her to know what a loser she'd been. She could at least postpone it. "Let me talk with Detective Sokolov about this new case of ours and I'll join you."

"Fair enough. I'll read your report." They were being terribly polite with each other, which was an improvement.

She went to Elise's cubicle and found her pulling papers out of her briefcase. "Will you join me, please?" She continued toward her desk with Elise following. "Brief me on what you've got so far on Cameron. Did you get anything done before your dinner last night?"

Elise stood at the cubicle door as Kay sat at her desk. "I ran a background check on Jim Cameron. He's a model citizen as far as the public record is concerned. No criminal record, no litigation, no financial trouble. He paid his taxes and returned his library books on time." Elise had apparently made a little joke. A corner of her mouth turned up.

"How about Brooke?"

"I ran the search on her later last night. She's clean also. No leads from the Accurint profiles."

"That would be more than we could hope for, I guess. I'm looking into her work situation, since that's where she spent most of her time."

"You think it's someone from work?" Elise looked doubtful.

"I have no idea," Kay said. "But I talked to a partner there yesterday and I got the feeling he was trying to steer me away from something. I'll dig harder."

Elise took a step backward as if she were ready to go somewhere. "The husband's signed a consent to search, so I'm headed over there to go through the place top to bottom. He spent last night at his mom's in Forest Park. He hasn't had access since we first arrived on the scene."

Kay nodded approvingly. "Good. Let me know when you're done. We'll talk to him again later today and we need to talk to some of their friends and family. I want to see what people say about them as a couple. Give me Brooke's best friend's number. I'll talk to her this morning. You start on the other names."

Elise left and Kay picked up the phone to tell Brooke Cameron's colleagues at the law firm she'd be in to talk with them later in the morning. She tucked her shirt in and adjusted her jacket before joining Jamie in the conference room. She sat in a chair across the table and met her gaze. She felt she was in her first day of school, wanting to make a good impression.

Jamie looked all business now. "Thanks for giving me your time. I have a few more questions."

"Sure."

"How confident are you the suspect is Kurt Becker?"

"We're assuming a lot, but the two things pointing to him are the strength of his motivation and the fact he broke parole and disappeared. It's almost certain he's gotten a new identity, and we know he has money to operate."

She drank from her coffee. "In other words, we have no real evidence."

Kay felt defensive, but knew why Jamie was skeptical. "The evidence will come. I'm still waiting to hear from my informant about Becker's new ID. And if we can find the stepdaughter, we can find the man." Jamie ran her fingers through her thick hair and tossed her pencil on the table. Kay plowed forward. "I'm the common denominator, and who else would have a vendetta against me? I might not have many friends, but I have zero enemies I'm aware of. Except for Becker." Why did she say that about not having many friends?

"You seem to be forgetting your ex-husband," she said.

"I'd appreciate if you'd refer to him by name, not as my ex."

"All right." Jamie looked at her calmly. Not patronizingly or sarcastically. She wondered if Jamie thought she was straight. Surely someone had clued her in by now. "It would help me if you could tell me more about him. From what I saw last night, he seemed a legit suspect."

Kay rearranged herself in her chair. "I don't know what more there's to say. Everything's in my report, including the information from his mother about his mental illness."

"Did you know about that when you were married to him?"

She frowned. "That's the sort of thing I don't feel is relevant."

Jamie nodded. "You're probably right, but I hate the idea of this creep terrorizing you."

Kay stayed silent. She hadn't put into her report that she'd felt terrorized by Griffin during the marriage, but she had said his temper was the reason she left. Jamie was reading between the lines. She was also correct. "The basic outline is enough to establish motive. He was crazy and I left. He was furious about it. Sixteen years later, he shows up, still crazy and furious."

"We haven't had any luck finding Erin Baran."

"I'm not surprised. Maybe we could talk to some of Anthony Baran's prison mates, see if they know anything about Erin."

"Already being taken care of," Jamie said. "You heard nothing from or about Becker the whole time he was in prison?"

"Not a thing." Kay looked out the conference room window and saw Lieutenant Sharpe marching toward them. She glanced at Jamie. "Incoming."

She turned her head to look as Sharpe darkened the door. "Adler, what are you doing here? I told you to stay clear of this investigation." He didn't seem angry as much as bewildered his orders weren't being carried out.

"Excuse me, sir," Jamie said. "But Detective Adler is a witness, a valuable one. She's going to have to be involved to a certain extent."

Sharpe sighed. "Make sure that extent doesn't lead to her taking over your investigation."

Jamie smiled. "I think I can hold my own, Lieutenant."

Sharpe left as quickly as he came. She and Jamie looked at each other. She knew Jamie could hold her own. Her self-confidence was evident. Kay's self-confidence was part of her reputation, but it far exceeded the reality. She doubted herself all the time.

Jamie continued her interview, getting her thoughts on what further investigation needed to be done. She kept notes and didn't question what Kay said. When she appeared to be finished, Kay said, "Is there anything else I can do to help you out?" She was going to be a fucking Girl Scout from now on. Jamie was turning out to be someone she could work with.

She closed her notebook. "There's something I'd like to take care of right now. I'm curious how our killer—let's call him Becker without totally committing to it—knows so much about you. I'd like to sweep your home for bugs. Your car, too."

"No way," Kay blurted. She didn't like people in her condo, maybe especially Jamie Sidwell, who laughed.

"You shift like the wind. I was getting used to the idea of us cooperating with each other."

"You can check my car, but I don't see how anyone could have gotten in my place. I live in a high-rise." She thought of Gerald the doorman. You wouldn't need to be Spider-Man to get into the building while he was on duty. He fell asleep regularly. And anyone could come in and fool a doorman by saying they were staying with one of the owners and showing a key. A good doorman would track down the owner and ask before letting a stranger in. But many like Gerald wouldn't bother.

"Where do you live?" Jamie said. She gave her address on Lake Shore Drive. "Really? I'm a couple doors down from you."

"Have you been there long?" she asked, pretending ignorance.

"No, a few months. It's probably why we haven't bumped into each other yet."

"I suppose." She hesitated a moment. "You can sweep my place if you want. It's better to be thorough."

She smiled. "Great. Let me make a call and we can drive over together."

A half hour later, a technician known as Radar was moving through the condo checking every nook and cranny with his detector. Cameras and recording devices were found in the living room and bedroom. "Fuck me," Kay said. She was furious. Her sanctuary invaded, her privacy violated. She flushed red thinking of every move of hers being observed, by either Becker or Griffin. "I wonder how long they've been there?"

"No way of knowing," Radar said. She watched nervously as Jamie looked around the living room. The bottle of Four Roses still sat on her coffee table with the dirty glass beside it. She didn't want her to think she was a lush.

"What do you think our killer might have heard?" Jamie asked.

This was embarrassing. "I'm here alone almost all the time. The only thing he would have heard was my side of a phone conversation, and I don't have many of those."

"Nothing else?" she said with a perfectly neutral voice. She may as well of asked, "No sex? For how long? Are you more pathetic than I thought?"

"Let's say nothing in the last couple of months. My mother was probably over here once or twice."

"What could he have heard from your side of a conversation?"

Kay invited her to sit at the dining room table, steering well clear of the sofa. "Not much. He could have figured out my parents are away on a cruise, which might mean he didn't intend to kill them when he set the fire. That points more toward Griffin. He didn't dislike my parents, which made him an oddity. He'd have heard me making arrangements to interview people or meet up with other detectives. Stuff like that."

"No phone chats with friends?"

"I'm sure he heard me talk with my friend Alice. She calls regularly." She realized Alice almost always did the calling and suggest their get-togethers. She'd have to change that. She had precious few friends to not treat them better than that.

They returned to the Area Four parking lot in Jamie's Lexus. A fucking Lexus. What gives with this woman? They found Radar at her very used looking Audi, dragging a long rod under the bottom of the car. He stopped to detach something from the carriage.

"Tracking device?" Jamie said.

"Yep. Someone's been keeping tabs on where the car is at all times."

"Holy Mother," Kay said.

"Did you find anything in the interior?" Jamie said.

"There's a voice activated recorder stuck under the driver's seat. I didn't want to remove it until you were here." Radar squatted by the open door of the car and pulled the device out from under the seat. Jamie put it and the tracker in evidence bags.

"Maybe we'll be able to pull prints from these, though I think he's more careful than that," she said. "Can we pull any signals off this?"

Radar shook his head. "It's a closed circuit so there's nothing to trace."

"I don't think it's a matter of being careful," Kay said. "He's already left us more clues than a careful bad guy would. He wants us to know it's the same killer, but he uses different disguises to keep himself hidden. I think he's feeling pretty smug. It would amuse him to see and hear us fumbling around trying to find him."

Jamie was leaning against her car. Kay glanced at the time on her phone. "I've got to go. I have this other case I'm on." She looked at her. She had to admit Jamie had presence. Her stance was strong, her eyes flashing with intelligence. Anyone would want her on their team. She tried to remember why she'd disliked her so much.

"I have to go, too. I'm the one following up on Baran's prison mates so I'm headed down to Pontiac."

Kay nodded. "Good. Wish I could be there myself."

"Arroyo and Simpson are at Becker's last known address to see if there's anyone there who can tell us anything."

She smiled. "Thanks for keeping me in the loop."

"If I were you, I'd want the same. In fact, you seem to be handling being taken off the case pretty well."

"It was inevitable." She took her car keys out. "I'll see you later, I guess."

"Also wanted you to know I talked to the FBI. Problem with trying to match up anything they might have seen nationally is there's nothing the victims have in common."

"No signature, you mean. In this case, I'm the signature."

"Right. They're working on it, they said. We'll see."

Jamie stepped aside so she could get into her car and watched her drive away. Kay switched her focus to her new case. She called Brooke Cameron's best friend to arrange a meeting at a downtown coffee shop. She switched to a cop car and drove to the Loop, which was more tangled with traffic than usual. Nearly every street was having work done. She was squeezed out of a driving lane into one of the new bus and bike lanes, forcing her to turn right, a feat made nearly impossible by the torrent of pedestrians crossing the street. It was the equivalent of a small town population spilling into the crosswalk each time the light turned green. Horns blared, bikes wove in between cars. She found it almost unbearable. There were too many people, period. She parked in an illegal spot and walked to Randolph and Wacker, where she found Judy Kline sitting at a small table in the back of the cafe. Her stomach rumbled at the smell of coffee and pastries. She kept forgetting to eat.

"Thanks for meeting me on such short notice," Kay said.

Judy was a tiny woman with long wavy hair. She wore an olive green business suit and carried a Coach purse. Her eyes looked red from crying.

"I shouldn't have even come into work today. I can't believe she's dead."

"I'm very sorry," Kay said, and she meant it. She thought of how she'd feel if anything happened to Alice. "Are you up to answering some questions?"

"Of course. I want to do what I can." Her hand trembled as she picked up her glass of water.

"Tell me about your relationship with Brooke."

"I'd say I was her best friend, mainly because I don't think she had many others. We saw each other for coffee and the occasional movie or shopping date, but it was hard to get time with her. She worked a lot at that stupid job."

"Why do you say stupid?"

"Because it took up too much of her time. No job's worth giving up a life for."

A server came by and they ordered coffee. Kay took out her notebook and wrote for a minute. "Did she confide in you?"

"Definitely. She liked to talk." Her eyes filled with tears. "Sorry. It keeps hitting me she's dead."

Kay put her hand on Judy's arm. "I know this is terrible for you. I won't take up much of your time. Can you tell me what she talked about?"

"Her job, for one thing, but recently she talked a lot about her husband."

"What about him?"

"They were having some trouble. Jim was very unhappy about her work hours. He's a school teacher, home by three thirty every day. She didn't get home until late evening so there were no dinners together. No time together." The server came by with their coffees. Kay didn't say anything as Judy pulled out a packet of stevia from her purse and stirred it in her cup. "Brooke knew he was unhappy, but she didn't seem capable of doing anything about it. She said she was growing tired of Jim's complaints."

"How mad do you think Jim was?"

"Do you mean do I think he killed Brooke? I don't know him, but I can't see it. I mean, it doesn't seem like something you'd murder your spouse over."

Kay knew there could be any number of reasons a spouse turns on the other. Her instinct about Cameron may have been off. "Was Brooke talking about separation or divorce?"

"She didn't say anything like that to me, but I haven't seen Brooke for a few weeks. We weren't phone talkers."

She said good-bye and left the cafe, taking her coffee with her. She drove across the Loop to the Spitzer Calden offices and parked illegally nearby. It was essential to drive an official vehicle in the Loop. It was nearing lunch hour, and the sidewalks were even more crowded with office workers fleeing the high-rises.

She exited the elevator on the main floor of the law firm. The lobby was empty and dead quiet. The same receptionist as the day before sat behind the console desk. She smiled brightly, which enhanced the lines around her eyes. She might have been in her fifties, but she was still gorgeous. Black hair, blue eyes, perfectly applied makeup, clothes that looked too expensive for a law firm receptionist. There was something engaging about the woman that made Kay feel they were already friends. She leaned slightly forward on the desk and smiled back.

"I'm Detective Adler, here to see Andrea Chen." She looked at the name plaque on the desk. "Caitlin."

"Oh, I know who you are. I didn't know you'd be back," Caitlin said, as if she would have worn something special for the occasion. The smile disappeared. "Are you close to finding who did this to Brooke?"

Kay saw real distress in her eyes. "Were you a friend of hers?"

"Yes. We were pretty close."

"You saw her outside work?"

"We had lunch together a lot, went to the theater when we could. I knew her well."

"I'm going to want to talk to you then. I'll check in with you after I talk to Brooke's colleagues." She could see this pleased her.

Andrea Chen came to get her and led her to another floor where cubicles were set up in a big open space, not unlike Area Four. "Is there a place we can sit and talk?" Kay said. "I'd like to get Bill Hertzig with us if we could."

Andrea found Bill and a small conference room. Comfortable leather chairs ringed the table. Kay took one at the head of the table and looked at Bill and Andrea.

"I know you've been told of Brooke Cameron's death. I'm here gathering background so we can find who did this to her."

"We're glad to tell you what we can," Bill said. He was a stocky man of about forty, his tie loose at his neck. He wore Dockers. Andrea was tall and very thin. She wore a pencil skirt and heels and looked at Bill as if she were already impatient with him.

"We're devastated about Brooke. But I don't know what we can tell you. She never talked about her private life," Andrea said. She seemed very buttoned up.

"That's not true," Bill said. "She talked about her weekends, on the rare occasion we had one. She mentioned her husband."

Andrea waved that away. "Mentioned being the operative word there. She never talked about her relationship with her husband, her family. I'd call her a very private person."

"We talked about the Cubs a lot," Bill said.

"I rest my case."

Kay looked at her notebook. "I talked with Ed Chalmers yesterday. He said Brooke was working with you on this case involving Eliann. Can you tell me about that?"

Bill and Andrea exchanged looks. "We can't talk to you about the case itself. We're covered by attorney-client privilege the same as the lawyers are," Bill said.

"I don't get that," Kay said. "I don't want to know state secrets. I simply want to know what the case is about."

Andrea looked embarrassed. "We've been told not to talk to you about it. Apparently, we're not to be trusted to know what's privileged and what isn't."

She could get the information herself from the Lexus-Nexus database, or probably from a quick Google search. The firm's reluctance to talk to her about it simply made her more curious. "I'm sure you can at least tell me what Brooke was working on at the time of her death. What brought her to New Jersey?"

"A whole group of us have been deployed to New Jersey for the last few weeks—the three of us plus four associates. All we're doing is sitting uncomfortably in people's offices, going through their files. We pull any document that's responsive to the plaintiff's discovery request, copy it, and put the original back." Bill looked at Andrea as if worried he'd said too much.

"It's called a document production and it's tedious as hell," she said.

"How much longer are you going to be there?"

They shrugged in unison. "There's no way of knowing. They keep coming up with new places old documents are stored. We'll probably die there," Bill said.

"When Brooke mentioned her husband, did she ever speak about trouble in their relationship?"

Andrea looked at her sharply. "Trouble? No, she didn't. That's exactly the kind of thing she wouldn't talk to us about."

"What was Brooke like to work with?" Kay said.

Andrea pursed her lips. "She was extremely professional. I never had any problems with her."

Bill looked at Andrea and waved his hand away, dismissing her comments. "I thought she was great. She was funny, ironic, easygoing, and she had so much energy she nearly trembled. She wasn't anxious, though. She accepted things as they came."

Kay closed her notebook and got up. "Thanks, Bill. You've been very helpful."

"Do you have any idea who may have done this?" Andrea asked.

"None. But we're just getting started." Andrea walked her back to reception and left her there. Caitlin looked at her with expectant eyes. She also had a lot of energy—she could feel it trying to burst through the confines of her life behind a desk. The lobby was empty.

"Can you talk now?" Kay said.

"Sure, if you don't mind the interruptions. I have to answer the phone." She wore a headset, and even that looked good on her.

"It sounds like you knew Brooke fairly well. Did she confide in you?"

Caitlin smiled. "Oh, yes."

"Tell me what was going on with her recently. Was there anything troubling her?"

Caitlin paused only a moment. "I saw her last Friday, when she got in from New Jersey, and we were able to have coffee together on my break. I'd say there were two main things going on. She was getting fed up with this place. She complained a lot about the lawyers she was working with and even more so about the client. She wouldn't talk specifics, but she didn't like the people at Eliann, what they stood for. This firm has many noxious clients. They're the ones with the deep pockets the partners go after."

"And the partner she worked for, Ed Chalmers?"

Caitlin frowned. "She hated him. He's patronizing and basically a whore to his clients. They worked together a lot, and she was getting to the end of her patience." The phone buzzed and Caitlin started talking in receptionist language while looking straight at Kay. She was feeling some sort of vibe from her. It was confusing. Caitlin pushed a series of buttons without looking at the equipment. "I'm back."

"What was the other thing?" Kay said.

Caitlin leaned toward her. "You might already know this, but she and Jim, her husband, were having some serious problems. She thinks, thought, he was having an affair."

Kay found this as surprising as a cold day in January.

"Why did she think that?"

"She thought he was overreacting about her work hours, but also realized she should probably make an effort. She was trying to figure out how to do that without quitting her job, but her hours only got worse. So the fights went on. Normally, Jim was home when Brooke got in from work, but that started to change. He said he'd started going to a bar to have some companionship, which sounds like a terrible idea to me."

This hit uncomfortably home. Losing a partner because you've starved them of your company, forcing them into an affair. It'd been two years since her last lover had left her for another woman. Maybe she'd handle things differently if she were ever to have another girlfriend.

"Do you know the name of the bar?"

"No, Brooke didn't mention it. She went to the bar one night to look for Jim, but he wasn't there. She went back home and Jim got in a couple of hours later. She asked where he'd been and he said he'd been at that bar."

"Did she confront him?" Kay said.

"No. I'm not sure why not. Maybe denial. Maybe ennui. She didn't think she could handle the blowup that'd follow. That was last week, right before she went back to New Jersey."

Ed Chalmers walked into the lobby and stopped in his tracks when he saw Kay. She straightened up and smiled at him as he gave Caitlin the evil eye.

"Don't get worked up, Mr. Chalmers. I was only flirting with your receptionist." She turned back to Caitlin and winked. "I'll catch you later." She walked to the elevators and Chalmers followed.

"Detective, we're eager to help your investigation in any way we can, but I have to insist you not speak with any of my employees without my being present. Is that understood?"

One of the elevators pinged and Kay held the door open with her hand. "That's not the way we work. No one here's being treated as a suspect. Is there some reason they should be?"

"Of course not."

"Then I suggest you not impede the course of our investigation." She stepped into the elevator and watched Chalmers scowl as the door closed on him. That was satisfying. She wondered if this would make him more or less cooperative. She'd find out soon enough. She got her car out of the garage and drove back to Area Four. She was starving and planned to pick up a sandwich on her way. Her phone rang.

"It's Elise. I think I found something."

❖

Kay pushed her tuna sandwich aside to look at the piece of paper Elise had found in the Cameron house. Sidwell and her team were out on assignment, so they spread out in the conference room.

"I found this in the bottom of a shoe box in Brooke's closet, under some tissue and a pair of high heels," Elise said. "I don't know what it means, but it has to mean something if it was in a shoebox."

"This is the copy you found?"

The document was opened flat in a clear plastic envelope. "Yes. You can see it was folded into quarters to fit in the box."

Kay started to read. It was an internal memorandum on Eliann letterhead. The colorful company logo was at the bottom of the page. It was from Nicholas Furman to the attention of Gerald Thompson, dated June 3, 1985, before email was commonly used.

As you may already be aware, R&D's final report to me on the ADP indicates a 1% chance of the device rupturing an artery in children due to its size. We have determined the minuscule odds of this happening warrant not passing this along to the FDA or our sales staff. If anyone questions you, please maintain lack of knowledge of the finding. No one knows about this outside R&D, who are prohibited from sharing findings of any of their research. NLF:km

"This must be the original." Kay turned the paper over. "You can see the slight indent from his initials."

"Why would Brooke hide this?" Elise said.

"Haven't any idea. It looks like the company didn't give a shit whether kids had their arteries ruptured by their ADP, whatever that is. I don't think that's something they want to get out."

Kay picked up her phone and Googled Nicholas Furman. She found his bio, which included a stint as CEO of Eliann from 1983-2011. "This was from the head of the company, no less."

"Why would anyone write this and make a record? That seems insane," Elise said.

"Can't answer that," Kay said. "Did you find anything else at Cameron's?"

"Nothing of interest."

Kay briefed Elise on what she learned from Brooke's friend and co-workers. "I'm going to follow up on this memo, and I want you to keep digging on Jim Cameron. You need to find out what bar he goes to and interview people there, find some friends of his, talk to his fellow teachers. We've got two viable threads here—her husband and her work. Let's find out which leads us to a killer." Elise turned to leave. "Wait. First you need to make a copy of this and get the original to forensics."

With Elise gone Kay stayed in the conference room and made a to-do list, which always calmed her. She wasn't happy about having a corporate investigation on her hands. She didn't trust big corporations or the law firms hired to protect them. But were they nasty enough to murder someone over a memo?

She was closing her notebook when Arroyo and Simpson walked in. Simpson carried a big bag of something fried. She could see the grease staining the paper. The smell made her stomach lurch.

"Christ, Simpson. You smell like a deep fryer."

He grunted as he sat down and started to take his food out. "You're welcome to some fries, Adler." He smiled sweetly at her before digging in.

"What did you guys find at Becker's apartment?"

Arroyo took a Saran Wrapped sandwich out of a brown paper lunch bag. "Only confirmation he lived there after he got out of prison. We showed his mug shot to a few neighbors and they recognized him. Didn't have anything to say about him, though. Are you back on the case?"

"No. I'm using the conference room for a little bit. I didn't think it'd been leased to Sidwell."

Arroyo grinned. "You two have never gotten along, have you?"

"I don't know. She's all right." She stood and left the room, feeling like an interloper. When she got back to her desk she called Petra Katsaros, a Cook County prosecutor friend of Alice's who occasionally joined them for drinks. She was always on the prowl when they went out, whether in a gay bar or straight. Kay explained she was calling for advice on product litigation.

"You're asking me as part of a murder investigation?" Petra said. "That seems bizarre."

"Bizarre would be one word. I need your opinion on something." She told Petra about finding the memo in Brooke's shoebox and read it to her.

"You can't make this stuff up, I swear," Petra said. "But this is actually a pretty serious thing. In lawsuits like this, the plaintiffs make discovery requests hoping to come up with a document like this one. The smoking gun, it's called. The company probably wasn't even aware it was there. It almost never happens, but if one is found among the thousands of other documents being produced, it has to be turned over to the other side. They can bury it among the other documents, but it's big trouble if it's discovered it wasn't produced at all. If the plaintiffs had this document, the defendant would pay a very large settlement to avoid trial. This memo shows intentional and willful disregard for the health and safety of the users of their product. And with children, no less. If it went to a jury they'd get hit with major punitive damages. The kind meant to hurt a company. The negative publicity could be equally as lethal."

"Any guesses on what Brooke was doing with this? It was an original."

"I can guess, for what it's worth. She could be hiding the document to protect the client, in which case she probably didn't tell the lawyers she works for, who would be obliged to turn it over. That would mean she has an almost unnatural loyalty to a client that probably doesn't know she exists."

"That doesn't seem very likely. I have a witness who said she didn't like the client."

"Then my other guess makes more sense. Say she found the document during the production and pulled it out to show the partner, not telling anyone else about it before she did. What if he read it and then swore Brooke to silence? Because she didn't entirely trust this partner not to destroy the document, she gave him a copy and kept the original."

"But what good does it do in her shoebox?"

"None. She might have been trying to decide what to do with it. She'd lose her job if she went around the partner in any way to release the memo—either to the other side or the press. This is all speculation, based on nothing."

"I understand. Interesting though. Is there a criminal case here?"

"If there is, it would be federal. I'll make a few phone calls."

They rang off and Kay jotted some notes. She had to decide whether to take this to Ed Chalmers or straight to the people at Eliann, who were likely to be well guarded. It seemed unreal any corporation would sanction the murder of someone to protect its reputation and avoid punitive damages, but people have been killed for far lesser reasons. She'd have to approach this carefully so the castle gates didn't slam down and cut her off completely.

❖

Later that afternoon, Kay and Elise sat in the living room of the Cameron house while Jim Cameron stood nearby looking exceedingly nervous.

"Please have a seat, Mr. Cameron," Kay said. "We'll try to make this quick."

He perched on the edge of a club chair. "I don't understand why you're here. I've already spoken twice with Detective Sokolov."

"And now I'm here to ask you a lot of the same questions. Bear with us. I know it's tedious, but you want to help us find who did this to your wife, don't you?"

Cameron nodded vigorously and sat more fully in his chair. "I do, absolutely. Please go ahead."

Kay brought him through his story from the time he told the school principal he was going home ill through the time the police arrived at his house. She looked at Elise when he was through to see if she caught any inconsistencies, but she shook her head.

"In an earlier conversation with us you indicated your marriage was a strong one and that you and Brooke loved each other."

Cameron was quick to respond. "Yes, that's true. We were happily married for over five years."

"That's one of the things I wanted to talk to you about. I spoke with a couple of people who claim Brooke was unhappy in the marriage."

He raised his hands as if in defense. "That's not true. We had fights like any couple does, but the marriage was solid."

"Weren't you fighting quite a lot over how much time Brooke spent on her job?" Kay kept her voice as conversational as possible. She didn't want him to feel she was about to arrest him for murder.

"Who told you that?" Cameron's eyes moved back and forth between Kay and Elise.

"I'll keep names out of it for the moment. Let's say I talked with a couple of her good friends."

"Brooke didn't have that many friends so Judy had to be one of them. She isn't a big fan of mine. I'm not sure what her problem with me is."

"You knew Judy well?"

"No, not at all. I picked Brooke up from a restaurant one night where she'd had dinner with Judy. When Brooke introduced us I got the big freeze from her. She barely acknowledged me."

"So you're saying Judy made up what she told me about your recent disagreements with your wife?" Kay looked at him blankly.

He paused before responding, as if reviewing his options. "Well, she wasn't totally wrong. I was unhappy that Brooke wasn't able to spend much time with me. I think it's important for a relationship, don't you? We've had words about it, sure. But it's not like it was threatening our marriage."

"Well, that's very interesting, since Brooke thought you were having an affair."

Cameron shot out of his chair. "That's ridiculous! I was not having an affair." He looked wildly around the room, as if seeking support, finally settling his eyes on Kay's. "That's absolutely false. She never said a thing about it to me."

"Is it true you started spending more time at a bar after you got off of work, rather than coming straight home?"

"I did stop by on occasion, but so what? That doesn't mean I was having an affair."

"What's the name of the bar, Mr. Cameron?" Elise had her notebook out. She hadn't been able to come up with the information herself.

He looked reluctant. "Are you going to go talk to the people there? It's embarrassing."

"The name?" Kay said.

"It's Riverview in Roscoe Village."

"Brooke told a friend she came home early from work one day and when she saw you weren't there she went to Riverview to find you. You weren't there either. When you came home later and she asked where you'd been, you told her the Riverview. Does that ring any bells?"

Cameron sat back down. "Wait a minute. Should I have a lawyer here?"

"That's your right, but we're viewing you as a witness, not a suspect. We're simply gathering information." Kay tried a placating tone.

"No, I think I've said enough. If you want to talk to me again I'll have an attorney with me. I'm sorry it has to be that way, but I know police always go after the husband. I don't want to be stupid."

Kay and Elise stood. "It always gets me thinking when a witness lawyers up," Kay said to Elise. She turned her back on Cameron. "We'll see our own way out."

They left the small house and got into the Audi for the drive back to Area Four.

"Is this unusual?" Elise said. "To have two legitimate suspects?"

"Yeah. Either could be behind the murder. And both are likely to have contracted a hit man to carry it out. Cameron's got a pretty tight alibi being at school, and he's not stocky like the man seen by our witness, and I can guarantee no lawyer or corporate hack would do their own dirty work. The man at the side door of their house was a professional."

It was end of shift when they arrived back at Area Four. Elise went to her desk to make more calls. Kay stopped to check out the coffee. Someone had left the burner on, so the empty pot had developed a nice sludge along the bottom. She rinsed it out and made some more. When she turned around to head to her desk, Jamie walked through the door. She was carrying a raincoat and her fancy leather portfolio.

"Still at it?" She walked over to the coffee station and stopped a couple of feet in front of her.

"Still at it. I have a case going."

"And I'm just back from Pontiac." She looked at Kay with sparkly eyes.

"Did you find out anything? Who'd you talk to?" Kay sounded eager, probably too eager. It mattered to her how she looked to Jamie, and when did that start? She wanted to keep her cool, not look as desperate as she felt to find the killer.

Jamie grinned. "How about we go grab a drink somewhere? I can bring you up to date."

A frizzle of something zapped through Kay. She couldn't identify the feeling, but there was no question of the source. She realized she'd been standing there not saying anything for a noticeable length of time.

Jamie cocked her head. "What do you say? I really don't bite, you know."

"Sure, I'd like that. But I have more work tonight."

"Me too. We'll try not to get hammered."

Jamie drove them to Wilde on Broadway, where they served a hundred different beers and whiskeys. A huge picture of Oscar Wilde looked out over the bar, which was getting busy with the after-work crowd. They found two bar stools. She studied the whiskey menu and ordered a Blanton's on the rocks, a fancier bourbon than Kay's Four Roses.

"So what can you tell me?" Kay said. She was turned slightly on her bar stool so she could face Jamie, who was turned toward her as well. It felt uncomfortably personal, unlike any prior interaction with her. Their knees were inches apart. She wasn't sure the discomfort was a bad thing.

"Unfortunately, I came up with zeros at Pontiac."

The drinks were delivered and Jamie drained half her glass. Kay sipped hers, not wanting to do anything embarrassing from the whiskey. Jamie signaled for another one, but Kay put her hand over her glass. "I'm not ready yet, thanks." Jamie didn't look concerned about how much she was putting down.

"It's been a hellish week, and it's only Tuesday," she said. "This bitch of a case has been dumped on me and my mom landed in the hospital." Kay felt stung. The bitch of a case was life and death to her. She turned to her drink. Jamie's face fell. "Oh, God, I'm sorry. That was a really stupid thing to say. I only meant—"

"Don't worry, I know it feels different when it isn't people you know getting killed."

"No, it was unthinking on my part."

She let her off the hook. "What's the matter with your mom?"

She drank from her second whiskey, a little slower this time. "Stage four breast cancer. She's dying."

Kay sat motionless. What the hell do you say to something like that? "I'm so sorry to hear that. Can't you take some time off?" The question was disingenuous. Now that she was assigned to the case, she didn't want her to leave.

She had a resigned look. "I could, but it wouldn't do anyone any good. They're moving her into hospice and she barely knows what's going on. Plus my mother doesn't like me much." She took a drink.

"That can't be true," she said, though she'd often wondered the same thing about her own mother.

"Trust me, she's made that abundantly clear. Last week she had her lawyers change her will to box me out. That seems a clear message to me."

Kay knew she'd been right—she was from money, and it sounded like a lot of it. The kind of wealth where having money problems means figuring out what to do with your money.

"I wanted to tell you about Pontiac. I was able to talk to two cons who were friendly with Becker, if that's the right term to use in prison. They ate meals together. Unfortunately, neither one remembers him saying anything about a stepdaughter, nor did he talk about any planned vendetta against you or anyone else."

"He's smart enough to not talk about anything like that. He knows a cop will show up sooner or later to talk to the people who knew him," Kay said.

"We have nothing to help us find him."

"You'll get there," Kay said. "If there's anything I can do on the sly, let me know." She tilted her drink to her.

Jamie stared at her for a moment. "Let's not talk about the case. Tell me something about yourself. All I know is you're a good detective."

She covered her surprise. Where was this leading? She was pretty certain Jamie was single, but it seemed beyond common sense that she'd be interested in another detective in her own area. And why did she think asking a simple question meant she was interested? Her phone rang. She turned the ringer off. "If I were to tell you about myself, it would mostly be about my life as a detective. It seems sometimes that's the sum total of my existence."

"I know all about that. How many times have you heard people say you need more balance in your life?" She smiled.

"Approximately eight hundred and thirty-two times. But right now, balance is about the last thing I could hope for. Until we catch who's doing this, I have no life at all."

Jamie was quiet for a moment. "We'll find this guy, Kay. I don't want anything to happen to you. I'll get the lieutenant to assign a team to follow you. If he's been following you, maybe we can pick him up that way."

She loathed the thought. "I reluctantly agree. I've never picked up any tail on me, but outside eyes would be better." She finished her whiskey. Jamie's gaze felt intense; if she locked onto it she'd be pulled into something she wasn't prepared for. Her phone lit up again.

"I have to get this. It's Elise."

"Sure." Jamie straightened up in her chair, and she wondered if a moment had been lost.

"What've you got?" she said into the phone. She could hear Elise breathe out.

"I don't know how to tell you this, but it's your ex-husband."

Dread came over her. "What about him?"

"He's been murdered. I'm at the scene."

She dropped the phone on the bar as if it were on fire. She wasn't a screamer. She didn't know how to react except to shove the phone toward Jamie, who picked it up and listened to Elise for a moment.

"Give me the address. We're on our way." She disconnected and squeezed the phone into Kay's hand. "Let's get to the scene," she said. "Sanderson just got himself off the suspect list."

She followed numbly as they trotted to Jamie's car, unable to comprehend that Griffin was dead. She'd loved him once, though the thought humiliated her. There had been times when she'd fantasized he was dead, fleetingly satisfying, but ultimately discarded. But she would never have wished for this. There had also been an earlier time in their relationship when Griffin was on a pedestal so high she'd need an eight-foot ladder to knock him off. After spending most of college looking for a connection with someone and finding only casual indifference, Griffin's laser like focus on her made her drunk with love. No one had ever put her needs and desires first for even a short while—not her parents, not any boyfriend.

Griffin seemed to anticipate everything. Before she could say she was cold, he'd take his jacket off and drape it around her shoulders. When she didn't feel like cooking, he'd surprise her with a dinner reservation. When she didn't feel like making love, which was rare, he'd hold her hand as they read themselves to sleep. She didn't have to go through the discomfort of saying no. She should have known, of course, that such effusiveness was not sustainable. With Griffin it was not only unsustainable, but as soon as they were married, it was shut off like a light switch. Was Becker trying to "help" her by killing the person who most irritated her? Wouldn't Griffin, along with the others, still be alive if it weren't for Kay? She wished Becker would turn his gun sights on her. Being killed didn't seem like the worst of her options.

Jamie raced the Lexus up Broadway, a flashing blue light suction-cupped to the hood. They were silent as she sped through red lights and took turns with tires screeching. She turned west on Granville and drove two blocks to a graystone three-flat with an English garden unit. The front of the building was crowded with police cars and ambulances. A cluster in plain clothes stood in a circle on the walkway leading to the front door, undoubtedly looking at the dead body. Jamie pulled the car up behind an ambulance and leapt out. Kay felt uncoordinated, as if a numbing agent had been injected into her legs and arms. She managed to get out of the car and stumble toward the body.

She could see Elise standing with a couple of Area Four detectives—Danny Perkins and Jen Hartwell. She and Jamie joined them. Everyone nodded at each other.

"What are you guys doing here?" Perkins said. "Looking for more work?"

Jamie's face was formidable as she looked at her fellow detectives. Everything about her was tense. "This homicide is related to a string of others we've been working. I'll ask the lieutenant to transfer it."

"Fine by me," Perkins said. "I have plenty on my plate already."

Hartwell gave her partner a sour look. She was short and stocky and had her hair cut by a barber. She wore a masculine cut blazer. She also had a husband and two kids, so go figure.

Jamie squatted next to the body, which lay facedown. "He was shot in the back?" She looked up at Jen.

"Looks like it. The ME and forensics are already done with the body, so we flipped it over. There's an exit wound in his chest. We haven't found the casing yet and it'll be dark soon."

Griffin was wearing athletic clothes and running shoes. Kay had never known him to be sporty. He might have been under orders to exercise by his psychiatrist. Kay knew from her bouts of depression that exercise was a good antidote. Dr. Google said so.

"Had he been running?" Jamie asked.

"We can only guess," Jen said. "So far we haven't found anyone who saw him coming or going. And no one who saw him get shot. A neighbor walking by saw the body and called nine one

one. Said he always looked at the yard because of all the flowers." Kay looked around and saw the whole front lawn had been landscaped and was overflowing with flowers in a riot of colors.

"He couldn't have been dead long. This block has too much foot traffic. How about the owner?"

"Haven't caught up with him yet." Perkins said.

Kay roused herself. "We have the bnb host's contact info in the file. I'll get Adam to track him down." She felt like she was waking up from a death nap and only now were things making sense around her. "Also, the fact that no one says they heard a shot makes me think silencer, just like in the other two murders."

"Makes sense," Elise said.

The paramedics took the body away, and Jen led the group down to the English basement where Griffin was staying. It was decorated in an English country cottage sort of way. The main room had pale blue walls, there was an abundance of throw pillows, and the tablecloth in the kitchen was yellow with lilac flowers dotting the cloth. Kay couldn't imagine Griffin comfortable in such a place, but she didn't know him anymore. He was clearly still unstable, but did he have more control of his harsh and angry side? Based on his outburst in the Area Four detectives' room, she didn't think so.

Perkins came into the main room from the bedroom, holding an overstuffed manila file folder in his gloved hand. "You'll want to see this, Adler." He dropped it onto the coffee table. "Looks like your ex-husband still had a thing for you."

The detectives gathered around as Kay sat on the couch, pulled on gloves, and opened the file. Taped to the inside cover was a photo of her from when they were married. She could see sixteen years had taken its toll. The younger Kay didn't have the crow's feet around the eyes, the line on the forehead, the short, layered hair. Instead she had teenager makeup on—blue eye shadow, eye liner drawn into a cat's tail. Her hair was midway down her back. She looked happy.

She could see that the rest of the papers all had to do with her. She didn't want to go through them in front of the other detectives. She looked at Jamie, hoping she'd understand.

"Perkins, would you bag that for me? We'll examine it at the area," Jamie said.

Perkins frowned. "Sure, Sidwell. I'm happy to do your grunt work." He went back upstairs to find a large evidence bag.

"He must be fun to work with," Jamie said to Jen Hartwell.

"Yeah. I can hardly wait to see his face every morning." She stepped back and looked around the small room. "I'll get started on the search, unless you'd like to do it yourself first."

Kay stood up. "We'll do it ourselves, thanks." She looked at Jamie. "I'll take the bedroom, his luggage."

Jamie looked hesitant. "You shouldn't be part of any search. This is your ex-husband and you've been taken off the case."

"So what? I'm here." She had her hands on her hips.

"I don't want anything contaminating this case, whether it be part of the Becker investigation or something completely random. You can't touch anything."

"Well, too late for that." She picked up the file folder and handed it to Perkins, who'd returned with a large evidence bag. She watched him slip it in.

Jamie looked at Elise. "I'm putting you in charge here. You can start the search with Hartwell and Perkins. I'm taking Detective Adler to the area and will be back as soon as I can."

Kay looked at Jamie in disbelief. Was she trying to humiliate her? All the detectives were looking at her, curious what she'd do next. If she blew up, it would only look a little desperate, because Jamie was right. She knew there could be hell to pay for her being actively involved in the investigation of the murder of her ex-husband. She could feel the heat in her face as she walked out the door. Jamie trotted up next to her.

"Are you pissed off?" she said.

Christ. Couldn't people leave things alone? Must everything be examined and discussed?

"I'm fine. Except for the fact another person has been killed because of me and no one will let me do a fucking thing about it."

"It's not because of you. It's because of Kurt Becker. You have to know that," she said. "At least we've narrowed it to one suspect."

They got in her car and headed back to Area Four. She stared out her window at the high-rises as they flew down Lake Shore Drive. All she wanted was to work, to do what she did best, to find the bastard. But she felt lost, almost catatonic. If a big fat clue dropped in front of her, she wasn't sure she'd know what to do with it.

They were silent and uncomfortable for the rest of the ride. She would lose it if she talked, and crying in front of Jamie Sidwell didn't feel like an option. When they got back to the Area, Jamie went directly into the conference room and started making phone calls. Kay walked to her desk, sat for about a minute, and then headed for the exit. She couldn't stay. Jamie raised her head as she passed through the room with her coat on her arm. She hadn't meant to look her way, but their eyes caught. Jamie gave her a tentative smile. Kay ignored her.

Kay lay on the couch with her forearm flung over her eyes. She was shaken by Griffin's death, but she'd left the bottle of bourbon in the kitchen. It was the worst time to drink simply because she wanted the drink so badly. Her father had avoided every emotion, especially worry and anxiety, by drinking them away. She wanted to do that. She couldn't do that. Her genetic propensity to alcoholism was coming to the fore, tempting her. She wouldn't give in. She'd drink only when she was in a decent emotional state. She'd start drinking beer.

She was going to have to cede the investigation fully to Jamie. She no longer thought she'd be the most effective investigator. She felt too hollow to be as objective and hard driving as she needed to be. Maybe she'd ask for some time off. She'd spend one more day on the Cameron case to see if she could break that open. If not, she'd ask the lieutenant for a week off and pass the case to Elise and a senior detective. She needed the time to clear her head and to warn everyone she knew. Was that the right thing to do? Terrify her friends on the off chance they might be the next to be killed? If it helped keep them safe, then it was. It was not going to increase her popularity any. She'd start with Alice, who would at least not hate her for it. She put the call in.

"Kay! I was going to call you tomorrow. You haven't been returning my calls. What's happening?"

"Things are hellish. I haven't been able to call back."

"Tell me."

She started to relax. Alice calmed her. She never felt like anything but herself when she talked to her. She was like family, though she wasn't sure that was a compliment. Now she was terrified for her. "Things are bad, and I need you to do something for me."

"Oh?"

"The man who killed Diane, and then another woman, and then set fire to my parents' house..."

"Jesus"

"He killed Griffin."

"What the fuck?"

"Remember when that woman was killed after a bullet went through a wall? My bullet, I should say. I think it's him. His modus is to attack people who are significant to me in some way. You're majorly significant, and I'm terrified you'll be next. You need to go into hiding while we try to find him."

"Hiding? You're joking."

Kay hardened her voice. "I'm dead serious. You need to leave town immediately—stay with a friend or relative. Stay in a hotel and I'll pay for it."

"Kay, I'm not leaving town. I have three major commissions I'm working on, all of them on deadline."

"Are you not understanding what I'm saying? This guy is killing people. Killing them, Alice. I should have made you go away sooner."

"I don't think you're in a position to make me do anything." There was an edge to her voice.

"Poor choice of words. I'm begging you."

Alice was silent for a moment. "Do you really think so?"

"Please do as I say. If something happened to you I really wouldn't be able to live with myself."

"Fuck. What's Mary going to say?"

"Bring her with. She can write her novel anywhere," Kay said. "Where are you now?"

"Home. We're both home."

"Stay there. The next time you go out the door you'll be on your way out of town. Promise me."

"I suppose we could go to my mother's in Florida. Do you have any idea how long?"

"None."

"I love you, but you've completely ruined my life," Alice said, a little lightness back in her tone. "I'll talk to Mary about it."

"Don't talk to her. Tell her. I'll check in later."

Kay rang off, feeling marginally better. She would make a similar call to Tom and Louise. She tried to think of others to warn, but she didn't have a long list of close friends. In fact, Alice was the only close friend among a large group of acquaintances, none of whom she'd seen recently.

Her phone rang while it was still in her hand. It was Gerald the doorman announcing Jamie Sidwell. A coconut falling on her head would've surprised her less. She told Gerald to send her up and jumped off the couch and into her bedroom. She tore off her sweats and threw them into the closet, then pulled on jeans and a button-down shirt in record time. She opened the door and saw Jamie walking down the hall toward her carrying a huge bag from Chipotle.

"I brought dinner," she said. "Thought you might be hungry."

She stepped back from the door and let her in. "You're the last person I expected to see, but I'm starved. Your timing's good."

"I didn't know what you'd like, so I got one of everything."

She took the bag and carried it into the kitchen. Jamie followed. "Why are you so surprised to see me? We work together. Something terrible happened today. I wanted to see how you're doing."

Kay didn't think she had any ulterior motive for being kind. She just was. They no longer had bridges to mend. They weren't keeping secrets from each other, they weren't competing for cases. Jamie didn't seem like she wanted anything from her. She looked relaxed, meeting her eyes directly, waiting for her to say something. Kay unpacked the bag and grabbed plates and forks. "Would you like a beer?"

"Yes. More than one." She took the plates and Kay brought the food and beers into the dining room. She quickly rid the table of the laptop and the files of material on the Becker and Cameron cases.

"My place looks a lot like yours. Are you a neat freak like me, or were the cleaners in?" Jamie said, trying to start a conversation.

"I'm definitely a neat freak. Practically OCD. There was a mess on the dining table only because my life is such a mess right now. I've been bringing work home."

"When don't we? I'm always thinking about work," she said.

"Same here. We're pathetic." Kay ate a burrito and kept her eyes on the plate. She felt nervous when their eyes met.

"We're going to find this bastard," Jamie said. She paused to take a drink from her beer. "But until we do, I'm worried about you."

"Worried in what way? I'm not about to crack up, if that's what you're thinking."

"Worried as in he'll take you down next. It seems inevitable that's what he's working toward."

Kay didn't respond. She thought the same thing. She almost wanted it to happen so the threat to others would stop. But living would also be good. They had to find Becker, and soon.

"We'll have a tail on you starting tomorrow," she said.

"What?"

"No arguing on this. We've been over it before. It's not only to protect you, but also because it may lead us to Becker. He's watching you somehow, though I don't know how since we removed the bugs he'd planted. It's possible we'll pick him out during surveillance."

She knew it made sense, but hated the idea of her colleagues knowing her every move. And what did Jamie mean when she said she personally wanted to protect her? She flushed and kept her eyes on the guacamole. "What did you come up with on the AirBnB search?"

"Exactly squat. I don't think the killer ever stepped into the apartment." Jamie paused. "I had to go through Griffin's collection of material on you. There wasn't anything in there that helps us."

"But lots of stuff about me." She looked at her steadily.

"True."

"Anything in there that surprised you?" She prayed there weren't any nude photos of her. She wouldn't put it past Griffin to have taken some while she slept.

Jamie finished her beer and looked at her. "I learned you graduated summa cum laude from ISU with a degree in English literature. I'm not sure that surprised me or not."

That wasn't so bad. "Anything else?"

"Most of it was press coverage of the cases you worked. I'd forgotten how the high profile cases seemed to always fall to you."

She grinned. "You jealous?"

She looked insulted. "Are you accusing me of being... competitive?"

She laughed. Every detective she knew wanted the high profile cases.

They were silent for a minute. It didn't feel awkward. "Do you plan on leaving here earlier than seven tomorrow morning?" Jamie said.

She shook her head.

"We'll start the shift then. We won't be intrusive. The goal is to not have you notice us, like any other tail. But we have to pursue every channel."

"I won't argue about it."

"Good." She pushed her plate away and drank more beer. "I was going to tell you my stalker story. Do you want to hear it?"

She nodded. She found she wanted to hear anything Jamie had to say.

"You might know her. She was in our academy class."

She looked up with interest. "Who?"

"Pamela Ahern."

"Oh, Christ. I can see that. She was weird, kind of creepy."

"I don't think I knew that at first. After we graduated and were assigned to different districts she started calling me. It's not like we had any kind of relationship at the academy. I couldn't really remember who she was. She called and said she'd noticed me and wondered if I'd have coffee with her. I thought, cool, a woman's asking me out. Why not check it out? I met her at Coffee Studio and knew it was a mistake as soon as I put the name and face together."

"What'd she do?" Kay said.

"First of all, she stared at me like I was a magic trick. She didn't want to miss anything. She didn't let five minutes go by before asking me on a real date—her place for dinner. The red flags were waving all over the place. I told her it was a busy time for me and I'd have to get back to her. Apparently, she took my not saying no as saying yes."

"Right. It wouldn't have mattered if you'd said no. It's like they don't understand the word." It was the same with Griffin after things had gone bad. She drank some beer, wishing she had a bourbon in her hand instead.

"She started calling and emailing constantly, and I not only said no, but threatened to report her to her sergeant. You hate to go that route with another cop, but this was crazy."

"How did it all end?"

"One night I was lying on my couch reading. I had a little house in Andersonville and I hung out mostly in the family room in the back. The sofa was against a window facing the yard. It's pretty quiet there. Just as I was turning a page—"

"What were you reading?" Kay braced herself for her response.

She closed her eyes for a moment. "That might have been when I was reading Dickens."

Dickens was a good sign. "Did you read all his work?"

"All the fiction. It took a while."

"I read the major novels and loved them. Then I started on Hardy and Eliot and they were even better." Jamie was the first cop she let know about her passion for reading. It looked possible she was the same.

She waved her hand in front of her face, as if swatting a fly. "You can't be serious. No one's better than Dickens among the Victorians."

Kay smiled. "I'm prepared to argue differently."

"I'd back *Bleak House* versus *Middlemarch* any day."

"I'm not sure how we'd settle that argument. Did you even read *Middlemarch*?" Kay said.

Jamie hesitated. "I started it. Couldn't get into it."

"Then we have nothing to discuss." She looked at her primly.

"I'm sure we can find plenty of books to argue about. I see Jane Austen on your coffee table, for instance."

Kay dropped her jaw and grasped the end of the table. "You're looking for serious trouble now, girl. Be sure you're ready for the consequences."

She held up her palms. "Thanks for the warning."

"Let's steer toward calmer waters," she said. "What happened with Pamela?"

Jamie gathered their plates and took them to the kitchen. She came back with more beer. "So I'm lying in the quiet reading Dickens when there's a sharp rap on the window, right by my head. I was so startled, I literally fell off the sofa. I scrambled up and looked out the window and there was Pamela on the other side, lit up by the motion sensor lights. She opened her coat and flashed me, completely naked underneath. I felt like I was in a seventies sitcom." She paused. "Turns out she was quite mentally ill and had to be removed from the department. She's been in and out of the hospital. I usually see her hanging around when she's out."

"Still?"

"She's never out for long. It makes you wonder how she got accepted in the academy."

"I've wondered about that with a lot of police. They have to have had connections."

"Lots of cops get in that way. It's Chicago," Jamie said.

They were silent for a little while. Kay picked up her beer. "Let's sit in the living room. It's more comfortable." She paused as she realized that sounded like a line in a seduction. Is that where this was headed? They settled on opposite ends of the couch. Kay sat with both feet on the floor, her legs straight, her body pointed forward. Jamie was leaning back into the corner of the couch, her body pointed at Kay. The air felt heavy. Expectant. Kay didn't know what she wanted to have happen.

Jamie put her beer down on the coffee table. She managed to move a little closer during the maneuver, which Kay saw as clearly as an incoming train. "This might not be the best time to say this," Jamie said, "but I'm clueless when a right time might be."

"Oh, God." Kay was looking at her, feeling half scared, half electrified.

She laughed. "I think you know what I'm going to say, which must mean the thoughts have been on your mind as well." She moved closer.

Kay put an arm out. "Don't say it."

"Why not?"

"I don't know exactly."

"Is it because of what happened to Griffin today?"

She realized she'd barely given that a thought since Jamie had arrived. "No, I don't think so. Apparently, I'm hard-hearted. That's a red flag, by the way."

She smiled. "I'll take that under advisement. Is it because you still dislike me the way you did before?"

"No. Not that." She felt desire start to flood her body.

"That leaves my last question, and I hope this is a no also. Is it because you don't feel what I feel between us?"

"I don't know what you feel, because I haven't let you say it. Nifty, eh?"

"You should be a lawyer."

"Insulting me won't get you far." She managed a smile.

"I found myself attracted to you the day I got assigned to your case," Jamie said.

This surprised her. "I thought we were fighting then."

"We were. But I couldn't stay mad at you." She inched closer. If she put her arm out straight, she could touch her.

Still, Kay didn't say anything. She wasn't being coy, she simply couldn't believe what was happening. Or how much she wanted it to happen. Instead of trying to move away, she relaxed her body and turned it fully toward Jamie. "You don't even know me."

"I know enough." She took her hand. "I'm not going to press you. I want to close this huge gap between us and kiss you, but I have to know you want me to."

Kay looked at her for a long time and then slowly bent forward. Jamie's eyes sparked as she drew closer. She didn't move until Kay's lips touched hers. The kiss was soft and tentative and quickly more assured. Jamie drew her close and she relaxed in her arms, excited and peaceful at the same time. The kiss went on a long time before she leaned back and took a deep breath. Then they kissed some more. She was at a low boil, the point where she had to decide whether to end things where they were or take them to where they were headed.

She stood and took Jamie's hand, pulling her gently to the bedroom, feeling the current between them, wondering how something could feel so good in the midst of so much bad. At the door, Jamie stopped.

"Are you sure? We don't have to rush."

Kay raised her eyebrows. "Are you calling me a loose woman?" She surprised herself with her teasing tone.

Jamie reached for her hand. "No! God, no. Loose is good."

"You're only making it worse," Kay said.

She looked dismayed. "I think I'm suddenly nervous."

"Then we've experienced complete role reversal, because I'm suddenly not." She looked into Jamie's eyes and saw desire and a little anxiety. "Do you want to turn back?"

Jamie stepped forward and wrapped her arms around Kay's waist, pulling her close for a searing kiss. They moved in an awkward tango toward the bed. As soon as the back of Kay's leg hit the mattress, she fell backward and pulled Jamie on top of her, who slid off to the side for a better angle kissing and exploring Kay's body. Her nerves seemed to be gone. Her hand moved slowly over Kay's shoulder, touched the small valley at the base of her throat, slid down and lightly over her breast. Kay gasped. Jamie's hand glided over the curve of her hip and across the top of her thighs. On the way back up, she unbuttoned Kay's shirt, still taking her time, lingering on each inch of skin exposed.

Kay was nearly unhinged. She rose and pushed Jamie onto her back, straddling her hips. "Slow is for later." She finished unbuttoning her shirt and ripped it off, along with her bra. She saw Jamie's eyes widen. "Fast is for now."

Jamie's hand reached up and trailed a finger across a nipple, squeezing it just a bit harder than gently, and Kay gasped again. She rolled off Jamie and started tearing her pants and underwear off and Jamie followed suit. When their naked bodies came together, touching from head to toe, it was like silk, it was a warm bath, it was burning, it was urgent. Jamie wasted no time now. Her fingers slid into Kay just as her mouth wrapped around a nipple. Kay lifted from the bed as if from electric shock. She knew if Jamie touched her in that one perfect spot, the top of her head would come off. She tried to slow her arousal, which was like reversing the course of a river. It was going one way only. Soon Jamie put her finger just there and Kay came with a roar. She'd never heard such a noise come out of herself. Before she had time to clear her head, Jamie slid between her legs and captured her with her lips, and soon Kay had her first multiple orgasm. Ever.

She lay boneless as Jamie gathered her up in her arms. She was physically stunned by the intensity of her response. Stunned emotionally at how different it felt from anyone she'd been with before. She could barely move, still breathing heavily with her mouth an inch or so from Jamie's breast. Her perfect breast. Desire surged through her again and she looked up at Jamie. "I want all of you," she said as she drew herself up. And then she had all of her, and every part was lovely.

CHAPTER EIGHT

O h, shit." Jamie shot up in bed, looking at her phone as if it'd betrayed her. "The alarm was supposed to go off at six thirty."

Kay lay on her stomach, her face in her pillow. "It did. You turned it off."

She scrubbed her face with her hands. "Now I'm going to have to do the walk of shame in front of the first shift surveillance guys, who naturally are Arroyo and Simpson."

"That'll keep them awake for a while."

Kay propped herself on her elbow and looked at Jamie's body. She'd touched every inch of it throughout the night, but in daylight she could see its beauty. Even her bedhead was appealing—locks of smooth, thick hair fell over her eyes. A red crease lined the side of her face from the wrinkled bedsheet. When she raised her arms for a languorous stretch, Kay saw a three-inch scar on the left side of her left breast. She reached out to gently touch it and looked into Jamie's steady gaze.

"Is this what I think it is?"

"I was going to tell you about it last night, but we didn't do much talking." She lay against the headboard, the sheet up to her waist.

"Breast cancer?"

Jamie nodded. "Runs in the family, I guess. I was diagnosed on my thirty-fifth birthday, almost four years ago. The timing was bad—my mother was going through chemo at the time. Then I had to have chemo. I don't think she appreciated sharing the stage."

Kay sat cross-legged and faced her, trying to rein in her thinking, which had already taken her to widowhood. She knew pre-menopausal patients had a dimmer prognosis, especially with a family history. "Can you tell me about it?"

Jamie smiled. "You look like you're at my funeral."

Kay took her hand. "Sorry. I have the world's worst poker face."

"You really don't have to worry. I'm fine, in total remission. It's like I never had it."

"Well, that can't be true," Kay said. "What was the diagnosis?"

"Stage II triple negative ductal carcinoma. Chemo, lumpectomy, radiation, and bam, I'm as good as new."

Jamie was a stoic, which usually meant an inability to show any vulnerability. Kay suspected she was the same. How would that work if they had a relationship? She didn't want to assume they were now a couple. Maybe Jamie thought of the epic night of sex as a one-off.

"Regrettably, I have to get going," Jamie said. "I'd rather Arroyo and Simpson not see me, and they start their shift in a few minutes."

"They'd love it. It'd give them something to talk about all day."

"You're more sanguine about them knowing than I thought you'd be."

Kay put her arms around her and pulled her close. "It's super sexy when you use words like sanguine." Jamie laughed. "But I have enough to worry about without caring about gossip in the area."

"Yeah. About that. Don't you think you should take some time off and lay low? I'd hate to see you get killed, now that I know how fantastic you are in bed."

Kay leaned forward for a short kiss. "I'm not going to lay low. Your whole plan of following me to catch sight of Becker would be moot."

"Moot? See, I said you should have been a lawyer. I didn't think I could convince you to sit and wait, so I won't try any longer. I feel better at least knowing some cops are watching you." She looked at her phone. "I have to go."

Kay put a restraining hand on Jamie's thigh. "I can barely believe last night happened."

"It was amazing." A moment's insecurity showed on her face before she smiled. "Don't you think so?"

"I do. But I'll have to get used to it, the idea of us being attracted to each other." Kay was leaning against the headboard, the sheet pulled up to her collarbone.

Jamie laughed. "Don't worry, we'll take things nice and slow."

"Like we did last night?"

"Exactly like that."

She got dressed while Kay made coffee. She handed a cup to her when she'd finished dressing. "At least you don't have far to go to get home."

Her mind seemed to be already shifting into work mode as she backed her way out the door, giving Kay a last kiss. Her eyes looked further away, less intimate.

Kay drove out of her garage a half hour later and could see Arroyo and Simpson in a surveillance sedan across the street. She waved and drove to Area Four. What did they now know, anyway? That she and Jamie slept together? That's as much as Kay knew herself. She didn't know if she meant for the one night to lead to something else. Maybe she was a player, though that didn't ring true. She needed to find out more about her before letting her attraction gallop away with her, like it had with Diane.

She called Alice and learned she and Mary planned to drive out of town that afternoon. She promised Kay she wouldn't leave the house until then. When she got to Area Four, thoughts of Jamie faded away as she focused on her work. Her first stop was Elise's desk. She was on Accurint, paging through Jim Cameron's file.

"I thought you said there wasn't anything in there?" Kay said.

"There isn't. I'm going over everything a second time, because we have next to nothing on Jim Cameron. We've gone through his cell record and followed up on all the recent calls. We've been through his email."

"That's not conclusive. He could have been using a burner phone, a second email address."

"Definitely," Elise said. "But of the friends and co-workers I talked to, only one—a teacher he had drinks with after school—said Cameron talked about his marriage being in trouble. He said he only mentioned it once, about a week ago, and it was very brief. Like he started to talk about it and then changed his mind."

"Get back to the friend and ask if Cameron ever mentioned any other bars he drank at. Maybe late night places. I want to find out what kind of people he was hanging out with. I have a hunch he was doing more outside the home than he's letting on. If he hired a hit man, he had to be in contact with someone who would have those kind of connections. Probably not the workers you find in a neighborhood tavern in the late afternoon."

Kay went to her desk to put her things down and then to the coffee station. As she was pouring she looked into the conference room to see if Jamie was there and saw Adam instead. Kay fixed her coffee, and when she turned back he was walking toward her.

"I hear our guy struck again last night," Adam said. "Sorry I wasn't around to help."

"It was my creepy ex-husband." Adam watched her, waiting for more. "But I didn't want him dead."

"Maybe we can pull out some further leads from this one. We've got shit otherwise." He poured some coffee.

"So what have you been working on? I don't see you much anymore."

"Sidwell has me chasing down a few things on her other cases. She wants the decks cleared."

"And that's okay with you?" It wouldn't have been okay with her.

"Whatever helps."

She took her mug and strode away. When she got to her desk she noticed her hand trembling as she put her full mug down. Her body was starting to break down. She'd always had nerves of steel. Now she only had nerves. Jangly nerves. Hours of sex had been a great distraction, but reality was flooding back in. She felt warm and took off the Tommy Hilfiger coat she'd bought at Costco.

She took out a copy of the Eliann memo and stared at it. What heartless bastards they were. She was going to take pleasure in knowing their failure to protect children would be revealed. She'd bring it to the press if she had to. But first she'd see if Ed Chalmers was a stand-up guy or not. She'd take it to him.

Jamie popped her head into Kay's cubicle. Her smile beamed like a flashlight. Kay tried to maintain a straight face.

"No fooling around at work," she whispered. She felt a flush of desire. "Really."

"Agreed. I'm here to report what we're up to," she said, watching as Kay's hand reached for hers. "No touching. I can't account for myself if you start touching me."

She pulled back. She hadn't meant to touch her. "Of course. What is it you want to tell me?"

"I've been trying to locate some of the associates of Anthony Baran, mostly those who spent time in prison with him and are now out on parole. I finally got hold of one, but he said he couldn't remember a single word Baran said. He did tell me about an ex-con who was supposedly Baran's best mate on the inside. I've put Adam on tracking him down. Maybe he'll know something about Baran's daughter."

"I talked to Adam a minute ago. He said he was cleaning up some of your cases."

"I talked to him thirty seconds ago, and he's back on the Becker case."

Kay tried to be optimistic. "It's a lead. That's good."

"It may be the best lead we've got. Also, the LT is sending more people to me. And I think he's going to force you to take time off and lay low. I can't say I'd be unhappy at that."

"I can say I'd be totally unhappy with that. I'm the way we draw Becker out. I'll go mad if I have to hide out in my condo." She started gathering her things.

"I'd come visit every chance I had," Jamie said.

"As tempting as that sounds," she said, watching her smile, "I'd still feel incarcerated." She pushed her chair under her desk and turned to leave.

"Where are you off to?"

"I'm going to rattle a witness. I'll take Elise with me." They were standing entirely too close to each other. She could hear Jamie's breathing. She could feel it. "You're killing me."

"Same here." She stepped away. "I'll catch you later. I'm glad Elise will be with you."

She watched her walk away and grabbed hold of the top of her chair. This was the worst time for her to suddenly find herself wildly attracted to someone. It was like a drug and it kept luring her away from the business at hand. She went into the women's bathroom and splashed water on her face. She did a deep breathing exercise she'd once learned from one of her department assigned psychiatrists. Then she went to fetch Elise and get down to business.

As soon as they exited the elevator at Spitzer Calden, Caitlin greeted them with a gigantic grin. They seemed like old friends now. She called Chalmers, and after a bit of a wait, his assistant came to escort them upstairs.

"I'm Angela, Mr. Chalmers's assistant," she said. "We met briefly the other day."

It was hard to believe it'd been only two days since she first talked to Chalmers. It felt like a different life ago. Angela led them past his office and into a lush conference room—the Ritz-Carlton to Area Four's Motel 6. A coffee service was laid on a credenza at one end of the room. She saw workers through the windows of the office tower across the street, staring at computer screens. She'd rather die.

"Mr. Chalmers wasn't expecting you, but he is here," Angela said. "He'll be with you in a few minutes."

Kay and Elise took seats opposite each other at the end of the table. After ten minutes, Chalmers bustled into the conference room and held out his hand to Kay. He wore a suit jacket this time. She introduced Elise and he sat between them at the head of the table.

"I'm not sure what I can help you with," he said. "I think we covered what I know about Brooke Cameron."

"I've come to discuss something else today. Elise, would you hand Mr. Chalmers a copy of the document?"

Elise took a single page from a file folder and slid it across the table to Chalmers. He scanned the document.

"Where'd you get this?" He looked startled.

"It was found hidden in a shoe box in Brooke Cameron's house." She watched Chalmers carefully, but he seemed genuinely surprised to see the document.

"Brooke showed me this document a week ago. I didn't know she'd kept a copy."

"She kept the original. I have that tucked safely away," Kay said. "Tell me everything about this. From my perspective, it looks like the kind of thing the company would want to stay hidden, maybe at any cost."

"You know I can't answer your question because of attorney-client privilege. I'm sorry."

Kay put her hands on the table and leaned toward him. "Mr. Chalmers, someone murdered Brooke Cameron. I'm trying to learn if your corporate client would be capable of ordering her death because she knew of this document. Remember that you're also an officer of the court. I'm asking you to cooperate with me and answer my questions."

Chalmers shrugged. "I'd love to cooperate with you, but the privilege clearly applies here. My hands are tied."

Kay was nearly convinced Chalmers and his client had no intention of producing that document and were anxious to make the threat of it go away. She didn't doubt for a second that enormous corporations would stoop as low as murder to manage their image and their stock prices. How to prove it was the problem.

"I'll have to ask you for the original of the memo. It's not your property," he said.

Kay stood and Elise followed. "That's not possible at this time. I'm holding the document as potential evidence. You'll have to lawyer that one out with the city attorneys. I'm keeping it in the meantime."

He watched them out with a thoughtful look on his face. He didn't seem panicked. Kay couldn't read him. As they drove back to Area Four she looked for a car tailing her, but couldn't pick one out. She wondered if Becker had figured out she was being followed.

"I want you to spend the afternoon tracking down that info on Jim Cameron. I'll try to come up with a new angle to approach Eliann and its lawyers."

She looked around the parking lot for Jamie's Lexus, but it wasn't there. She tried to dismiss her disappointment. The whole thing was absurd. She couldn't let the desire she felt interfere with her work, but she wasn't sure how possible that was.

❖

Kay thought better of going back to the area. Lieutenant Sharpe could be lying in wait for her, ready, if not eager, to put her on enforced paid leave. She'd play hide-and-seek as long as possible. She reversed direction and drove out of the lot, headed to Panera for a salad and then home. The lieutenant called while she was eating. She let the call go into voice mail and then played back the message. She was either a coward or a procrastinator. His voice barked out of the phone:

"Adler, I want you to get to your place and stay there. That's an order. I'm putting you on paid leave starting immediately. Dan Holden is taking over your cases. I'm sending him over for a briefing. Call me. That's an order, too."

Oh, Christ. Did they all think she was Becker's next target? She didn't see it. He was having too much fun torturing her by attacking others. If he killed her he'd have no more sport. She called the lieutenant and told him exactly that.

"Really, Adler? Is this something you're willing to be wrong about? Because that would be a terrible mistake. I'm not willing to take that risk."

"Isn't it mine to take?" she said coolly.

The lieutenant's voice grew harder. "You're a detective in my area. To the extent I can protect you, I'm going to do that. Are you at home?"

"For the moment," Kay said.

"Don't leave there. Let Sidwell find this guy while you stay safe."

"I'm fine with her running the investigation. That's not my objection to this. I'm the one thing that can draw Becker out. It's crazy to take that off the table."

"I'm not using you as chum," he said.

"What your asking is ridiculous. You can't put me under house arrest." There was a pause. "Lieutenant?"

"I'm mulling over how to do that. Good idea."

"Funny." It probably would be much easier to agree with the lieutenant than to argue with him. They both knew she'd do as she liked. "All right. I'll agree to the paid leave. Send Holden over and I'll brief him on the Cameron case."

"I'm always suspicious of you suddenly agreeing to anything. This is serious stuff, Kay."

"You think I don't know it's serious?" she said. A cork popped and she was furious. "Three people are dead because of me. That's about as serious as it gets. Fucker."

"Excuse me, Detective?"

She hung up. She meant that Becker was the fucker, but let Sharpe think what he wants. He was a fucker too. There'd be hell to pay for that, but it wasn't on her list of things to worry about. She felt like a fly with her wings pulled off. She had fewer and fewer ways to find the killer. One thing was certain. She wasn't going to sit in her condo while someone found him for her, even if that someone else was Jamie.

An hour later, Kay finished up her briefing with Dan Holden. He sat at her dining table and made the chair seem spindly beneath him. He was nearly as broad as he was tall, all of it muscle. He worked out a lot with Sharpe. He wasn't the smartest detective in the area, but he was a plodder, and plodders eventually got what they were after.

"How the hell am I'm going to follow up on this memo? It doesn't seem likely Eliann's CEO is going to invite me for a sit-down."

"I'm sure that's true. I'm also sure Chalmers has talked to them and they won't say a word without their lawyer present. But you have to try."

Holden had a buzz cut and he kept skimming the palm of his hand across the top of his head.

"Tell me again why you think a corporation would order a hit on someone holding this memo?"

"I don't know if I think it's true as much as it's a viable theory. If Chalmers and his client really didn't intend to produce the damning memo, then they'd want the only other person who knew about it eliminated."

Holden shook his head. "Maybe I haven't grown cynical enough yet. I find that idea shocking. Killing someone over a document?"

"More like killing someone over the many millions it will cost them if the memo gets out. Plus the horrendous publicity."

Holden stood. "Okay. I'll check in with Sokolov on the husband angle. Don't worry about anything. I've got you covered."

"Thanks, Danny," Kay said. She was secretly glad she didn't have to rattle the corporate tree. She hated dealing with those guys. They protected their corporate interests over those of human beings, and she could never respect that. She hoped Eliann got nailed by that memo.

She saw him out and turned to face her living room, as if assessing a jail cell. It looked good in that regard, but it still was a jail. Or at least the lieutenant would like it to be. As soon as she could figure out her next move, she'd be out the door. She thought of calling Jamie to let her know she'd been yanked off duty, but as she picked up the phone it rang. Her heart rate went up a tick when she saw her name on the screen.

"Sidwell," Kay said, keeping her voice business-like.

"That's me, checking in to see how the prisoner's doing."

"Ack. I'm not a prisoner. He can't shackle me to a chair in my own home."

"I don't think it would make any difference if he did. You'd leave your place with chair in tow." She seemed amused.

"That's funny," Kay said.

She paused. "I know this is very tough on you. Unfortunately, the lieutenant has asked me to keep an eye on your movements."

"I thought you'd want to do that anyway. Am I reading too much into last night?" She kept her voice light, but she wanted to know. What did last night mean?

"Not at all. I'd love to keep an eye on you."

"I might consider staying put if it were for sex. Is there anything you can do about that?"

"Jesus, Kay." She let out a long, loud breath.

"Too much?" She held her breath.

"It's not that it's too much. It's that it isn't enough."

She grinned. "What're you suppose to report to the lieutenant?"

"He wants to know when you leave your condo and where you're going. We're keeping two men on you at all times. Doesn't that make you feel safe?"

"It makes me feel like I'm suffocating. I assume we can come to some sort of arrangement where you don't feel you have to tell Sharpe every little thing," she said.

"The problem is the detectives who will be tailing you. They report directly to the lieutenant. How about this? I keep you completely in the loop about what we're doing on the Becker case and you keep your head down."

"No chance."

"Come on, Kay. I don't want to lose you."

That lay in the air like a big bubble that would pop at any second. She wasn't sure what to say.

"I mean I'm just getting to know you," she said. "And I like what I know so far. A lot." Her voice wasn't tentative as much as careful, as if she were concerned her words might backfire.

Kay softened her voice. "That's very good to hear. A relief, actually."

"I don't want last night to be it," she said. "I'd like to see you tonight if I could."

She laughed. "Well, you'll know where to find me."

"Does that mean you'll stay put?"

"At least for today. To tell you the truth, I'm not sure where I'd go. Have you had any luck finding Anthony Baran's prison mate?"

"Some. We've gotten an address for him as of this morning, but no cell number or work address. Adam's waiting for him in front of his apartment. We have his mug shot to go by."

"I hope he comes home soon. Becker could strike again at any time."

They rang off. She walked over to her couch and looked at it with disdain. It was Wednesday, the middle of the day. She felt she couldn't possibly sit on it. It's not that she was opposed to relaxing during the day. There were weekends and other days off when lying down with a game on the TV and a bowl of popcorn in her lap was pure pleasure. Or she'd binge watch Netflix and feel slightly hungover from it. That was all good, as long as she had work to go back to. This leave could last one day or a hundred, an impossible scenario for her to even imagine. She would go insane.

She forced herself to sit and picked up her book. She was rereading Jane Austen and was halfway through *Pride and Prejudice*. She felt uncomfortable reading in the daytime. It was a pleasure earned by working. The book was like comfort food—warm, filling, satisfying, but even Elizabeth and Darcy couldn't settle her down. She popped up and went to the kitchen to make coffee. The bottle of Four Roses sat on top of the refrigerator, and she noted it was still a quarter full. She hadn't been guzzling, even with all that had been going on the past week. She looked at the clock on her oven. It was only two. The afternoon stretched impossibly before her. The real problem with having this time was it gave her the opportunity to really think about the lives that had been lost. Every time she did, it felt like a belt was being pulled tight around her chest. And every time she thought of Jamie, which was frequently, she felt guilty for not concentrating on the problem at hand.

Her phone rang and she trotted to the dining table to pick it up, anxious now for any distraction. Or maybe not. It was her mother. She was so bored she picked up.

"Hi, Mom. Having a good time?"

"Where the hell have you been? You haven't returned a single text of mine." Her mother sounded like this failure on Kay's part had been a major inconvenience. Kay had often felt throughout her childhood that she was a major inconvenience to her parents.

"I've been here. I'm busy with a big case."

"Your father wants to know if the fish are okay," her mother said.

The lie came easily. In the lifelong tally of truth versus lies told to her mother, lies were leading by a mile. "The fish are doing great." She could hear her mother telling her father the fish were fine. She could only imagine what his reaction would be when he learned of their fiery death.

"We're having a horrible time here," she said. "I've been thinking about coming home early."

"What? Why?" Panic. Dealing with her parents now would put her over the edge, leave her drooling in the corner of her bedroom.

"The weather's been a nightmare. The ship's been pitching about like you wouldn't believe and your father's been sick for two days. Me, I don't get sick. I have good sea legs."

"You can't come home, Mom. Think of all that money you'd be losing. What's the weather forecast?" Kay was trying to keep any sense of urgency out of her voice.

Kay could hear her mother call out: "Martin, do you know the forecast?" He grunted something back. "He's looking. Now tell me about you."

"Nothing to tell." She didn't want to tell her about Jamie, but it would distract her. "Well, maybe something. I think I met a woman I like."

Her mother snorted. "I can't wait to hear about this."

Kay proceeded to embellish a pretty bare bones story, making it sound like she and Jamie were far more involved than they were. Maybe she was projecting? Whatever the case, her mother was over the moon.

"She sounds like a good match," she said, much to Kay's surprise "This is big, Kay. Don't screw it up."

This was the exact advice she was giving herself, but hearing it from her mother caused irritation to rip through her like a gale. She breathed in and out.

"I'll bring her by as soon as we can manage it," Kay said. If she asked Jamie to meet her parents at this stage, she'd run screaming in the opposite direction.

The weather report came back temperate, so her mother agreed they would stay through the whole cruise. Kay hung up tremendously relieved. She looked at the time again. Only two fifteen. At this rate she would be certifiable by four thirty.

She forced herself to lie on the couch and watch a movie, and then fell asleep halfway through.

❖

It was past five when she woke up, stunned by sleep. She was still in her business suit, now rumpled and uncomfortable. She got up to splash some water on her face and change into sweats. But what if Jamie came over? Are sweats and tube socks what she wanted her to see her in? She pulled out her good jeans and a silk T-shirt before shoving them back in the drawer. She wasn't going to dress for anyone when her world was falling apart. You got a free pass in these circumstances.

On her way to the kitchen for coffee, she stopped by the window overlooking the lake and stared out. The days were getting longer, but there was a tint to the sky that said dark was a couple of hours away. Her phone rang. Kay looked at the unknown number on the screen and took the call.

"Is this Detective Kay Adler?" a deep male voice said. Kay felt a rush of fear flood through her body. She could tell an official voice when she heard one.

"Yes. Who's this?"

"Officer Charles Wilson. I'm at Northwestern Emergency with Alice Denton. She asked me to get hold of you."

Kay's stomach dropped, like an elevator with its cables cut. Not Alice. Please, not Alice. "Tell me what happened."

"She was shot in the chest, but the shooter's aim was off. Looks like she'll be okay, but they're taking her into surgery now."

"On my way."

She was barely coherent when she called Jamie and told her what happened. She scrambled to get her car and drive to the hospital. She couldn't think. She was driving like an automaton, unaware of what her body was doing. She wondered if Mary was at the hospital. She and Mary weren't very close, but now she'd loathe her, the angel of death who'd nearly gotten Alice killed. She clung to the fact that Alice was alert enough to ask for her, which must mean she wasn't in any danger. She didn't know how much to believe from the officer.

She drove through the mammoth Northwestern University medical campus downtown and pulled into the ER driveway, threw her keys to the valet, and raced in as fast as the sliding doors allowed. She had her star out when she went to the triage nurse at the front desk.

"Alice Denton. Tell me what bay she's in."

"Bay twelve. But I think she's been sent up to surgery."

Kay pushed through the doors into the treatment area. People in different colored scrubs walked quickly this way and that, carts trundled by, patients lay in beds lining the hall. She reached bay twelve, but when she drew the curtain back she found it empty. A doctor walked by and she grabbed him by the arm of his gray coat. The gray meant he was a senior physician, not accustomed to being grabbed by anyone. He shook her off.

"I'm sorry, Doctor. I'm trying to find the woman in this bay, the shooting victim." She held up her star.

He was tall and reed thin and closely resembled a white crane. He raised his beak to look at her after examining her identification. "She's up in surgery."

"How bad is it?" She hunched her shoulders, bracing for the news.

"She suffered a penetrating wound that luckily missed her pulmonary artery and aorta. It did hit the lung. The surgeon will repair the lung and any effected vessels. The patient should be fine."

"Oh, thank God."

"It's a serious injury, but entirely survivable." He started to move past her, but Kay blocked him.

"Do you know if anyone was here with her? There should have been police officers at least."

"They're all in the fifth floor waiting room. Her partner is there as well." He walked away without excusing himself.

Kay followed a labyrinthine path of green dots on the floor that led to the hospital's main elevators. She needed to talk with Mary, but she hoped Officer Wilson was also there. She wanted the official version of what happened, not Mary's anguished one. Guilt was starting to swamp her as she realized how stupid it was not to have gotten Alice out of town earlier. She got out on the fifth floor and followed more markers to the waiting room, an open area that held about a dozen chairs and a Keurig machine. Mary was standing next to an officer who was jotting down some notes. Her normally cheerful face was pale with fear. Another cop sat in a nearby chair, his radio crackling as he leafed through an *Oprah* magazine. A civilian sat in a chair in the far end of the room, his head hanging over his knees as he stared at the ground. Mary saw Kay, and she looked like she couldn't decide whether to hug Kay or kick her.

"How could you let this happen?" Mary said loudly. "She might die because of you." Apparently, she'd opted for the kick. Another officer entered from the hallway.

"Detective Adler," he said. "I'm Officer Wilson."

Kay didn't address Mary but motioned Wilson to join her in the hallway. "What can you tell me?"

"We got a call at 1615 about a shooting at the Morse el stop up in Rogers Park. We found the victim in a storefront under the tracks."

"That's where she has her pottery studio," Kay interrupted.

"Right. She was faceup on the floor, a bullet hole in her chest but still conscious. This gentleman here," he pointed at the man staring at the ground, "was next to her. He called nine one one. You can talk to him if you want. It seems he walked in on the suspect."

She felt a ray of hope. Not only did the victim live, but there was an eyewitness also. Becker was unraveling. He'd not been scrupulous about his own safety up until then, but shooting someone in a storefront in the middle of the afternoon seemed unhinged. It might have been part of his message, telling her he could do anything he wanted and she couldn't stop him. So far, that'd been true.

She walked over to the man in the chair. He was about her age. His shaggy black hair hung over his face. He wore a plain green T-shirt and mustard yellow jeans. When he raised his head as she approached, she saw his jet-black eyes and cupid's mouth. He was a tad short of good-looking. She knew Jamie should be the one interviewing him, but it was impossible not to start. She sat in the chair next to him and introduced herself. She now wished she'd chosen the other clothes to wear. She didn't look very detective-like in sweats. "What's your name?"

"Barry Abramo. Is there any word about Alice?"

"No, I think she'll be in surgery a bit longer. Will you tell me what happened?"

He ran his fingers through his hair and then angled his body toward her. "I'm a friend of Alice's from graduate school. I knew she had the studio on Morse. I've stopped in a number of times when I saw she was there. Her wheel's in the back, but the front room always has its light on when she's there and the door has a bell so she'll hear whenever anyone enters. So I was walking back from the Jewel with my groceries and saw the light on, thought I'd stop in. I went through the front room and was entering the hallway to the back room when a man ran right into me. He shoved me to the side and was gone. I ran to the back room and found Alice on the floor. That's when I called nine one one." His delivery was even, but she could see he was shaken.

"Tell me everything you remember about the man. What he wore, what he looked like, what his gun looked like."

"It happened in an instant. He was moving fast."

Kay called up both artists' sketches and Becker's mug shot. "Did he look like any of these?"

Abramo stared at the picture for a long time. "I'm sorry, but I don't think so. I only saw his face for a nanosecond."

"How would you describe him, as best you can with that quick glimpse."

"The only thing I really noticed was his red beard and hair. The beard was huge—it must have come down below his chest. Mountain man style. And his hair was super long, too. Frizzy and sticking out every which way."

"Anything about his facial features?" Abramo looked at her as if he were failing a final exam. "He wore sunglasses, but I don't remember anything about his face."

"Did Alice say anything to you?"

"Not at first. I thought she was unconscious, but then she turned her head toward me and whispered that I needed to call Mary and you. You were both on her speed dial. That's when the cops arrived. I gave her phone to the police to handle calling people. After that she seemed to become confused, and by the time the ambulance arrived she wasn't able to communicate. Do you think she'll die?" he said, clearly fearful.

"I think she'll be fine. The doctor I talked to said so. You'll need to talk to some other detectives and make a statement, so stay put for a while longer."

She stood and saw Mary staring at her from across the room. She walked over expecting a difficult conversation. "I should have gotten you both out of town sooner. I'm sorry, Mary."

She shook her head. "No, I'm sorry I yelled at you. You did warn us. It was Alice who ignored you. I pleaded with her to not go to the studio before we left town, but she insisted she needed to get some things done before she could leave. When the police called to tell me, I was almost not surprised."

"She's always been contrary," Kay said. "I'm going to stay here until she's out of surgery, if that's okay with you."

Mary hugged her. "I'll be glad for the company."

Kay caught sight of Jamie hurrying down the hall toward her. She had Adam in tow. She caught them up on everything she knew.

"That fucking bastard," Jamie said, angrier than she'd ever seen her. She stood beside Kay and wrapped an arm around her. "Are you okay?"

There's a way people say things that lets you know there's more than friendship going on. She saw Adam's eyes widen as he figured out they were together. Jamie rubbed her hand up and down Kay's back. It was too much; she had to step away. "I'm okay. It's Alice who's been shot. I'm not going to say how I'm doing until she's out of surgery."

"Of course," she said. "We'll talk to the witness. What's his name?"

"Barry Abramo."

"Yes, and then we'll go to the crime scene. Elise and Arroyo are there now. The canvassing is underway. Someone must have heard something or seen him run out of the place."

"He has to be using a silencer," Adam said. "In all of these incidents there should have been at least one witness who heard a shot, but we have no one."

Jamie turned toward Adam and asked him to get hold of the detectives at the crime scene for an update. Kay caught a flash of annoyance crossing Adam's face before he turned to go make the call. She guessed he didn't like having his comment ignored and being ordered to do another menial task. She didn't think therapy was helping him any. When he walked away to make the call Jamie took her by the elbow and led her into the hallway. They stopped next to a cart full of dirty dinner dishes. "He's escalating, agreed?"

"Absolutely," she said. She was essentially divided in half. One side was thoroughly shaken by Alice being shot and was focused only on the surgery. The other side was a fully engaged detective. "This is the most personal of all his attacks, except for the fire at my parents' house. Somehow he knew that Alice was close to me, closer than the other victims by a fair amount."

"Have you checked for bugs at your place?"

"Since yesterday you mean? I haven't even had time to get my lock changed."

Jamie frowned. "I'll take care of that first thing in the morning. I think he's starting to lose it. This attack was ill-conceived and high risk. Any number of people could have seen him go in or flee the premises, let alone hear a gunshot, though he's a genius with disguises. It almost doesn't matter if anyone's got a good look at him."

They didn't say anything for a while. Kay wanted to fall into her arms. It had been so comforting before. But the half that was on duty denied her that. "Don't worry about me. Go do what you need to do."

"Are you going to stay here?"

"Yes."

"Then I'm going to arrange for these two officers to stay with you. I'm pretty sure Becker is lying low, but he's completely unpredictable."

Kay decided not to argue. She didn't want to be obstreperous every time she asked for some cooperation. She respected Jamie, knew she would catch Becker if anyone could.

"I'll be here. Let me know if anything develops." Kay turned away just as Adam approached with phone in hand.

"I talked to Elise and told her we'd be there soon. One storekeeper saw a man racing from the studio, but he didn't get a close look. So far they haven't been able to locate anyone else who heard or saw anything."

Jamie frowned. "Naturally. I swear he wears an invisibility cloak. Adam, you go interview the victim's partner and I'll take the witness. Then we'll head up to Rogers Park."

Adam stood there as Jamie and Kay stared at him, until he finally realized he was being dismissed. He walked over to talk with Mary.

Jamie turned to her and placed a hand on her shoulder. "Kay, I need to see you. Maybe come to your place when things shake out tonight. What do you think?"

"I don't need watching over."

"That's not why I want to come over. Why do you always push back?"

Kay looked up at her and shrugged. "Habit?" A habit at odds with the heat generated by the hand on her shoulder. She could feel it coursing through her system like a stiff bourbon. "I need to see you, too. As soon as possible." She wanted to lean in for a kiss.

"I'll be there."

Jamie walked over to Barry Abramo while she found a seat and settled in, prepared to wait however long it took to hear how Alice was.

❖

Four hours after the operation began, a surgeon walked into the waiting room to talk to Mary. Kay joined them at the coffee machine as the doctor made a cup. She was a sturdy woman, on the short side, no makeup, hair sticking up as if she'd been electrified. None of that mattered. She had the cool, supremely confident bearing you expect in surgeons and which Kay always found attractive. She introduced herself as Samantha Levy.

"Surgery went very well," she said. "We had some vessels to repair in addition to the bullet wound, but she'll fully recover. Plan on ten days or so in the hospital and she's good to go."

Kay let out a breath as if she'd been holding it for the past hours. She asked if they could see Alice, and Dr. Levy nodded her approval. "Short visit," she said, before striding away. Kay and Mary waited an hour while Alice was in recovery and then went up to ICU to be with her. Six very ill people lay trussed up in medical equipment, including Alice, who had an IV line running out of her arm and monitors beeping all around her. She was completely helpless. Mary approached the head of the bed first and carefully took Alice's hand. Her eyes were closed and she looked like death warmed over, but that was to be expected. It reminded Kay of how close Alice had come to being killed. A matter of less than an inch. She was standing behind Mary when Alice's eyes fluttered open.

"I'll go get the nurse," Kay said. Alice's face was perfectly calm and she looked alert.

"No, don't. I want to look at you both." Her voice was raspy and barely above a whisper.

"How do you feel, babe?" Mary said.

"A lot better than before. Kay, come here." Mary stepped back as Kay leaned toward Alice's face.

She blinked back tears. "I'm so sorry, Alice. I don't know how you'll ever forgive me."

"Forget that. I want to tell you what happened."

"Do you have the strength for that?" Mary said.

"I think I'll pass out soon and who knows how long I'll sleep. Kay needs to know this now."

She felt a beat of excitement. "Only do what you can, Alice." She tried to scoot up a little but couldn't manage it.

"I don't know how much this will help, but the guy who shot me was talkative before he pulled the trigger. Mostly, he talked about how much he's grown to hate you and how much he loves watching you squirm. He was absurdly pompous."

"What was his voice like?"

"He had a lisp and it almost seemed like he was showing it off. He'd say something with a lot of s's and stopped to admire the sibilance."

"Was it deep, high?"

"Medium." Her eyes fluttered. "He had flaming red hair and beard. Hair everywhere. And he wore sunglasses."

Another disguise, almost a sleight of hand trick. Overpower with the hair so the facial features aren't noticed.

"I've seen him before in the neighborhood. I think he lives there," Alice said.

Kay almost yelped. They were getting close, she could feel it. "That's fantastic, Alice. It's a huge lead." She pulled her phone out and showed Alice the artist's sketches and mug shot of Becker. She studied the mug shot for a while. "He didn't look like any of these at a glance. All I could see was red hair everywhere." She took a deep breath as if struggling for air. A nurse appeared and put an oxygen line in her nose.

"That's it, ladies. She needs to sleep. One of you can sit by her bed if you want."

Alice's eyes shut like the lid of a lead box. Kay left Mary to sit with Alice and started retracing her steps out of the hospital. She realized she was hungry and thirsty, but more than that she was recharged for the hunt. While waiting for the valet, she called Jamie and left a message sharing what Alice said. She didn't think they had enough to institute a dragnet to find Becker, nor did she think that would do anything but drive him underground and out of the city. Her preference was to use some of her informants in the neighborhood to show the artist's sketches around. Jamie probably had her own CIs and they could also employ plain clothes cops to cover more ground. At least they had a small region to concentrate on, the same area of Rogers Park that Becker lived in when he first got out of prison was also near the Morse el stop. It was home turf for him. But they had the severe disadvantage of not knowing what he looked like. She was surprised to hear he'd worn the red hair disguise while going about his business in the neighborhood. But he couldn't appear as Kurt Becker. That was too risky.

She let herself into her condo and headed straight for the Four Roses. She didn't deserve a drink, but she needed one and wouldn't deny herself. She lay on her couch with her phone and drink resting on her chest, waiting to hear from Jamie, waiting for the alcohol to do its job. It was close to ten o'clock. She finished the drink in two swallows and put the glass on the coffee table. Another drink would mean she had to get up for the bottle. She fell asleep instead.

She didn't know how much later it was when her phone blasted her out of a sound sleep, like an explosion next to her ear. She stabbed at the green button and accepted the call.

"It's Jamie."

"Ah."

"What's that mean?"

"It means I was asleep. Where are you?"

"I'm about to enter the lobby of your building. Can I come up? The doorman's not here."

"Of course. See you in a minute."

When the knock on the door came, she opened it to find Jamie leaning against the doorjamb, holding a pizza and a six-pack of beer. Her face seemed to sag a bit from fatigue, but she wore a crooked smile.

"I don't know if you're hungry," she said, "but I'm starved."

Kay motioned her in and took the pizza. "I'll get plates. And I'll have one of those beers." She walked toward the kitchen before turning to look up at her. "Thanks. I'm very glad you're here."

"That's a relief. I thought it was fifty-fifty."

She hunched her shoulders. "I have a terrible reputation, don't I?"

Jamie laughed. "Maybe, but it doesn't bother me."

"How reassuring you are." She led the way to the kitchen where they got plates and beers and moved to the living room. When they got settled on the couch, Kay jumped to business. The mushy stuff would have to wait. "What have you done about the information Alice has given us?"

"I've gotten a half dozen plain clothes on the streets looking for him. They're working off all the sketches and the mug shot. We can't do a dragnet when we don't know what he looks like."

"Agreed. I'll call my Roger's Park CIs and put them on the street."

Jamie drank her beer. "The information puts us closer to him than we've been. But he's still out of reach. And I think he's one step away from going for you."

"That's possibly true," she said, unconcerned. "It's also true he may have already gone underground, given Alice survived the attack."

"He may not know she's alive."

"He'll know. The *Trib*'s already got it on their website. It'll be in the paper tomorrow."

Jamie took a couple of enormous bites of pizza and followed it with more beer. Kay watched her. "Other than having a specific area to look for him in, we're at the same impasse. I still haven't been able to connect with Anthony Baran's prison buddy. I've had someone watching his apartment building for over a day now."

"And if we do find the daughter through him, it seems unlikely she'll help us find Becker. It was her mother I killed that day," she said.

"But we have to try."

"Yes."

They were silent for a while, as if too exhausted to talk more about Kurt Becker. Kay knew she was. Jamie's brow was knitted, but she couldn't be as distraught as she was. It wasn't her best friend who'd been nearly killed. She reminded herself that it wasn't any reason to be angry at her, but she suddenly felt furious.

She went to the kitchen to get the bourbon and brought two glasses back with it. They landed heavily on the coffee table, just this side of being slammed down. Jamie watched her.

"What's going on? You look like you want to shoot someone."

"I do. If Kurt Becker were in front of me I'd gladly shoot him again, and this time I'd kill him." She started pacing. "I have to be there when we catch him. I have to be able to look him in the eye before I pull the trigger. You can look the other way. He needs to be eliminated."

Jamie stood and caught her hand. She ripped it away and turned on her, fury painting her face in high color. "I'm not the enemy here," she said.

"Did I say you were?"

"No, but it feels like you'd shoot me as easily. You're going to burst an aneurism if you don't calm down." Jamie stood and reached for Kay's hand.

"I hate it when people tell me to calm down," she said. She felt the anger start to drain away, like adrenaline does after a car accident. She didn't mean to make Jamie feel attacked, but she lacked nuance. Things were becoming black and white. She took a few deep breaths and looked up at her. "So much for rehabilitating my reputation."

Jamie stepped closer. "Of course you're angry. You should probably be whacking furniture with a Nerf bat. But don't let yourself stay in that state too long. It's not productive. Plus, I want you to be nice to me."

She relaxed her shoulders. She felt lighter than she had a minute ago. She took a step toward her and she opened her arms. When they were wrapped around her she felt safe. She'd been vulnerable and secretly terrified for what seemed like weeks. Completely new emotions for her. Jamie made her feel less alone, her effect both a balm and an infusion of strength.

"Starting now, I'm going to be nice to you. We're off duty. We're like any two people who've just met," she said.

"And how's that?"

She stepped back from the hug. "Curious and nervous. Excited."

"Yes, all those. You're very distracting." Jamie gently took her hand and led her to the couch. "Let's kick back and watch a movie or something."

Kay sat close to her, their hips touching. "I think I'd like the something."

"You have impressive stamina. Aren't you exhausted?"

She stayed quiet, wondering at the woman beside her. She first experienced her as cool and haughty when they were thrown together on a murder case. She'd seen her stand up to the lieutenant, dress down a subordinate. She knew she was strong and had backbone. But none of it explained this patient, understanding woman. She wasn't a pushover or a sap. She was someone she could be herself with. That was new. And then there was her body, which was on fire and leaning toward Jamie as if pulled by a magnet.

"I'm tired," Kay admitted. "But so what? My opinion is tired sex is better than no sex." She opened a couple of buttons of Jamie's shirt and slid her hand inside, smiled at the sharp intake of breath. "It's time for bed."

Chapter Nine

K ay opened her eyes to find Jamie standing next to the bed, slipping into her shoes. She looked at Kay, as if she'd heard her wake.

"I'm not running out," she said. "But I have to get to work."

"What time is it?" She raised herself against the headboard, leaving her breasts uncovered. The sun was fully up, sneaking past the bedroom window blinds.

"Seven forty-five."

Her eyes popped all the way open. "Shit. I never sleep this late." Jamie sat on the bed and took her hands.

"And why shouldn't you? First of all, you're on leave and you don't have to get up. Secondly, because I know you'll discount the first, you're still exhausted. Yesterday was upsetting and last night…"

"Was spectacular. I gladly sacrifice my body in the interest of sex."

Jamie had a half smile on her face. "You know this isn't about the sex, don't you?"

Kay looked at her steadily, keeping her expression neutral. She didn't want to show how much she hoped that was true. Was she talking relationship? Jamie squeezed her hands. "This isn't the right time to talk about it," she said. She rose and picked up her jacket from the back of a chair, where it had been tossed the night before.

"You're probably right," Kay said, hiding her disappointment. "What are you up to this morning?"

"First thing is to see how Alice is doing. If she's up to it, I want the artist to do a sketch of Mr. Redhead. She had a good look at him."

"Maybe her artist's eye picked up more detail."

"Let's hope. Then I'll get the new sketch to everyone patrolling for Becker in Rogers Park."

She got out of bed, threw her robe on, and walked Jamie to the door. "I don't know what the hell I'll do all day."

Jamie held her by both shoulders and leaned in for a kiss. "I'll bring you a jigsaw puzzle. Whatever you like. But please don't leave here. I think anything could happen today."

Kay nodded her agreement, knowing it was a lie. She planned on seeing Alice and patrolling for Becker. She hoped this was a lie Jamie could tolerate. As soon as Jamie was gone she dressed and left the building, bringing her coffee with her. Her police escort was nowhere in sight, perhaps pulled to take care of more urgent matters than watching Kay's building. Since Jamie was heading toward the hospital to see Alice, she headed north to Rogers Park. She started to cruise an area within a four-block radius of Alice's studio, looking for the different versions of Becker, looking for other cops looking for him. The sidewalks were crowded with commuters headed to the Morse el stop to get downtown. She didn't expect Becker to be among them, so she set herself up on the outer edges of the radius. Several hours later, she felt she'd picked up all the police cars and plainclothes officers looking for Becker, but no sign of Becker himself. She was glad Jamie had secured the extra bodies, which was never easy to do. But the brass couldn't downplay their need. Becker was a serial killer and they couldn't be stingy with resources without calling the holy wrath of the press down on them.

She'd called earlier to check in with Alice and give her the heads-up about the sketch artist. Now it was midday and she headed to Northwestern to see her. She was still in the ICU, but she was sitting up, her color good, and she swore at Kay as soon as she saw her.

"You crazy bitch. You're supposed to be home. It's so like you to walk around with a big target on your back."

Kay grinned. "Wow, you're ready to rumble. How much longer in the ICU?" The room was busy with nurses and techs, carts and chatter, machines beeping, and the low moan coming from a patient clearly ready for more pain meds.

"Another couple days and then to a step down unit for a couple days. It seems extreme."

"You were shot through the lung, you know. It's a big deal."

She made herself comfortable in the chair beside the bed, then took Alice's hand and kissed it. "I'm so, so glad you're okay. You have no idea."

Alice smiled. "I get it. I'd feel the same if it were you." She took a drink from her sippy cup. "Your girlfriend was here this morning."

"Stop it. She's not my girlfriend." Kay could feel herself flushing. Alice laughed.

"Whatever. But if you don't try to make her your girlfriend you've turned the corner into hopeless. She's hot."

Kay changed the subject. "What about the sketch artist? Were you able to give him details on what your shooter looked like?"

"Yeah, I think so. He was here a long time. Your woman left before he was done."

"She's not my woman." She pulled out her phone and texted Jamie. *Curious about new artist's sketch. Can you send it to me?* Within five minutes, it appeared on her phone.

She sat with Alice until Mary came at two and then headed back to Rogers Park. She studied the new sketch. Like the previous one, it bore no resemblance to the Becker she'd seen fourteen years earlier. Alice had been able to describe the nose and chin more specifically, and she looked for similarities in Becker's mug shot. They looked alike, the first tenuous link they had that the killer was actually Becker, but it didn't help them. She knew

Jamie would have forwarded the sketch to everyone working the Rogers Park lead. She sent it to her own CIs, who she was paying to patrol the streets. Also to the CI she used for forgery and fraud investigations, who'd come up empty when he'd earlier canvassed his contacts. She'd also given him the old mug shot of Becker with his original face. If there were any hits, the information would be expensive, and she couldn't ask the department for funds since she was supposed to be on leave. She didn't care. She'd give everything she had to find Becker.

Another couple of hours went slowly by as she drove up and down the streets. Her phone rang. The display showed the name of her forger CI.

"What have you got, Billy?"

She heard a chuckle on the other end. "You never were much for the social niceties," he said.

"It's a crisis situation. I don't have time to make you feel good."

"Maybe this will help you. I sent out that new sketch of the red-haired dude and got lucky. One of the guys remembers him because of the hair, and was able to tie it with the mug shot you sent."

Kay's heart nearly stopped. "No shit. Gimme, gimme."

"It'll cost you. He wants a couple grand to give us the name and address."

"Fine. I want every photo of this guy, including those on his original ID," she said. She nearly had him now. "I need it all, as quickly as possible."

"No problem, but there's my two thousand dollar finder's fee on top."

"I personally guarantee it, but we need the info now, Billy. I can't pay you until tomorrow when I can get to a bank."

"That would be cool with me, but my contact's not going to produce until you pay."

She looked around the commercial strip she was on, as if a branch of her bank would magically appear. It was a little before five. If she hurried she could get to a teller. "Where can I meet you to hand off the money?"

Billy named a place in Lincoln Park, a neighborhood far south of Rogers Park. "I'll be there in forty-five minutes, maybe sooner. How long before we can get the new identity info?"

"It'll take me half an hour to get to him. I can read it to you from there."

She raced down Clark Street to a Chase Bank she knew of in south Andersonville and got in as they were starting to close. She made the withdrawal and headed at speed to Lincoln Park. Billy was as unlike her other informants, as a yacht is to a fishing boat. As Lincoln Park is to Rogers Park. His specialty as a criminal was white collar crime and he looked like he would mix seamlessly with the CEOs of the companies he'd fleeced. Unfortunately for him, an embezzlement scheme had gone awry. She was working financial crimes at the time and made the arrest. Part of his plea bargain was being an informant, a role he'd warmed to over the years. She could rely on him to look into the things she asked for instead of lying about it, as many of her CIs did. When she pulled up to the corner of Lincoln and Dickens in front of the Carnival grocery, he was waiting for her, licking a Fudgsicle. He was dressed in gray flannel trousers and a thin blue sweater. She handed him the cash through the car window. "Half an hour," she said.

"On it," Billy said. He jumped into a BMW. Apparently, his financial troubles were behind him.

She stayed in the illegal parking spot while she called Jamie. No answer. She texted her to head to Rogers Park ASAP, address to come. Then she made her way to Lake Shore Drive and drove again to Rogers Park, looking at the clock on her dashboard every two minutes. At the thirty-eighth minute, Billy called. "I got it. Ready?"

"Wait. I'm driving. Can you text it to me? I need name and address."

"Sure."

She took a peek at her phone as soon as she heard it ping with the incoming text. Becker's new name was Andrew Paulson, with an address six blocks west of the Morse el stop at Ashland. She called Jamie again and she picked up.

"I was just calling you back," she said. "Where are you? I hear driving sounds."

She tried to modulate the excitement she felt. "I might have something. Meet me at Ashland and Morse."

"Wait. What is it?"

"Maybe a sighting. I want you to check it out with me." She hung up as she exited Lake Shore Drive and headed up Sheridan to Morse. Jamie kept calling her back. Then she texted, *Do NOT do anything stupid!*

Kay drove past the address, a brick, six-unit apartment building. Lights in the first floor unit he lived in shone brightly in the growing twilight. She parked out of sight down the street. She knew they'd be lucky if Becker still lived there, but they were on his tail. Becker might be narrowing his focus for a strike at Kay, but at the same time they were narrowing in on him.

Jamie texted she was at the corner of Morse and Ashland and she gave her the address of the house she was parked in front of. Soon she pulled her car up to Kay's so their driver's sides were next to each other, cop style. She was in the same suit she'd seen her in that morning.

"You didn't go home to change?" Kay said. "That surprises me."

"Why?" She looked down at herself.

Kay shrugged. "You seem meticulous, like a wrinkled shirt wouldn't be comfortable for you."

"Fussy, in other words."

"I wouldn't say fussy. You're always well dressed though. It's a compliment." She smiled, worried she'd said the wrong thing.

"I'm going to file that in the things to talk about later drawer. What's going on here?"

A car squeezed by Jamie on the street, honking in irritation. They could see the driver's angry face as he passed.

"I hate honkers," Jamie said.

"Me too. I've pulled over some really obnoxious honkers."

"Good for you." She nodded.

Kay looked into her eyes for a measured moment, a drop of time to connect before getting on to business.

"My CI knows most of the forgers in the city. We got a hit from one of them when he showed the new sketch around. Andrew Paulson's his new name and we have an address. We no longer have fuck-all."

She looked more interested than excited, part of that calm exterior. Kay gave her the address.

"So, right behind us?"

"It looks like he's there. All the lights are on. I want to go up."

"Hell, yes." Jamie reached for her radio. "I'll call for backup."

"No backup," she said sharply. "That involves too many people and we're going to miss our opportunity. Let's go up there together and knock on the door."

"No. Not without vests and some uniforms."

"I shouldn't have even called you. We're wasting time." She was blocked in by Jamie's car, but opened the door to get out anyway. It clunked against her sedan.

"Hold on a second. Christ." She drove her car to the end of the street and parked in a tow zone. A few seconds went by before she climbed out and motioned Kay over. She trotted to her car.

"I know you're a badass, Kay. You don't have to prove it to me." She opened the trunk and hauled out two Kevlar vests, handing one to her. "I called for two cars. They should be pulling into the alley any minute. As soon as two of the officers join us out front, we can go up. Now put the vest on."

Kay shoved her arms in the vest and covered it with her jacket. "We may as well have megaphones to announce our arrival. I thought you had more guts than this."

Jamie grinned. "I have guts enough to not be an idiot. I understand you're desperate to get this guy caught, but let's do it right."

She knew she wasn't acting professionally. She felt wild as they closed in on Becker. She marched quickly to the apartment building with Jamie behind her, meeting up with two officers in front. She led them all to the entry and pulled burglary tools out of her pocket. Jamie frowned.

"I keep them in my glove compartment. It's amazing how often they come in handy. I'm only going to pick the building entrance. I'm not going to break into his apartment." She was reading the names next to the buzzers at the entryway. "His name's not here." She sounded like it was hard to believe.

"He's probably not living here. Why would he live at the address on his ID? He's smarter than that."

She turned back to the door and stuck one of the tools in the flimsy lock. It clicked open in a matter of seconds. The door on the other side of the foyer was locked also, and she made quick work of it as well.

"That's impressive, but we could have simply rung the buzzer."

She held the door open. "Element of surprise." She led them silently up a short flight of stairs to the first floor apartments. They took position on either side of the south unit, guns drawn. She rapped sharply on the door. "Chicago Police," she said loudly. "Open up." They heard movement inside before the door was opened wide and a woman well into her seventies stood in front of them with her hands on her hips.

"What the hell?" she said. She was wearing Cubs clothing from the cap on her head down to her slippers. Kay could hear the game on the TV. They all lowered their weapons.

"I see you're ready for the baseball season," Kay said.

The woman started to smile but quickly returned to her fierce look. "What's the matter with you?" she barked. "Let's see some identification."

Kay and Jamie showed their stars, which the woman examined carefully. "Ma'am, if you'll give me your name, I'll tell you what's going on," Jamie said.

"I'm Camille Rizzo, not that it's any of your business."

"Thank you," she said. "Detective Adler and I are going to step inside if that's okay with you. We're looking for some information you may be able to help us with."

Camille stepped away from the door and ushered them in. Her expression was now more curious than annoyed. She led them into a small living room that was as undecorated as a monk's cell. The only things in the room were the large flat screen TV, a huge La-Z-Boy chair, and an uncomfortable looking settee. She collapsed into the La-Z-Boy and pointed Kay and Jamie to the settee. The Cubs were up to bat on the TV across from her. She levered the chair into an upright position and took a can of beer out of the built-in cup holder. This was command central, with a phone and remote control on the table next to her, piles of sudoku and crossword puzzle books, a half eaten sandwich, and a worn paperback with a shirtless man wearing a kilt on the cover. She picked up the remote and turned the sound off the game.

"Are you any relation to Anthony Rizzo on the Cubs team?" Kay said. Rapport building was easy with the Cubs-obsessed.

Camille's eyes lit up. "I wish! He's my favorite, of course. Are you a fan, Detective?"

"Lifelong." She took her notebook out and rested it on her knee. "We believe a man named Andrew Paulson lived in this apartment, probably right before you moved in. Does the name mean anything to you?"

Camille took a drink and replaced her can in the cup holder. "Would you like a beer?"

Kay shook her head, though she'd have loved a beer. "We're working, but thanks. Can you tell us anything about Andrew Paulson?"

"I moved in here a few months ago. The place was vacant when I first looked at it, so I never saw him. I know it was him who lived here though. There was a note in a kitchen drawer asking me to forward any mail."

Kay tried to contain her excitement. "You have a forwarding address?"

"Who is this guy? A murderer or something?" Camille said.

Jamie leaned toward her with her elbows on her knees. "We really can't say at this point. But you're being extremely helpful in our investigation. How about if we get back to you after we've wrapped this up? I'll be happy to tell you the whole story."

Camille looked at her shrewdly. "I suppose that'll have to do." She levered herself out of the chair. "Let me get the note. I don't know why I didn't throw it away. He never did get any mail." She walked out of the living room.

Kay looked at Jamie as they waited. "We can't be this lucky."

"Probably not. Becker's not going to leave bread crumbs the size of boulders."

Camille came back and handed over a page from a small spiral memo book. It simply said "Andrew Paulson, PO Box 474, Chicago, IL 60626," which was a Rogers Park zip code.

"May we keep this, Mrs. Rizzo?"

"Sure. What do I care? Maybe it'll help." She climbed back into her chair.

Jamie tucked the note into an evidence bag and put it in her pocket.

Kay stood. "I'm going to the post office. Would you arrange a rotation so we have twenty-four-hour coverage?"

Jamie frowned before turning to Camille, who was watching them with wide eyes. "Mrs. Rizzo, is there anything else you can tell us about Andrew Paulson?"

"Not a thing." She sounded regretful.

"Then we'll leave you to your Cubs game and thank you for your time." Kay could see Camille was charmed by her. So was she. They left the apartment and sent the uniforms away, stopping to talk in front of the building. The sidewalks were busy with people coming home from work. The streetlights were on. Kay could see the lowering sun in the west, blinding her as she looked up at Jamie.

"You're not going to the post office," she said. Her tone wasn't particularly friendly. "The more you're out there the more a target you are."

"Oh, Christ. That again? Do you seriously think I'm going to go home when we're finally closing in?"

Jamie looked like she was counting to ten. "As soon as we finish arguing about this I'm going to get surveillance at the post office. Would you like me to also call the lieutenant and tell him you're interfering with my investigation?"

She narrowed her eyes. "You wouldn't."

"Try me. I don't have time for this. You're ridiculously stubborn."

Wordlessly, Kay took off her Kevlar vest and handed it to her. Then she turned and walked away. She heard Jamie behind her. "Is that the way you handle conflict? You leave? Good to know."

She slowed her pace, angry but curious what more she had to say. Jamie approached and placed an open hand on Kay's forearm. "Chances are high enough he'll try to kill you that any fool would be really afraid. I'm not trying to block you from the investigation."

"That's exactly what it feels like."

Jamie's voice hardened. "What do you think you can do to help? We don't need you to watch the post office. There are plenty of other cops who would be better at it than you. There's no place for you now. You're in the way."

"Fuck off," she said as she turned her back to her. She got into her car and slammed the door. Jamie watched as she peeled away from the curb. She was either with her or against her, and it looked like she was against her. Too bad. She had had hopes for their relationship. She thought because she was a cop she understood what drove her. It'd seemed like she did. But she couldn't be with a woman who tried to keep her from doing what had to be done. She had an inkling she may be overreacting, but better Jamie understand fully she was the decision-maker in her life. There was no give on that.

She detoured to a Starbucks before heading to the Rogers Park post office. When she entered the room with the PO boxes, she saw a plainclothes cop had already arrived and was looking at the door of box 474. There was no window in the box to tell if it was empty or not. She identified herself and told him to find out about the contents from one of the post office employees. She waited for him. He came back to report the box was empty, which could mean Becker had already been there that day, or it could mean nothing. Maybe he rarely got mail. The name for the box was Andrew Paulson. Because the room was separate from the customer service area, no one knew when he came and went.

"My instructions are to sit in my car in the parking lot and watch for this dude to arrive, so I better go do that," the officer said.

"Understood." Kay checked to make sure he had the updated artist's sketch of Becker on his phone before leaving. It felt stupid to sit in her car waiting for Becker when the plainclothes guy was doing the same thing, and he'd never leave without Jamie's order. She decided to go home to change clothes and get something to eat and then make arrangements for a rental car. Becker knew her Audi; cruising in it was not the best choice. There wasn't much she could do other than that. The post office was their remaining lead.

Adam called while she drove south to Lakeview. "I thought you'd want to know we ran a search on Andrew Paulson. Not surprisingly there isn't much record on him. He has a charge card, but the only charges are for gas and groceries, both up in Rogers Park, both within the last couple of days."

"Good. Maybe someone can identify him."

"We're headed up there in a minute," he said.

"Is there an address associated with the card?"

"Jamie tells me it's the address you just visited."

Kay paused. "You already reported this to her?"

"Well, yeah. She's the one who gave us Paulson's name. She's the lead, Kay, but I thought you'd want to know."

She knew she should be grateful to him, but she felt more like an outsider than ever. "Did anything else come up?"

"He has a driver's license, but no violations. Not even a parking ticket. There's a car registered to him, again using the Ashland address. I've put out a BOLO for the car, but I'm pretty sure it's not on the streets. Not unless he's an idiot."

"What kind of car?"

"An ancient Geo Prism. It has to be a total piece of shit," Adam said. "Is there any way he knows we've found this new identity for him?"

Kay turned off Lake Shore Drive onto Belmont. "God knows. He seems to know everything."

She disconnected and threw her phone onto the passenger seat as she pulled into the parking garage of her building. Her spot on the second level was near the elevator, which was good, but she had to go from there down to the lobby to cross over to the elevators up to her unit, an irritation each time she did it. She wanted a house one day, where she could pull up to her door and not worry about how to get bags of groceries from a tight spot in the parking garage to her thirtieth-floor home. She walked through the lobby and past the doorman's station. The "back in fifteen minutes" sign was on the counter, which probably meant Gerald was on duty. The other doormen usually took their breaks when a maintenance man could cover for them. She waited in the lobby for the elevator and nodded hello when her next-door neighbor, Rufus Sinclair, emerged. Rufus played a cop on a TV series that filmed in Chicago, and never failed to mention it when he saw her.

"Kay! Good to see you. We're filming tonight. I'm headed to the west side for a scene where I'm checking out a dead body in an alley."

"Sounds fun," Kay said dryly.

"I've always wondered about something. Real police don't have much of a reaction, right? Not after seeing so many victims."

She stared at him but didn't respond as she let the elevator door close. Rufus was close to the truth—cops did become inured to the sight of a dead body. But she fought hard for each one of them, for justice for every killing. She didn't trust herself to not blow up at Rufus.

She opened the door with the key to the newly installed lock. It was nearly dark. She heard a thud as she stepped in, like something heavy falling on a carpet. She drew her gun out of instinct and swung her arms to the sound. She saw a silhouette standing in front of the window, the lights of Lake Shore Drive and the harbor outlining a male figure. Six feet tall. Slender. Her heart leapt into her throat.

"That's disappointing," he said in a deep voice. "I've been here so long your entrance startled me, and there went your bottle of booze off the coffee table. Completely ruined the surprise."

As her eyes became adjusted to the dark, she saw Kurt Becker, undisguised, more polished looking than in his mug shot. She held her gun steady on him and saw his aimed directly at her. She wasn't surprised to see a silencer attached. She breathed in deeply.

"I'm sorry I kept you waiting, Mr. Becker. I wasn't aware you'd be dropping by." The couch and coffee table were between them, and behind him was eight feet of empty space in front of the TV. She could see his expression clearly. "I see my new lock wasn't an obstacle for you," she said. He had a slight grin on his face, as if he'd moved his bishop into checkmate. Her gun was as big as his. She didn't think he had anything to be smug about. One of them was going to die, that seemed certain.

"I'm a man of many skills," he said. "Your new deadbolt wasn't a problem. Neither was your doorman, who wasn't there when I came in. You're not very secure here, are you?"

He was edging sideways as if to walk around the sofa to be closer to her. Kay tracked him with her gun. "Stop where you are. I don't mind shooting first."

He stopped. They were twelve feet apart, can't miss distance. Each aimed at the other's heart. "Whose arms will tire first, I wonder?" he said. "I had a lot of time in prison to do push-ups. A lot of time in prison to do a number of things. Like think about what you did to me, for instance."

Kay kept herself locked into his gaze. His eyes would give him away if he was going to fire, but for now, they looked amused. This was fun for him. The whole goddamn thing had been a holiday, an extreme adventure vacation designed for his pleasure. "If you want me to talk about your wife's death, I think I'll take a pass."

His smile faded. "Oh, I agree. There's not much to say about that. You shot her and she died. You may as well have shot me while you were at it. My life ended when hers did." He moved his gun in small circles, as if outlining his target.

"Did they have courses in disguise while you were in prison? You seem to be quite skilled."

"I don't think I'll share all my secrets with you. It's been fascinating to watch you over the last couple of weeks, to come to know what you did, who you saw, how you thought." He smiled.

She continued to stare but didn't engage him further. Anything could provoke him to shoot, and she had no plan for how to disarm him. He might be right about it coming down to whose arms tired first, and she hadn't done a push-up since the academy. She felt her arms grow heavy and gripped her gun tighter.

"The only thing that has kept me living was my plan to avenge Dina's murder, and you've seen how well I've executed it. Maybe you know a little of the pain of losing someone for no reason, though none of the people I killed were as close to you as Dina was to me. I'm not a monster like you." He looked at her as if she were someone to be pitied. "It seems there aren't many people who are close to you at all. Must be fear of intimacy. I read a lot of self-help books while in prison and that comes up time after time. I'd say you're very guarded and don't let people in, which is no way to live. Even though it nearly killed me when you murdered Dina, at least I can say I loved deeply. I can recommend a few titles if you're interested in working on your problem. If you're alive to work on it, that is."

Kay ignored him. The last thing she'd do is discuss her relationship abilities with Kurt Becker. She'd never talked about that with anyone, and he certainly wasn't going to be the first. Did his weeks of watching her reveal something to him that she didn't see herself? She shook off the thought and tried to ignore the growing ache in her arms.

She was a few feet in from the door. If she shot and dropped to the floor behind the couch, there was a reasonable chance his shot would miss her. She wasn't ready to die.

"Let's talk about how we're going to get out of this situation," she said. "We can stand here staring at each other until one of us shoots, but I suspect we'll both be shot when that happens. Is that how you see this ending?"

He shrugged, his gun remaining steadily aimed at her. "It's true I'd rather have been able to shoot you when you walked in the door, but I can live with the situation. I've told you already life doesn't have much meaning for me after Dina. It doesn't matter whether I die here or not."

That wasn't good news. A man who was willing to die was a dangerous man. She collected herself and said in a light tone of voice, "That's kind of sad. You're a young man, with plenty of life behind bars ahead of you. I, on the other hand, would very much—" Kay shot him in the chest as the words came out of her mouth, dropping down and scrambling onto her knees behind the couch. She heard Becker fall to the floor. She listened for any sound, but there was none. She waited another minute before crawling around the sofa to see if he was dead. He lay on his back, splayed out on the rug as if he was making an angel in the snow. His gun was under the coffee table, flung there as he fell. Kay got to her feet and kept her weapon trained on him as she approached. She nudged the body with her foot. No response. She knelt and held her fingers to his carotid artery. No pulse. She looked at his shirt and saw she'd made a perfect shot to the heart, which surprised her given her arms had begun to tremble. She sat on the rug beside him and lay her weapon to the side.

She was entirely spent. The thought of calling 911 and putting in motion the great procedural circus of the police department felt overwhelming. The adrenaline that had been so high during the confrontation disappeared like water circling a drain. She sagged, her shoulders dropping and her head hanging over her chest. She scootched back so she could lean against the wall below the window. Soon a sob welled up in her chest and pushed its way out, despite her frantic attempt to keep it inside. She started crying, overcome with wracking sobs that completely outmatched her.

Why cry now? The man who'd made her life a nightmare for the past week was two feet away, dead, the threat over. She had no regret killing him. She was glad it was she who'd done it. But she cried as if she'd lost someone dear. She was more terrified by how out of control she felt than she'd been when Becker held a gun on her minutes before. She was only glad this happened before the police started pouring in.

When she finally quieted, she lay on her side. She needed a tissue but felt too weak to get to the box on the coffee table. She lay there snuffling, feeling nothing, more tired than she ever remembered being. She could easily fall asleep, were that not such a bad idea with a dead body in her living room. She thought of Jamie and felt ridiculous for having been mad at her. She'd been right about Becker wanting to take her out next. But she'd been entirely wrong about her home being the place to hide from him. One out of two wasn't bad. She heaved herself up and walked to her bag, which she'd dropped to the floor when she first walked in the door. She dug out her cell phone and sat at her dining table.

Jamie answered on the first ring. "Please tell me you're safe and at home."

"Okay. I'm safe and at home. But there are complications."

"Of course there are." Her voice sounded light, relieved.

"I'm sorry we argued. I couldn't stand the idea of anyone else taking Becker down."

"Couldn't?"

She paused. "He was waiting for me here when I got home."

"Jesus Christ. Are you okay? I mean you must be. What the hell happened?" Her voice was gratifyingly frantic.

Kay told her everything she could remember. It was all a little hazy to her. "So I'm here with the body and I've got to call it in." She snuffled before she thought to stop herself.

"Are you crying?" she said "Killing a man is a huge thing."

"I'm not crying. I was happy to kill him." She snuffled again and felt mortified.

"You're a bad liar, Adler. And more macho than I'll ever be. Sit still. I'm on my way over."

Before Jamie could arrive, four uniform officers burst through the door with their guns drawn. Someone in the building must have called 911 after her weapon fired. Her ears were still ringing from the sound. She'd hoped she had a little more time before the parade began. One of the cops pointing his gun at her was Officer Carey. He lowered his weapon and motioned for the others to do the same. "What's going on, Detective?"

"Oh, you know. This and that. You'll find a dead body over by the TV." She was so tired she held her head up with her hand, elbow on the table, as if she were bored out of her mind. Carey and the others walked quickly to the body, radios crackling.

"Is this the guy you've been after? Sidwell's case?"

"That's the one. She's on her way over, but you might as well sound the alarm."

Carey radioed in an officer involved shooting and posted one of the uniforms in the hall outside the condo. He sent another down to the lobby to direct incoming police and forensics, the EMTs, brass, and undoubtedly the internal affairs guys, who must be sick of her by now. She stayed at the dining table, resigned to letting events unfold around her. Jamie walked through the door and examined the body before joining her.

"I'm surprised he wasn't in disguise." She sat with Kay at the dining table.

"Not me. He wanted me to have no doubt who was going to kill me."

Jamie looked at her closely. "You're sure you're okay? You look a little pale."

"I'm tired. Why don't you go do what you need to do and I'll make coffee."

She nodded. "Okay. But I think you should spend the night at my place."

Kay smiled weakly. "You're not mad at me?"

"Was I mad at you? I don't remember. Bigger things have happened since. What do you say?"

She was relieved to have a place to go, and even more relieved that things were back to normal between them, though their relationship was only a minute old, not long enough to establish a normal.

"It's about time I see your place," she said. "But I have to warn you it might only be sleep tonight."

Jamie smiled. "Of course. Sex didn't even enter my mind."

"Now who's the liar?"

"Whether I thought about it or not doesn't mean I expected it." She squeezed her hand and turned to meet the great number of people who'd already made their way in.

Kay got up to make coffee and drink some water, staying out of the way as best she could. She was pouring another cup when Jamie came in to let her know the brass had arrived and she was needed. She didn't think she had the energy to face what came next, but she had no choice.

❖

After twenty-four hours of interviews with detectives, her lieutenant and captain, internal affairs, and the mandatory psychologist, Kay was cleared to return to work. It was Saturday, so she had a couple of days before starting. It was the second night in a row she'd spent with Jamie. The crime scene in her condo had been cleared, but she was in no rush to get back. She had to arrange for her big oriental rug to be cleaned, Becker's blood having mixed in with the deep reds and oranges of the pattern. It was probably ruined. She had to clean and remove the detritus of a crime scene. But the truth was she didn't want to be alone, which she found shocking. She always wanted to be alone.

They were flat on their backs in bed after some vigorous morning sex.

"I wonder if you'll be skittish if I tell you something," Jamie said.

"When am I skittish?"

Jamie turned on her side and leaned on an elbow. "Whenever I've tried to talk about us, you've cut me off or changed the subject."

Kay looked at her levelly. "Here's your chance then. I won't say a word."

"I'll want you to say something. Don't leave me hanging here."

"Where?"

Jamie blew out a breath. "Where I'll be after I tell you I think I'm falling in love with you."

She hadn't expected that. She knew Jamie liked her, even that she wanted to be with her. But this made something jump inside.

"Okay," she said lamely, buying time. "Is it possible to fall in love this fast?"

She frowned. "I guess if you're asking, then you don't feel the same way."

"I don't know. I wouldn't assume that." Jamie look discouraged, so she took her hand. "This is what I do know. Since Becker's death, I think about you all the time. Before that I only thought about you a lot of the time. I'm sure you understand."

She nodded and watched her closely.

"I'm happy when I'm with you. I want to make love every time I see you. And I miss you when we're not together."

Jamie smiled. "Some might call that being in love."

"Despite my advanced age, I don't have much experience with love. None of my relationships, if you can call them that, lasted very long. There's another red flag for you. You're the first woman I've felt this intensely about. Call it what you will." Jamie leaned against the headboard and drew her close. They lay quietly, peacefully.

"Why don't we leave it at that? It's enough to say we want to be together."

Kay kissed her and then wiggled out of her arms. "I'll go make coffee." Jamie sighed and let her go. She walked through her enormous living room. Like hers, the windows faced the lake, but Kay had two to her five. A baby grand piano was tucked in a corner of the room, with a Bach sonata spread open on the music stand. The more she learned about Jamie, the more a mystery she became. There was an L-shaped couch in front of a gas fireplace. The rug in front of it looked hand loomed in subtle shades of gray. Expensive. A TV was mounted above the fireplace, but she had a feeling it wasn't turned on much. The coffee table was piled with books—Marilyn Robinson and Carol Anshaw were on top of the two stacks. Facedown on the floor by the couch was a copy of *Middlemarch*. She smiled. She was sure Jamie came from well-to-do parents, went to an expensive private college, and disappointed her family by becoming a cop. She didn't know of any legacy cops who'd even try to read George Eliot.

She stood wrapped in Jamie's robe, contemplating the matter of coffee. She'd watched her make it the day before and set out the necessaries for doing it on her own. It'd been complicated and tedious, involving timing and plunging, but the coffee had been fantastic. She craved a cup and she wanted it quickly. By the time she had two mugs in hand and was headed back to the bedroom, Jamie was up and dressed and walking toward her across the living room. They met on the couch and settled in.

"What'll you do with your day?" Jamie said.

"It's Saturday, so I'll probably avoid errands. I'll go see Alice, take a run. I have to get back to my place. I can't hide out here." She brought her mug to her lips and kept her focus on the coffee table in front of her.

"You're welcome to hide out here as long as you want. You know that, don't you?"

"Why don't we go out tonight? Becker's dead and we're together—we should celebrate."

"I don't know where I rank in that dual celebration, but I'll take it," Jamie said.

Kay stood and pulled her up. "You figure out the where and when. I have to go home." She looked around the room. "Though I've got to say, I love this place. How'd you afford it on a cop's salary?"

Jamie gave her a measured look, not entirely happy with the question. "If you're implying I'm bent, I'll have to ask you to take it back."

Kay looked up at her, her gaze steady. "That's not what I meant. I'm simply asking how you got this condo. Shit, this is coming out all wrong. It's none of my business."

Jamie stepped away from her and took her coffee cup into the kitchen. Kay followed. She put it in the sink and turned around to lean on the counter, looking like she couldn't decide what to say. For once, Kay kept her mouth shut.

"Normally, I'd say it isn't any of your business, but since we just got finished talking about having a relationship I think I should explain. To make sure you know I'm not on the take, if for no other reason."

"I don't think you're on the take. Not for a minute. I'm sorry I even brought it up." She didn't break her eye contact with her.

"I don't know why I find it embarrassing to admit, but my family has a lot of money, going back a couple of generations, and I have a large trust fund. It's not something I want people to know."

Kay didn't know what to say. Her new girlfriend was rich. Her first thought was to not have her mother find out. "I have a lot to be embarrassed about in my past, but if I came from family money, that wouldn't be one of the things I regretted. I think it's great. It's good to be fortunate."

She saw Jamie's face relax. "You're the first cop I've told this to."

Kay moved toward her and reached her hand out for hers. "Now you've told me and we don't have to talk about it again if you don't want to." She leaned over and gave her a kiss, the kind you'd give a spouse on the way out the door in the morning.

Jamie smiled. "I'll call you later about tonight."

Kay got dressed and left, elated about the relationship and exhausted by all the sharing. She could easily get used to having copious amounts of sex, but she'd never get used to all the sharing.

It felt alien, as if she'd woken up in an AA meeting or a therapist's office. She had no experience of it.

She walked down the street to her own building. Gerald was behind the desk. He turned from his newspaper and gawped at her.

"Jesus H., girl. I hear you've been killing people in our building." He gave her an approving look.

"Only the bad guys, Gerald. You don't have to worry as long as you stay on my good side." She stopped in front of his desk. It was hard to tell, but his face, which had no visible bone structure, seemed to be smiling. She'd never seen him smile before.

"Oh, I intend on doing that, Detective."

She left him and walked to the elevators, deciding not to mention that the bad guy got up to her place because Gerald wasn't manning his desk at the time. She knew she should bring up security concerns with the condo board, but the thought made her hunch her shoulders. Condo administration was a hotbed of politics and she steered wide of it.

When she walked into her place, it felt like burglars had been through it. Nothing was missing, but everything was slightly off. The unread *New Yorkers* on her coffee table had been neatly stacked, the bottle of Four Roses moved to the center of the table, with the dirty glass beside it. Her blinds were drawn. The computer and papers in the dining room were pushed together in the middle of the table. Only her bedroom seemed untouched, though she didn't doubt someone had been through every drawer, which meant they'd gotten a good look at her plug-in Hitachi Magic Wand. She couldn't think about it.

Despite all the lovemaking with Jamie, she felt like her body hadn't been exercised in ages. The running path along the lakefront was crowded on Saturdays, but she had to go. She changed and left the building, crossing Lake Shore Drive through the underpass and falling into step on the path behind a plump, middle-aged man who wore purple spandex shorts that looked like they were squeezing the life out of him. A yellow fanny pack bounced around his hips, which were wide like a woman's. As she passed, she made the mistake at taking a look at him. His penis was perfectly outlined beneath his shorts, as if he were wearing a Speedo. She sped up and tried to rub the image from her mind.

She felt creaky and short of breath. The sky was perfectly clear and she regretted not bringing her sunglasses. Runners wore short sleeves, the air finally feeling like spring. Usually, she ran as far as downtown and back again, but it didn't feel like she'd last that long today. As she made her way through Lincoln Park as it approached Fullerton, she stopped at the water trough to take a long drink. She was listening to Patricia Barber on her headphones and wondering if Jamie liked jazz too. Suddenly, an arm flashed around her from behind and a knife plunged into her abdomen, just as she was turning away from the fountain. She felt it move to the left as if gutting her. Her hands went to her belly and were quickly drenched in the blood. She staggered back and looked wildly around her, but it was impossible to identify her attacker in the stream of runners moving along the path in both directions. She didn't feel pain. She didn't feel anything until she found herself sitting on the ground and terror washed over her. A runner stopping for water saw her clutching her middle, saw the blood, and screamed.

"Call nine one one," Kay said, before she fell flat on the gravel path. Her mind was barely processing, but one thought was clear. Becker was dead. Who was trying to kill her?

Chapter Ten

K ay opened her eyes to a pale green room saturated with fluorescent light. A woman stepped into her view and she tried to focus on her.

"Where am I?" she said, sounding like a drunk waking from a blackout.

The nurse smiled and patted her on the arm, as if she were a very old person. "You're in a recovery room at Northwestern Memorial. You've had surgery to repair a knife wound in your abdomen."

She may as well of been speaking Swahili. None of what she said made sense. Her name tag identified her as Sharon, who glanced at the monitor next to the bed. It told her practically everything there was to know about Kay and she seemed content with what she saw.

Kay tried to speak and nothing came out. She tried again and sounded remarkably like someone who'd smoked fifty years. "What wound?" she managed. She was starting to feel that all wasn't well down there, but she didn't feel pain. More like a giant rubber band was squeezing her belly. She didn't remember getting any wound, let alone from a knife.

"You were stabbed, Detective, but I'll let the doctor tell you all about that. For now, you'll rest here for another hour and then we'll take you upstairs. You can have someone sit with you, if you'd like."

Stabbed? "I don't need to rest. I want to go home." She tried to rise from the bed, and a searing pain pierced her midsection. She grunted and fell back. "Fuck."

"Exactly," Sharon said. "You got hurt pretty bad. You're not going anywhere anytime soon. We'll give you some pain meds as soon as the doctor sees you." She patted Kay on the knee and walked away.

"Wait." She was starting to feel panicky and alone. "Could you see if there's anyone out there for me?"

"Sure. I'll be right back."

As she waited, glimpses of what happened started to return. She'd been running on the path, then drinking from the water fountain, then down on her ass with blood gurgling through her fingers. What the fucking fuck? Her brain couldn't contend with what it meant. It could be a random maniac who attacked her, couldn't it? Becker was dead. She couldn't have been the target. She started to feel sick, whether from the thought of a killer still out there or from the anesthesia. She didn't know. She didn't know anything.

It seemed like ages before the curtain around her bed swept back and Jamie appeared. "Here you go," Sharon said, her smile much brighter now. "I'll be back to check on you." She walked out, leaving Jamie standing next to the bed, her face pale. She stared at Kay as if she were at her wake.

"I'm not dead yet, you know." Kay saw she was devastated and tried to smile.

"Thank Christ." She looked around and found a stool to sit on. She held her hand. "Can you tell me what happened?"

"Not exactly. It feels very hazy. I didn't see it coming, I know that. I couldn't tell you if it was a man or a woman. I never saw the person." Kay felt toxic, as if she had a bad hangover.

"We only have the witnesses who saw you after the attack. No one witnessed it, not that we've found so far."

They were silent a moment. "Please don't tell me you think this has something to do with Becker," she said. "I don't think I could handle it."

"It can't be a coincidence, Kay. The chances are vanishingly small you'd be a random victim after what you've been through."

She pulled her blanket up around her neck. "But a second killer? I think I'm going to throw up."

Jamie looked sympathetic. "It's a lot to take in."

"No, I mean I really am going to throw up." She looked around and found a kidney-shaped bowl by her bedside. She grabbed it and got it under her chin just in time. She heaved, but she had nothing in her stomach to expel. Her wound screamed every time she retched. Sweat was breaking out on her forehead. If Jamie still wanted her after this, she'd be ready to marry her.

Jamie held her forehead until she was done and then took the pan to the other side of the room. As she walked back to the bed, the curtain slid open and a doctor walked in. She wore a long gray coat with a blue silk dress under it. Her hair looked like it'd just been professionally blow-dried and her makeup was appropriate for a night on the town. She couldn't imagine the woman up to her elbows in blood. Trailing behind her were four medical students, the pockets of their short white coats overflowing with paper and pens, pagers and phones. They looked barely old enough to legally buy a drink. Jamie stepped back as the doctor walked around to get a close look at Kay.

"I'm Dr. Bosworth," she said, as she drew the sheet and blanket down the bed, exposing Kay's legs up to where they ended. The hospital gown was twisted around her waist. She saw Jamie back away another step and the medical students step forward. The doctor moved the gown farther and removed the bandage, examining the surgical site. She glanced at Kay. "I don't know the story, but someone stabbed you and made a bad job of it. You have a slicing wound. The knife entered to the left of your stomach and pulled toward the left hip. He sliced up a lot of muscle, but other than a knick on the small intestine, he missed anything vital. You're lucky. Stomach wounds can be very nasty."

"I can't tell you how lucky I feel," Kay said. She stared at the huge dressing wrapped around her belly.

Dr. Bosworth ignored her. "We took you into surgery. You lost a lot of blood, so we transfused you. I repaired the tears to the muscle wall and put a couple of sutures into your intestine. How's your pain?"

It was getting worse with time. "I wouldn't say no to a pain pill."

"The nurse will fix you up with some morphine."

The doctor looked at Jamie. Kay could see the slight change in her demeanor and knew in a flash she was gay. Her face had moved from business like to flirty. "What are we looking at in terms of recovery? Will she be here long?" Jamie said.

Dr. Bosworth cocked her hip and smiled. "How lucky she is to have you to worry about her. She's going to be fine. A few more days here, and then about ten days at home. We'll check on her to see whether any rehab is needed, but I doubt it."

Kay tried again to raise herself from the bed but slumped back immediately. "She is right here, Doctor."

The doctor turned back to her and the smile faded. "We'll move you to a room in a few minutes and you can get comfortable. I'll see you first thing in the morning." She turned on her heel and marched out of the curtained area, the students behind her like ducklings.

"I'm not staying here a few days. That's ridiculous." She tried to get her gown straightened out and gasped as pain shot through her.

"You physically can't go anywhere, so you might as well accept it. And it's probably the safest place for you," Jamie said.

Kay looked at her miserably. Another killer was too much. She only hoped she was the sole target. "Are you assigned to this case?"

"I will be. I'm going to get the team together to go over everything from the beginning. Someone's been working with Becker, and you're not safe until we figure out who that is."

Kay thought it was hopeless. At least with Becker they knew who they were looking for. Now they were clueless. She closed her eyes and gritted her teeth as another wave of pain surged through her. "Maybe I'll remember more and get some sense of who attacked me. It's still blurry."

A nurse came in and injected something in her IV line. "Here's your morphine. You'll feel better in a moment." She left as quickly as she came.

Kay shut her eyes and felt the opiate at the top of her head and followed it as it worked its way down her body. By the time it got to her knees she was nearly asleep. She cracked open one eye and looked at Jamie. "I have a whole new understanding of junkies," she said, before passing out.

❖

Kay woke the following morning to blinding sunlight. The windows of her private room overlooked the lake, which shimmered under the blue sky. It looked like a summer day, but it was still April, a month that seemed to be lasting an eternity. She didn't know what time it was, but from the position of the sun she could see the morning was well advanced.

There was a breakfast tray on the table next to her bed. Cold toast, warmish yogurt, and a banana on its last legs. If she'd been hungry she would have been disappointed, but her stomach was still dodgy. She picked up her remote control and raised the bed until she was in a sitting position. The more upright, the more her wound hurt. She backed off to a modest slant. Everything was uncomfortable. Her gown was bunched up around her waist again, she was in pain, and she had to pee. There was another kidney-shaped bowl on her table, but she was pretty sure it wasn't intended as a bedpan. She looked at the call button on her remote, but tossed it aside. She'd get to the bathroom herself. She wasn't going to use a bed pan. It was like admitting complete defeat.

She raised the bed back up and looked at the guard rails that ran along two-thirds of the bed. She had to scootch down to the foot of the bed to swing her legs over. With the first slide of her butt, she gasped as pain scorched up her side. She moved her legs farther down the bed and slid her butt after them. Same pain, followed by a sharp yowl. When she was in place, she swung her legs over and put her feet tentatively on the floor. She was sweating. Her gown was wide open in the back. Her feet were freezing and she felt like someone was holding a sharp poker at her belly. She clasped the guard rail and put some weight on her legs. They held firm, so she stood erect and let go of the rail. She was damn well going to ask for more morphine the second she got back in bed. She tottered to the bathroom like a person walking on bound feet. Each step was precarious, but somehow she managed to get in and out of the bathroom. As she took her first step back to the bed, Jamie walked in carrying a bag. She stopped in her tracks.

"This can't be right," she said, stepping forward to take Kay's arm. "What are you doing up? You look like hell."

"Thanks." She continued to move to the bed.

"You're completely gray. Are you supposed to be out of bed?"

"No one's been in to see me yet, so I can't tell you." She lunged for the guard rail like a man overboard reaching for a rope. Sweat was dripping into her eyes.

Jamie's face was grave, as if she were watching an execution. "My guess is not. I'll go get a nurse."

"We can call from here. Help me get back in bed." Jamie lowered the guard rail and helped her into the bed. Tears were leaking out of Kay's closed eyes.

A nurse walked in as Jamie was adjusting the sheet around her. He was paper thin, with purple hair and a giant hole in his earlobe where one of those savage, distending earrings once resided. You could fit a small Maglite through the opening. He looked at Kay with dismay.

"You're awake," he said, reassuringly observant. "And you don't look great. Time for your pain meds."

Kay wanted to raise her paws and pant like a dog getting a Snausage, but she felt immobilized by pain and exhaustion. The nurse sank the drug into her IV line and she waited for the blessed relief. She'd have to avoid painkillers when she finally got home—she liked the feeling too much.

"The doctor's right behind me, so we'll change your bandage after she removes it and takes a look. Do you need anything, angel?"

Angel? That's a first. She shook her head and kept her eyes closed, waiting for the drug to fully kick in.

"I brought you some things," Jamie said. She reached into the bag and pulled out a *People* magazine, a big bag of Twizzlers, a bag of Fritos, and a brand new copy of Jane Austen's *Persuasion.* "I can go to your place for some clothes and whatever else you want."

Kay opened one eye and looked at the small pile on the table. "I see you're concerned about my nutrition." She smiled wanly. "Maybe you can read to me later. *Persuasion's* one of my favorites." She was drifting off when Dr. Bosworth entered the room with her entourage. She couldn't tell if they were the same students or not. They flanked behind her, pens and paper ready.

"Good morning," the doctor said. Cheerful, but brisk. It was a Sunday morning and she was still dressed to kill. Maybe she couldn't help herself. She smiled warmly at Jamie, then drew the covers away from Kay and moved her gown clear from the bandaging. She was unconcerned how much flesh was exposed for Jamie to see. Carefully, the doctor undid the bandage and peered at her wound from close range. She probed with her fingers, felt the skin all around the sutures. "It all looks good. Clean, tight sutures, no sign of heat around the wound." She motioned her troops forward and they all peered over her to study the surgeon's work. Her pubis was on display, but the drugs helped her not care.

"How long will I be here?" Kay said.

"I'm not positive yet, but I would guess another two days. You'll need someone to help you when you're at home, at least for a week or so. I'll have a nurse come in and bandage you up again," she said. "You'll see another doctor during rounds this evening." And she was gone.

They looked at each other. "Two days doesn't seem like enough time to me," Jamie said.

"It's about a day too long as far as I'm concerned." Her body was completely relaxed, as if she were melting into the bed. Her eyes fell shut.

When she woke, Jamie was still there, dozing in the chair. Her mouth felt like a dry river bed and her head throbbed, but she stayed still and watched her. Jamie was made of stronger fiber than she was. As girlfriends go, Kay'd brought more trouble than one could dream up, but Jamie seemed to take it in stride. She realized she trusted her. So much goodness in a person would normally make her suspicious. Maybe she was lucky for once.

She reached over for her sippy cup and knocked over the bag of Fritos. Jamie jerked awake.

"What time is it?" Kay said softly. She reached over for her hand.

Jamie looked at her watch, a gleaming, complicated thing that undoubtedly cost thousands of dollars. "It's a little after two. I should be going."

She was silent for a moment, disappointed. "Have you made any progress?"

"Everyone's at the area, trying to find something we haven't thought of before. Obviously, Becker wasn't the end of it."

"It's the daughter. Becker's stepdaughter. It has to be. I remember the attack more clearly, and it wasn't a big person who snaked that arm around me. Her motivation's the same as Becker's, if not stronger. I killed her mother. That's even more primal than losing a spouse."

"Yeah, I was thinking that myself this morning," Jamie said. "When I wasn't thinking about how much nicer my bed is with you in it."

"Sweet talker. If there wasn't a crazy person out there trying to kill me, you wouldn't be able to peel me off of you." She raised her bed and realized the pain was not nearly as bad. "We know Becker was the instigator, and maybe Erin's been part of it the whole time. She must be trying to finish the job."

Jamie moved uncomfortably in her chair. "How to find her is the problem. I have Elise going through everything we have on Erin Baran, which so far is only her birth certificate."

"It's almost impossible to have so little on the record. Maybe she changed identities like Becker did. I wish I'd caught a glimpse of her yesterday."

Elise came through the door and stood at the foot of the bed. "I have news I thought you'd like to hear."

"Hello to you too," Kay said, shifting farther up the bed.

"Sorry. How are you?"

"Fair to middling. Why aren't you tracking down Erin Baran?" Jamie said, her tone none too friendly. Elise looked cooly at her, unruffled by the reprimand. Kay approved of her growing confidence.

"I'll get back to it as soon as I leave here." She turned to Kay. "I just heard from Detective Hansen, who interrogated Jim Cameron this morning. We took a call from a teacher at his school who poked a big hole in his alibi. She said she saw him get into his car a full hour before he claimed to have walked into the house and discovered his wife's body. This would give him plenty of time to get home, shoot Brooke, return to school, and then talk to the principal about being sick. Hansen rode him hard on it and Cameron confessed. He hadn't pulled the trigger himself—he hired someone from the dark web, as he called it."

"So why did he leave school early and potentially blow his alibi?"

"Because he's an idiot, I guess. He wanted to watch from his car across the street."

Kay blew a soft whistle. "Good work, both of you. Did Cameron say why he killed his wife? Working too many hours seems an inadequate cause for murder."

"That's the thing about murderers, isn't it? Any excuse is sufficient if your mind is running that way. Anyway, he confessed. That's all we need. Hansen's working on finding the hit man." Elise hitched up her shoulder bag. "I'll get back to work now." She walked quickly out the door.

Kay looked at Jamie. "I was hoping it was the corporation contracting a professional hit. The husband as murderer is so boring."

Jamie looked at her with surprise. "Let's say the morphine is doing the talking for you, shall we?" They sat in silence for a long minute before Jamie reached into her jacket and pulled out a small Smith & Wesson revolver. Kay raised her eyebrows. "I have an officer posted outside the door, but I don't like to leave anything to chance. Keep this under your covers and use it if you have to."

She nodded and took the gun. Shooting someone in a hospital was not a good option, but she was too weak to defend herself otherwise. She placed it next to her right hip. "Thanks. I'm sorry I brought all this down on you."

Jamie stood up and leaned over to kiss her forehead. "It's my job, Kay. But even if it wasn't, I'd do whatever I could." She touched Kay's cheek. "I'll be back later, I hope. I'll even read Jane Austen to you."

"Now I know you're serious," she said. Her eyes were getting heavy.

"A bunch of police have been up here since yesterday. I'm not sure who's out there now. Do you want to see anyone?"

Kay felt the color drain from her face. Her eyes were wide open, her pupils tiny. "Oh, fuck me." She threw her covers off and tried to swing her legs to the side of the bed. No dice.

"What are you doing?" Jamie said. She pushed Kay back against the bed, but she resisted.

"You've got to get my phone. It's life or death." She felt wild with panic. "My parents come home from their cruise today. They don't know their house burned down."

"Oh." She reached into a cabinet by the bed and found the phone in a plastic bag of her belongings. "What will you do?"

Kay looked at the screen and gasped. "There's a message from my mom. More like six of them. Their flight lands at four and she wants to know if I'll be picking them up. I'll call and tell them I'm gravely wounded so they'll come here before going to what they think is their home. They'd want to see their wounded daughter first thing, don't you think?" She wasn't entirely sure they would.

"You'd hope so."

"Better yet, why don't you call them, say you're the woman I've been dating, and explain how seriously injured I am. My mother, at least, will want to come straight here to meet you."

Jamie laughed. "I'll pick them up. Should I call now and leave a message?"

"Yes, and then call again when they land to make sure they got the word." Kay looked at her phone for the flight information her mother had texted her.

Jamie picked up the phone and pressed "Mom" on Kay's favorites list. "What are you going to tell them when they get here?"

"The truth, including my involvement in it, which won't win me any points. I'll have to ask them to stay at my place while they sort things out." The thought was completely enervating.

"Are you sure you don't want to stay with me for a while?" Jamie smiled. The look on her face became serious as the call connected. Sounding exactly like a girlfriend and not a detective, Jamie left a voice mail letting Kay's parents know what happened to Kay and that she'd pick them up. She told them to call when they landed, she'd be in the cell phone lot waiting. When she hung up she looked at Kay. "Try not to worry. There's nothing they can do to you."

"If only that were true." She tried to get comfortable in bed, but her body had seized up like a cramp.

When Jamie left, she tried to calm her breathing. She was taking quick, shallow breaths, the signs of an anxiety attack. She pressed the call button for the nurse. What could be a better treatment for anxiety than morphine? Surely it was time for another dose. She tried to get out of bed so she could move around. The nurse arrived as her bare feet touched the linoleum floor—female, easily six feet three inches tall, raw boned, and stone-faced. Undoubtedly she'd been the center for her high school basketball team.

"What are you doing?" she said as she came around to Kay. Her name tag identified her as Tamber, a possible combination of Tammy and Amber, as if the mother couldn't decide between two such beautiful names. She slammed the guard rail down and lifted Kay's legs to swing them back in bed. "You're on bed rest, no exceptions."

She let herself be maneuvered back into place. "I was testing the waters. Sorry." She felt sweat trickle down her face—pain or anxiety? Tamber bustled around and looked at the monitor to note Kay's vital signs, like she expected dire news after her attempted walkabout. "It's time for my morphine, isn't it? I'm in a lot of pain."

Tamber looked at her watch. "You're blood pressure's a little elevated," she said, not without some satisfaction. "And you look like you've run a marathon."

"The morphine?" Kay said.

"Nope. It's still an hour before you're due. I suggest you lie back and try to relax."

"Right. You're not in a Doomsday scenario with your parents. They'll be here soon."

Tamber hung a new bag of saline on Kay's IV pole. "Then you'll want to be as alert as possible." She tried out a smile.

"Oh, no. I want to be as drugged as possible. And honestly, I'm in a lot of pain. It feels like someone's got the wound in a vise grip."

Tamber looked at her blankly. "I'll send a message to the doctor. We'll see what she says."

Kay closed her eyes. She knew by the time the doctor got back to Tamber, it would be time for her regular dose. The wait would be hard, but much harder was waiting for her parents to arrive. At 4:45, Jamie texted. *I'm waiting in the car while your parents are wandering around what's left of their house. I told them what happened, thought it would make things easier for you. They insisted on coming here first. ETA at hospital 5:30.*

She was now officially in love with Jamie for delivering the hard news. She'd get her pain meds before they arrived, thank all that is holy. She was going to need to be relaxed to handle her mother. It was all about her mother. Her father mimicked whatever emotional state she was in. He didn't have access to any of his own emotions, other than anger and irritation. That meant she would have two irate parents in front of her who didn't care how badly Kay had been wounded.

Tamber finally came in and injected the morphine in Kay's IV line. She didn't feel the effect as much as she had the first time, which was disappointing. She was too anxiety ridden to relax, though the morphine took an edge off. By five thirty she was desperate for her parents to arrive, if only to end the horrible anticipation. She'd rather be yelled at than think about being yelled at.

Jamie walked into the room with her parents right behind her. They stopped at the foot of the bed. The first thing Kay thought was her parents looked old. They were only in their sixties, but they looked much older, particularly her mother. She seemed tiny in her knit travel suit, the shoulders of the jacket appeared to be resting on a hanger, not flesh and blood. Her face was tanned, but you could tell the skin was a whitish gray right under the topical color. Her father looked lost. His eyes kept shifting from place to place with nowhere to settle. It was unnerving. His big frame seemed slightly stooped since she last saw him. Their house was gone—what did she expect?

Jamie ushered Kay's mother to the chair next to the bed and left the room to find another. Kay raised the back of her bed as upright as possible. Her parents were silent, which was the most unnerving of all. Neither looked at her.

"I would give anything to bring the house back," Kay said. "I'm so, so sorry this happened."

Her mother opened her purse and slowly reached in for her cigarettes, pulling them out and then rooting around for a lighter.

"Mom, you can't smoke in the hospital. Seriously."

She lifted her head and looked at Kay, her eyes suddenly like steel. "Forty years. That's how long I lived in that house with your father. And he's spent his entire life there, with his parents and grandparents before him." Kay glanced at her father and saw his eyes had regained focus. He stared directly at her, his lips held tightly together.

"It was my house too, Mom. I know what a loss this is."

She waved that away. "From what I understand, this happened because of you." She threw the cigarettes back in her bag and slumped against her chair. Kay wasn't sure she'd wanted to tell them that part, but at least it took the decision out of her hands. Jamie came in with another chair and offered it to her father, then stood at the foot of the bed.

"Things are about to get ugly," Kay said to her. "You probably should go."

Jamie ignored her and looked at Kay's mother. "I heard what you said as I walked in, Mrs. Adler. As I told you before, you can't blame Kay for this."

"Why not? It's because of her our house was burned down." She looked narrowly at her.

"Believe me," Kay said. "She can, and not without reason."

"That's right." She looked mildly satisfied.

"I don't understand the need to cast blame," Jamie said. "The man who burned down your house was after Kay for a police action she participated in a long time ago. She didn't do anything wrong. You haven't even asked about her wound. She was nearly stabbed to death."

Kay's parents stared at her. She was sticking up for Kay, trying to protect her. Is this what being truly cared for felt like? Jamie was the opposite of her mother, and thank God. Many of the women she'd been in relationships with had had some of her mother's characteristics, and not the better ones.

Her mother turned her gaze back to her. "This is your new girlfriend? You have her trained well." That was a showstopper. Kay was mortified, Jamie looked more surprised than angry, and her mother seemed pleased to get a reaction.

"Listen," Kay said, trying to control herself. She didn't know whether to be hurt or angry. "You're in shock. You've only just found out. Let Jamie drive you to my condo. You can stay there while we get things sorted out."

"I'd rather stay in a hotel," she said. Her arms were crossed, her lips pursed.

"Mom, please don't be this way. I know you're incredibly angry, but don't spend your money to make a point. I won't be staying at my place, anyway. You'll have it to yourselves."

She could see a corner of Jamie's mouth move up. At least one person was happy. Her father stood, eager to get moving, while her mother rose as if her joints hurt.

"All right," she said. "Give me the keys."

"I'll call and have the doorman let you in. I'll have to get you a set of keys." She looked up at Jamie, who nodded.

"I'm sorry you were wounded, but you seem all right. The fire, though, is too much," her mother said. Her father trailed her out the door, while Jamie moved to the side of the bed and took her hand.

"I had no idea you had difficult parents," she said.

"Their house burned down. I suppose anyone would be difficult," Kay said softly, unconvincingly.

"I'll get them settled at your place and make another key for the new lock. Then I'll get a uniform posted outside, to be safe. Luckily, you'll be in here another few nights so things have a chance to calm down." She leaned over and kissed her.

"Being my girlfriend must suck."

Jamie laughed. "It's not dull, that's for sure. I'll call later." She kissed her again and left. Kay grabbed the remote and put the bed back in an angled position. Her wound was throbbing. She hadn't really thought her mother would blame her for losing the house. She felt guilty, but shouldn't a mother reassure her? Be sad for the loss but not angry at the messenger? Kay had lapsed into her recurring mistake—hoping her parents would actually act like parents. What did she expect? Something. She always hoped for something.

CHAPTER ELEVEN

K ay walked into Area Four two days after being released from the hospital. She moved stiffly—her normal gait made her wound ache. Her discharge instructions were to stay at home for a week and move as little as possible. Jamie seemed weary when she asked her to do as she was told for once in her life. It hadn't been her experience that she stayed put when she was supposed to. Kay knew she was once again a target and even more vulnerable because of her injury. The thought didn't scare her. She was used to it, in the resigned way one becomes used to having eczema or a painful elbow—annoying but not threatening. After Jamie left for work that morning, she'd eased herself into sweatpants. Her sutures were at waist level, and blue jeans were impossible. She knew she couldn't start working yet, but she had to see what was going on. She felt distanced from work, like she'd been quarantined.

Lieutenant Sharpe stood at the coffee station like a tree trunk. He was not a coffee man. He was a green tea guy in the morning, with generous portions of Gatorade during the rest of the day. He had an array of vitamin supplements lining the credenza behind his desk and had been known to offer Kay some vitamin D when she was particularly cranky. When he saw her walk toward him he raised a hand as if stopping traffic and put his mug down.

"What in the everlasting hell are you doing here, Adler?" He sounded like he'd just seen a paraplegic get up and walk.

She stopped in front of him and peered at the coffee pot. There was an inch left, undoubtedly viscous and bitter. She poured a cup. "Don't worry, boss. I'm not here to work. I thought I'd stop by and see how the investigations are going."

Sharpe pulled the tea bag out of his mug and stirred it slowly as he looked back at her. "You're like a mole who keeps popping her head out of the ground. Apparently, nothing can kill you."

She smiled. "I'll take that as a compliment, though I've heard better." She looked around and saw Adam and Elise in the conference room. "I'll check in with those two and get out of your hair."

He took her by the elbow and pointed her the opposite way. "No. You're going to leave. I don't want to see you back here until you're physically recovered and the person who attacked you is found. Are we clear?"

She looked wistfully at the conference room, wanting nothing more than to drink bad coffee and talk about the case with the others on the team. Elise and Adam saw her and waved. "Now that I'm here, Lieutenant, it can't hurt to touch base, can it?"

The grip on her elbow tightened and he began walking with her toward the exit. "Jamie told me you're staying at her place."

Kay flushed. She wasn't ready to make their relationship public. But so little of her life had been private recently. She was getting used to that too.

"Now you're going back there and not leaving until we tell you it's safe. That's an order," he said, peering at her intently. "Keep your gun nearby."

Elise and Adam walked up. "You're leaving? Without saying hello?" Adam said.

"Blame it on the boss. He's throwing me out."

Sharpe let go of her elbow. "Fine. You have five minutes. Then you go." He turned toward his office and walked away. Kay took a sip of the atrocious coffee and looked at Adam over her mug.

"How're you feeling? You look a little shaky," Adam said.

The pain in her side was growing worse the longer she was out. She hadn't wanted to take pain pills while she was driving, but now she felt hot and uncomfortable. "I'm fine. Any news on Erin Baran? It looks like I'll be locked in until she's found."

Adam looked at Elise. "Nothing yet. Jamie called Baran's grandmother, and she confirmed what she told you, that she doesn't even know her granddaughter. We've been checking north side high schools to see if we could find where she went. Finally found her at Lane Tech."

Kay smiled. "That's where I went. That's good work." She glanced around the room. "Is Sidwell here?"

Adam grinned. "We heard you're staying at her place." Kay stared at him until the smile went away. The silence was loud. Elise changed the subject. "We also hear your parents are staying at your place."

"Is this what you do all day? Talk about me? No wonder there're no leads yet."

"You know it's not like that," Adam said. "Everything about you is relevant to our investigation. We're not gossiping."

A couple of detectives entered the room and glanced at her as they passed. They didn't know her, but everyone knew about her. She felt like she had the mark of Cain on her forehead. She turned back to Elise and Adam. "My folks are still at my place, but they're moving into an Airbnb tomorrow. The housing is covered by the insurance. Now tell me about the high school."

"All we know is Erin went to Lane from 2000-2004," Elise said. "Jamie is over there now talking to the teachers who may have known her. She doesn't see the principal until later this morning."

Kay nodded. "That's a start. Good. What are you two doing?"

"I'm still scouring the Internet," Adam said.

"And I'm heading out to talk to Anthony Baran's prison friend to see if I can learn anything else about Erin. Maybe we missed something the first time we talked to him."

Kay was approaching whimpering level, and she wouldn't let anyone ever see her whimper. "Okay. I'm going to move along. Would you guys keep me up to date?"

"You're going straight to Jamie's, aren't you?" Adam said. "You're looking worse by the minute."

She walked to the coffee station and put her mug in the sink. "I'm fine, I told you. I have to stop a few places before I check on my parents."

"What places? I'm not sure you should be driving yourself," Elise said.

"You're both worrywarts. I'm buying groceries and making a Target run." She turned to leave and then turned back again. "And don't tell Jamie I was here."

❖

Kay loaded six Target bags into the trunk of her Audi. Underwear, slippers, light jackets, toiletries. Her parents needed everything. Their suitcases were filled with leisure wear for a Caribbean cruise, not a cool and rainy Chicago April. The Airbnb they were moving into was furnished and had a full kitchen, so they didn't need plates and silverware and pots and pans—all the things we use every day and don't think of until they've been melted down into ash and plastic goop and molten metal.

She drove out of the crowded Target parking lot in Uptown and headed down Broadway to her building. The rain was coming down steadily, and pedestrians were scurrying along the sidewalks. Her phone was on the seat beside her and she saw it flash awake with an incoming call from Jamie. She'd be able to tell she was driving, so she ignored the call and avoided the lecture. She planned to be in her guarded condo long before she got home. She looked at the screen again and saw a text from her pop up. She kept one eye on the road and read. *Urgent. I know who Erin Baran is. Call me now.*

Kay turned left onto Roscoe and pulled into a hydrant zone. She hit Jamie's number on speed dial and she picked up before she heard it ring.

"You aren't going to believe this," she said.

"Probably not."

"I saw a photo of Erin at the high school. It's Elise. Our Elise."

Kay didn't say anything. She couldn't. There was a short circuit in her system.

"Are you there?" she said.

"Holy mother. Are you absolutely sure?"

"I'll text the photo to you. She looks young, of course, but it's a spitting image of Elise."

"It explains some things. Becker had his bugs in my car and condo, but he seemed to know about my movements beyond what they could have picked up. Things that Elise could've heard from me or nosed around for. Jesus. Do we know where she is?"

"I've tried to call her and she's not picking up. Adam said she left the area right after you did. I won't ask what you were doing there. She's probably on the run since she knows I'd find a photo of her at Lane Tech."

"Who's out looking for her?"

"I'm on my way to her apartment. The lieutenant doesn't want to put out a BOLO since she'll hear it on the radio. He's getting things covered at the airport and train stations."

Kay felt something drop in her stomach, a literal gut feeling. "I know where she is. You've got to turn around."

"Explain."

"Elise was there when I said I was going shopping for my parents and then on to my condo. She's gone there. She has my parents, I'm sure of it."

Jamie's voice was cool, while Kay's had a rising trill to it. "I'm on Elston at Irving Park. With lights on I should be there in less than ten."

"Don't call in backup. Not yet. I don't want this to be a hostage situation without me with them inside. I have a plan, but I need to get in there alone to divert Elise's attention away from them. Meet me in the garage of my building."

She threw the phone down and took in a gasping breath. Her wound was incredibly painful, but what made her ill was the thought Elise could kill her mother as some sort of eye for an eye revenge. She pulled the car onto the street and drove quickly to her garage. Nine minutes later, Jamie pulled in. She had the garage attendant valet her car and climbed into Kay's. She drove up three levels to her assigned space.

Jamie stared at her. "You look like you're about to keel over. Whatever you're thinking of doing, you probably can't do in your condition."

She felt physically able to confront Elise, but her emotions were about to uncork. She parked in her spot. "You can save your breath. I'm going in. Here's the plan."

Kay got out on the thirtieth floor and pointed her cart full of shopping bags toward her condo. There was no police officer in sight—Elise could easily have ordered him off his post. She unlocked the door and backed in, as if she didn't suspect anything. She didn't hear a sound other than its squeaky wheels. When she'd pulled it in farther and shut the door, she turned and saw Elise standing by the dining room table. Her parents were sitting on the same side of the table, facing the windows, their hands behind their backs and their mouths taped shut. Elise had a gun pointed at her mother's head.

"Let go of the cart and keep your hands up," Elise said. She turned the gun on Kay, who stood inside the entrance and summoned whatever talent she had as an actor. She looked surprised and horrified.

"It's you?" she sputtered. "What the fuck?" She took a step into the living room and Elise waved her gun at her.

"Stay exactly where you are, Adler. I have three targets to shoot and it doesn't matter to me where I start."

"Take it easy," Kay said. "I'll do whatever you say. But can I make a suggestion? Why don't you shoot me and let my parents go? I'm the one you really want."

"Shut up," Elise said. Kay glanced at her parents, whose eyes were wide with fear. She tried to give them a reassuring look, which was impossible in the circumstances. Her mother's eyes started darting around. She squirmed in her chair and made crazy noises behind the tape.

"I know I'm supposed to be shocked to discover it's you, Elise. I mean Erin. But now that I know it all makes sense. Can I come closer so we can talk about this?"

Elise's face was expressionless. "You can shut up, like I said. Keep one hand in the air and drop your weapons. Including your backup gun." Elise pressed her weapon against her mother's temple, whose eyes rolled to the top of her head. Her father seemed catatonic.

"I'm not wearing my BUG today. See?" She pulled her right pant leg up. "I'm going to reach into my jacket for my service weapon." Elise watched her closely as she slowly pulled her gun from the holster on her hip. She stooped and placed it on the wood flooring. "I don't want to drop it and have it go off. It's racked and ready."

Elise's mouth turned up on one side. "Were you expecting some trouble?"

"Considering how off guard I was when you stabbed me, I though it prudent."

"Not my best work, I have to admit," Elise said. "That was meant to put an end to all this."

"And yet, here we are." A stiff wind had come up along with a lashing rain. Drops were hurled against her windows, making loud, staccato sounds in the room. She looked at Elise. "So where do you want me?" So far she hadn't addressed her parents, though their eyes were fixed on her.

Elise moved to the end of the table closest to Kay, placing her parents behind her. She motioned with the gun, which had another blasted silencer on it. "Come over here and sit across from your parents." Kay advanced with her hands out in front of her, skirting around Elise and taking a chair facing the kitchen. Elise's weapon followed her closely. "Put your hands on the table and don't move them." She did as she was told, calmly looking from her mother to her father.

Elise remained standing. "In some ways, this has turned out more satisfying than had you died on the running trail. Can you guess why?"

"I'm not an idiot, Elise. This whole thing started because I killed your mother, many years ago now. And here we are with my mother. I get that."

Her mother tried to get up, ungodly muffled screams coming from behind the duct tape.

"I'm not sure you do get it," Elise said, pushing her back down. "From the way you've talked about your parents, I don't know how much you care if they're dead or not."

That got her dad's attention. He turned his eyes on Kay as if to say, "I knew it."

"Of course I care," she said. "But I might not be as obsessed with my parents as you are with your mother. You've thrown your whole life into getting revenge. I'd say that qualifies as having mommy issues."

Elise swung her pistol and hit Kay above the ear, opening a cut that started bleeding profusely.

"Ow. Christ!" She glared up at Elise. "That was a cheap shot. I didn't realize you were so sensitive."

"You're right about one thing. At this point I'm wasting time with you." She placed the gun against her mother's temple and the screaming began again. Her father tried to get up and knock the table over toward Elise, but she shot him in the shoulder before it had raised more than an inch off the ground. Kay remained impassive. Her father roared behind the duct tape and fell back in his chair.

"Again, it seems to make more sense to shoot me instead. No one's going to care about this eye for an eye thing you've set your mind on. If you kill only me, you'll spend a long time in prison, no doubt. If you shoot the three of us, you'll never see outside again."

"You're presuming I'll get caught."

Kay looked past her and saw Jamie standing behind Elise in the kitchen. Her weapon was aimed at her back. Unaware she was there, Elise jabbed her gun tighter against her mother's temple, as if she were about to shoot, and Jamie shot her in the back of her hip. She cried out and crumpled to the floor, dropping her gun. Jamie stepped forward and picked it up. Her parents had been scared into silence. They stared at her with eyes like saucers. Her father's shoulder was bleeding, but he seemed impervious to it.

Kay looked at Jamie, who was kneeling beside Elise and putting cuffs on her wrists. She didn't struggle. She lay facedown, grimacing. Kay looked at her curiously before turning back to Jamie.

"Were you trying to make the rescue more dramatic? You got here a lot later than I was expecting."

She looked up at her. "It would have helped if you'd given me the right key to your back door. You gave me the key to your new lock and the back door didn't open with it. I had to get the super."

"Oh." Kay gave her an apologetic smile. "Tell them to send two buses when you call it in. My dad's been shot, too." She went to the kitchen to get a pair of scissors and cut open the plastic ties binding her parent's hands and ignored the blood dripping down her own face. She wished she could keep the duct tape over their mouths, but her mother had hers off in a second.

"Your father's been shot," she said ferociously. She turned to her father and ripped the duct tape off him. "Do something!"

"Jamie is calling for an ambulance now. Everything's going to be fine." She went to her father and looked at his wound. The bullet hit right at the joint of the shoulder, which had to be painful. He looked at her suspiciously, as if he didn't know her. And still he didn't say anything. She grabbed a clean towel from the kitchen and pressed it against his wound, which was streaming blood.

"You've ruined my life, Kay. I don't know how we'll get over this." Her mother was standing behind her father, her face twisted with fear and anger.

"Sit down. I'll bring you both a drink."

Jamie was on the phone in the kitchen, calling in the troops. Kay joined her there and reached for the Four Roses.

"Do you want a drink?" Kay said. "I could use one." She poured an inch of bourbon in a tumbler and drank it back.

Jamie smiled. "Good plan, by the way."

Kay shrugged. "It worked." She poured more bourbon in her glass.

Jamie looked at her thoughtfully. "You don't seem particularly happy or relieved." She drained her glass.

"I'm numb. Can't feel a thing. I dread dealing with my parents. First the house burns down, now this. They're furious with me." She took back the bottle.

"I don't get that," she said. "You saved their lives. None of this is your fault."

"They'll think you saved the day, which you did, but I'm to blame for the whole fucking mess. That's the way it is." She grabbed the bottle and a couple of glasses. "Why is it the idea of someone trying to kill me didn't scare me at all, but going back into that room is terrifying?"

Jamie pulled her close for a hug, which brought her perilously close to tears. "I don't know, but I think you should find out."

She had no reply to that. She wrenched herself from her arms and returned to the dining room, plunking the bourbon on the table. They all drank up.

Chapter Twelve

D r. Bosworth finished probing the sutures along Kay's wound. "Everything looks good," she said in a clipped tone. She was probably disappointed she'd shown up without Jamie in tow. "You're two weeks out and exactly where you need to be." She turned abruptly and started typing notes into the computer in the small exam room.

"Can I go back to work?"

"No," Bosworth said, typing away. She didn't elaborate.

Kay sighed. She was too tired to bother getting mad. "Perhaps you'd tell me how long I'll be off work, if it's not too much bother, that is."

The doctor shot her a quick glance and returned to her typing. "Another week."

Christ, she'd go crazy by then. The first week off had been dominated by the confrontation with Elise and her complicated reaction to it. She felt deep relief to be rid of the killer, and a surprising sadness at losing the Elise she thought she knew. The second week, she'd been as restless as a horse at the starting gate. There wasn't an inch of her place that hadn't been cleaned. A third week would be brutal. She drove home as if she were returning to prison after a furlough.

Jamie came over at five. She'd been spending most nights at her place, returning to her own to grind out the days. She opened her door as if she was a hungry zoo tiger and Jamie the keeper bringing dinner. She grabbed her by the sleeve, pulled her in before pushing her against the closed door and kissing her soundly.

"I can't tell if this means you've had a good day or a bad day," Jamie said.

Kay took her hand and led her to the kitchen where she poured them each a drink. "Tolerable day, but I'm not looking forward to tonight."

Jamie was wearing finely tailored heather gray pants with an asymmetrical black blouse. Kay's jeans had holes at the knee. "It's not going to be that bad. Your mom seems to like me."

"Don't presume anything. She's cagier than a cold war spy. She may act nice to you, but there's an agenda there somewhere." She poured another drink.

"What possible agenda could your mother have for me? Can't it be as simple as her thinking we're good together?" Jamie said.

"That's extremely relative. She's not anti-gay, but she simply can't conceive of a universe in which a woman would not want to be with a man. I don't think it feels quite real to her when she sees me with a woman." Kay quickly caught Jamie's eyes. "Not that she's seen me with many women, and not for a long time."

"Why did you take such a long break from relationships? I'm curious."

"I'm not sure, other than I was sick of the same thing happening over and over. First a woman would think my job was exciting. Exciting to be associated with. Then, when she saw how involved with my work I am, she'd become jealous and start nagging me."

"And this feels different because I'm also a cop?"

"I think it's different in every way." Kay's voice was soft.

"I do, too." Jamie looked thoughtful.

"What?" Kay said. "You're making me nervous."

"I'm thinking about us working together at Area Four. Do you think it's a good idea?"

"We'll have to wait and see. I suppose if you get on my nerves you can always transfer to another area."

"You don't think we'd make the most amazing crime busting duo ever?" Kay laughed. "I'm not kidding. We'd be legendary."

She shut her up with a kiss. "You're awfully sure of yourself."

"With your brawn and my brains, we'll be unstoppable," Jamie said. She looked rather serious.

"I'm wondering if you're unstoppable, as in will you ever shut up about this?"

Jamie relaxed and took Kay into her arms. "I want to be around you. That's what matters."

She picked up her glass and drained it. "Come on. We have to get to my parents' place. Now that detente has been reached we have to pay the price for peace. We'll see how much you want to be around me after spending an evening with the Adlers."

Jamie pulled her up from the sofa. "I'm not worried about it."

Kay looked at her with pity. "Oh, honey. You really should be."

About the Author

Anne Laughlin is the author of four previous novels published by Bold Strokes Books. She is a four-time Goldie Award winner and has been short listed three times for a Lammy Award. In 2008, Anne was named an emerging writer by the Lambda Literary Foundation and returned to their retreat in 2014. Her story, "It Only Occurred to Me Later," was a finalist in the Saints and Sinners Short Fiction Contest. She has attended writing residencies at Ragdale, Vermont Studio Center, and others.

Anne lives in her hometown of Chicago with her wife, Linda Braasch.

Books Available from Bold Strokes Books

A Date to Die by Anne Laughlin. Someone is killing people close to Detective Kay Adler, who must look to her own troubled past for a suspect. There she finds more than one person seeking revenge against her. (978-1-63555-023-8)

Captured Soul by Laydin Michaels. Can Kadence Munroe save the woman she loves from a twisted killer, or will she lose her to a collector of souls? (978-1-62639-915-0)

Dawn's New Day by TJ Thomas. Can Dawn Oliver and Cam Cooper, two women who have loved and lost, open their hearts to love again? (978-1-63555-072-6)

Definite Possibility by Maggie Cummings. Sam Miller is just out for good times, but Lucy Weston makes her realize happily ever after is a definite possibility. (978-1-62639-909-9)

Eyes Like Those by Melissa Brayden. Isabel Chase and Taylor Andrews struggle between love and ambition from the writers' room on one of Hollywood's hottest TV shows. (978-1-63555-012-2)

Heart's Orders by Jaycie Morrison. Helen Tucker and Tee Owens escape hardscrabble lives to careers in the Women's Army Corps, but more than their hearts are at risk as friendship blossoms into love. (978-1-63555-073-3)

Hiding Out by Kay Bigelow. Treat Dandridge is unaware that her life is in danger from the murderer who is hunting the woman she's falling in love with, Mickey Heiden. (978-1-62639-983-9)

Omnipotence Enough by Sophia Kell Hagin. Can the tiny tool that abducted war veteran Jamie Gwynmorgan accidentally acquires help her escape an unknown enemy to reclaim her stolen life and the woman she deeply loves? (978-1-63555-037-5)

Summer's Cove by Aurora Rey. Emerson Lange moved to Provincetown to live in the moment, but when she meets Darcy Belo and her son Liam, her quest for summer romance becomes a family affair. (978-1-62639-971-6)

The Road to Wings by Julie Tizard. Lieutenant Casey Tompkins, air force student pilot, has to fly with the toughest instructor, Captain Kathryn "Hard Ass" Hardesty, fly a supersonic jet, and deal with a growing forbidden attraction. (978-1-62639-988-4)

Beauty and the Boss by Ali Vali. Ellis Renois is at the top of the fashion world, but she never expects her summer assistant Charlotte Hamner to tear her heart and her business apart like sharp scissors through cheap material. (978-1-62639-919-8)

Fury's Choice by Brey Willows. When gods walk amongst humans, can two women find a balance between love and faith? (978-1-62639-869-6)

Lessons in Desire by MJ Williamz. Can a summer love stand a four-month hiatus and still burn hot? (978-1-63555-019-1)

Lightning Chasers by Cass Sellars. For Sydney and Parker, being a couple was never what they had planned. Now they have to fight corruption, murder, and enemies hiding in plain sight just to hold on to each other. Lightning Series, Book Two. (978-1-62639-965-5)

Summer Fling by Jean Copeland. Still jaded from a breakup years earlier, Kate struggles to trust falling in love again when a summer fling with sexy young singer Jordan rocks her off her feet. (978-1-62639-981-5)

Take Me There by Julie Cannon. Adrienne and Sloan know it would be career suicide to mix business with pleasure, however tempting it is. But what's the harm? They're both consenting adults. Who would know? (978-1-62639-917-4)

The Girl Who Wasn't Dead by Samantha Boyette. A year ago, someone tried to kill Jenny Lewis. Tonight she's ready to find out who it was. (978-1-62639-950-1)

Unchained Memories by Dena Blake. Can a woman give herself completely when she's left a piece of herself behind? (978-1-62639-993-8)

Walking Through Shadows by Sheri Lewis Wohl. All Molly wanted to do was go backpacking...in her own century. (978-1-62639-968-6)

A Lamentation of Swans by Valerie Bronwen. Ariel Montgomery returns to Sea Oats to try to save her broken marriage but soon finds herself also fighting to save her own life and catch a murderer. (978-1-62639-828-3)

Freedom to Love by Ronica Black. What happens when the woman who spent her lifetime worrying about caring for her family, finally finds the freedom to love without borders? (978-1-63555-001-6)

House of Fate by Barbara Ann Wright. Two women must throw off the lives they've known as a guardian and an assassin and save two rival houses before their secrets tear the galaxy apart. (978-1-62639-780-4)

Planning for Love by Erin Dutton. Could true love be the one thing that wedding coordinator Faith McKenna didn't plan for? (978-1-62639-954-9)

Sidebar by Carsen Taite. Judge Camille Avery and her clerk, attorney West Fallon, agree on little except their mutual attraction, but can their relationship and their careers survive a headline-grabbing case? (978-1-62639-752-1)

Sweet Boy and Wild One by T. L. Hayes. When Rachel Cole meets soulful singer Bobby Layton at an open mic, she is immediately in thrall. What she soon discovers will rock her world in ways she never imagined. (978-1-62639-963-1)

To Be Determined by Mardi Alexander and Laurie Eichler. Charlie Dickerson escapes her life in the US to rescue Australian wildlife with Pip Atkins, but can they save each other? (978-1-62639-946-4)

True Colors by Yolanda Wallace. Blogger Robby Rawlins plans to use First Daughter Taylor Crenshaw to get ahead, but she never planned on falling in love with her in the process. (978-1-62639-927-3)

Unexpected by Jenny Frame. When Dale McGuire falls for Rebecca Harper, the mother of the son she never knew she had, will Rebecca's troubled past stop them from making the family they both truly crave? (978-1-62639-942-6)

Canvas for Love by Charlotte Greene. When ghosts from Amelia's past threaten to undermine their relationship, Chloé must navigate the greatest romance of her life without losing sight of who she is. (978-1-62639-944-0)

Heart Stop by Radclyffe. Two women, one with a damaged body, the other a damaged spirit, challenge each other to dare to live again. (978-1-62639-899-3)

Repercussions by Jessica L. Webb. Someone planted information in Edie Black's brain and now they want it back, but with the protection of shy former soldier Skye Kenny, Edie has a chance at life and love. (978-1-62639-925-9)

Spark by Catherine Friend. Jamie's life is turned upside down when her consciousness travels back to 1560 and lands in the body of one of Queen Elizabeth I's ladies-in-waiting...or has she totally lost her grip on reality? (978-1-62639-930-3)

Taking Sides by Kathleen Knowles. When passion and politics collide, can love survive? (978-1-62639-876-4)

Thorns of the Past by Gun Brooke. Former cop Darcy Flynn's heart broke when her career on the force ended in disgrace, but perhaps saving Sabrina Hawk's life will mend it in more ways than one. (978-1-62639-857-3)

You Make Me Tremble by Karis Walsh. Seismologist Casey Radnor comes to the San Juan Islands to study an earthquake but finds her heart shaken by passion when she meets animal rescuer Iris Mallery. (978-1-62639-901-3)

Complications by MJ Williamz. Two women battle for the heart of one. (978-1-62639-769-9)

Crossing the Wide Forever by Missouri Vaun. As Cody Walsh and Lillie Ellis face the perils of the untamed West, they discover that love's uncharted frontier isn't for the weak in spirit or the faint of heart. (978-1-62639-851-1)

Fake It Till You Make It by M. Ullrich. Lies will lead to trouble, but can they lead to love? (978-1-62639-923-5)

Girls Next Door by Sandy Lowe and Stacia Seaman eds. Best-selling romance authors tell it from the heart—sexy, romantic stories of falling for the girls next door. (978-1-62639-916-7)

Pursuit by Jackie D. The pursuit of the most dangerous terrorist in America will crack the lines of friendship and love, and not everyone will make it out under the weight of duty and service. (978-1-62639-903-7)

Shameless by Brit Ryder. Confident Emery Pearson knows exactly what she's looking for in a no-strings-attached hookup, but can a spontaneous interlude open her heart to more? (978-1-63555-006-1)

The Practitioner by Ronica Black. Sometimes love comes calling whether you're ready for it or not. (978-1-62639-948-8)

Unlikely Match by Fiona Riley. When an ambitious PR exec and her super-rich coding geek-girl client fall in love, they learn that giving something up may be the only way to have everything. (978-1-62639-891-7)

Where Love Leads by Erin McKenzie. A high school counselor and the mom of her new student bond in support of the troubled girl, never expecting deeper feelings to emerge, testing the boundaries of their relationship. (978-1-62639-991-4)